Should I

I slowly pulled open the pouch of runes and slipped my hand inside, expecting to feel the cool smooth stones.

Heat burned at my fingertips and a shock shot up my arm, making all my nerves tingle. With a yelp, I quickly withdrew my hand.

"What's going on?" I muttered.

Someone touched my shoulder.

I yelled and shot to my feet. The outcrop was slick, and in my haste I was dangerously close to the edge.

With a scream, I felt myself sliding into nothingness . . .

The Ophelia and Abby Mysteries
by Shirley Damsgaard

SHIRLEY DAMSGAARD

The Seventh Witch

AN OPHELIA AND ABBY MYSTERY

AVON

An Imprint of HarperCollinsPublishers

This is a work of fiction. Names, characters, places, and incidents are products of the author's imagination or are used fictitiously and are not to be construed as real. Any resemblance to actual events, locales, organizations, or persons, living or dead, is entirely coincidental.

AVON BOOKS
An Imprint of HarperCollins*Publishers*
10 East 53rd Street
New York, New York 10022-5299

Copyright © 2010 by Shirley Damsgaard
ISBN 978-0-06-149347-8
www.avonmystery.com

First Avon Books paperback printing: February 2010

Avon Trademark Reg. U.S. Pat. Off. and in Other Countries, Marca Registrada, Hecho en U.S.A.
HarperCollins® is a registered trademark of HarperCollins Publishers.

Printed in the U.S.A.

10 9 8 7 6 5 4 3 2 1

Acknowledgments

Writing the Ophelia and Abby mystery series has been a ride of a lifetime, and has given me the opportunity to meet and work wiht some amazing people. This book is no exception.

My agent, Stacey Glick—without your faith in the series, the past five years would have never happened! More thanks than I can express for your guidance and for all your hard work! I'm so glad that your're in my corner!

My editors, Emily Krump and Wendy Lee—Emily, you made what could have been a difficult trasition easy! Thanks for your insight! And Wendy, though we only worked together a short time, I really appreciate your input on this Book!

Sharon Robinson and Lydia Wiley—my Southern ladies and private tour guides! I thank you not only for all your help, but also your friendship! I hope you approve of your characters! (Sharon, I tried to do just as you asked, but it was hard!)

Sallie, Lisa, and Oreon—thank you so much for your kindness, your hospitality, and the information you shared with me!

Joanna Campbell Slan—once again J., you held my hand through the whole process and listened to all my angst! I honestly don't know what I'd do without you!

June and Paul Steinbach—my go-to people for everything to do with medicine, murder, and mayhem! Thanks for helping me get it right! (And if anything *is* wrong . . . it's my fault!)

To all the readers of the series—you have no idea how much your kind words mean to me! Your emails help get me through the day!

And of course, my family and friends. What can I say but thanks for putting up with me, especially when I'm facing a deadline! Love you all!

The Seventh Witch

Prologue

The clock on the top of the rough hewn dresser ticked away the final moments of the old woman's life. It had been a long life—a life full of struggle and loss. But she'd be joining the one who'd died so many years ago, leaving her alone to raise three rowdy boys. Even though she'd brought them up to be tough and mean, only one of those boys had survived the wild ways of their youth. He now sat, surrounded by kin, in the corner of the small bedroom. With his head down, he studied the shadows cast by the kerosene lamps across the planked floor.

Would he be finally free, free from the old woman's control once she crossed to whatever reward waited for her on the other side? No. It was his curse and his punishment to spend his life under a woman's thumb. Next it would be the one who waited to take his mother's place as head of the family—his niece, the daughter his mother never bore, his mother's heir. She shared the way of the mountains with her grandmother. She understood things he could barely comprehend. Resentment snuck through his thoughts. It wasn't fair. It wasn't right to always bow to a woman—he'd been forced to do it for over sixty years. He could try and wrest the power from her, but like everyone else, he'd grown to fear *her* as much as he did his mother.

The sudden whisper of cotton dresses and the muted sound

of heavy work boots sliding across the bedroom floor made him raise his head. His niece strode into the room with easy, confident steps. Her straight brown hair framed her thin face while her dark eyes burned into those gathered around the bed. With heads down, they all backed away from the bed, leaving his niece as the only one at his mother's side.

She knelt and lifted his mother's frail hand from beneath the homemade quilt. Wrinkled eyelids flew open and eyes hard as stones searched the younger woman's face. Fingers twisted with arthritis grasped her hand with a strength that belied the spirit slowly oozing from the old woman's body.

"Do you see it?" croaked the ancient voice.

"Yes." The younger woman's eyes burned hotter as she gripped her grandmother's hand. "What do you want me to do—tell me and it's done."

"Revenge," gasped the old woman.

"Granny, the death price was paid over fifty years ago."

The white frizzled head, lying on the down pillow, moved back and forth in a slow pattern. "Not enough . . . more." A tear leaked from the corner of the old woman's eye. "So much lost . . . husband . . . sons . . . power that should've been ours."

"I know, Granny, I know," his niece replied, her voice low and soothing.

"I failed," the old woman wheezed as her thin chest rose and fell in her struggle to draw air. "Protect you . . . I had to protect you." Her hand gripped the younger woman's. "Your legacy . . ."

"Hush, Granny." The younger woman stroked her grandmother's gnarled hand. "I *won't* fail . . . I promise." The dim light reflected in her eyes, turning them black, and the shadow of her kneeling body seemed to grow as if the spirit fleeing the old woman's invaded hers. "They'll pay . . ." Her voice trailed away while the ticking of the clock filled the room. "They'll pay with blood."

At his niece's words, his mother's eyes drifted shut. One last breath and her chest stilled forever.

His niece stood, placed a soft kiss on his mother's wrinkled cheek, and quietly crossed the room to the dresser. Taking a shawl, she draped it across the old wavy mirror hanging on the wall. Then she opened the glass door of the clock and stopped the swinging pendulum. A heavy silence suddenly fell upon the room. She turned, and with one last look at the quiet form lying in the double bed, she marched out the door.

One

The mountain sang to me and I heard its song with my heart. Each sound—the early morning birdsong, the stream rushing over stones as it hurried down the mountain, the whisper of the wind through the pines—reverberated deep in my soul.

Standing on the outcrop of rock and looking out over the valley, I watched the sun streak the clouds with gold, pink, and lavender while the morning mists swathed the rolling peaks in blue. Below me, clusters of houses littered the valley once owned by my many times great-grandfather, Jens Swensen and his wife, Flora Chisholm Swensen. The houses all belonged to various cousins who could trace their lineage back to Jens and Flora. I easily spotted the red tin roof of Abby's childhood home gleaming in the early morning light. A thin plume of smoke rose from the fieldstone chimney, and even at this distance, I could smell the faint tang of wood smoke in the fall air. A smile tugged at my lips as I imagined my elderly Aunt Dot bustling around the kitchen, in her cotton housedress, her blue hair frizzed around her head, firing up the old woodstove to prepare breakfast.

After arriving so late last night, I'd been reluctant when Abby first suggested we hike up the mountain at this ungodly hour, but now I was glad we had. I felt peace, a sense of belonging, standing here as the first rays of sunlight warmed my chilled face. Hugging myself, I closed my eyes and let the knot that had been firmly lodged in my stomach since we left Iowa dissolve.

It wasn't that I didn't *want* to come to North Carolina for Great-Aunt Mary's 100th birthday, but the idea of spending an extended amount of time in her presence made me ill at ease. The woman was spooky. Her pale blue eyes had the habit of focusing on a spot right behind you, and it made the back of my neck prickle. I had to fight the desire to whip my head around and take a look. But I knew if I did, all *I* would see would be empty air. Great-Aunt Mary is a medium, and I'm not. I'm just a psychic with a talent for finding things, not seeing spectral images. With Great-Aunt Mary, I could never shake the feeling that at any moment a ghostly hand might suddenly reach out and grab me. The whole thing gave me the heebie-jeebies.

I opened my eyes and scanned the houses below. My parents were staying in the house with the gray roof. The image of my mother sleeping peacefully beneath a hand-stitched quilt made the knot start to form again. I loved my mother, I truly did, but Margaret Mary McDonald Jensen was a woman who'd never had a question she was afraid to ask. To call her assertive was a gross understatement. And since I'd adopted Tink, she'd become an expert on child rearing. Forget that she only raised one child. It appeared she was reading every book ever written about the care and feeding of teenagers and could quote them chapter and verse, which she did, often. I'd already received several doses of her advice via the telephone, and I couldn't imagine what it was going to be like being one on one with her during this visit.

A light touch on my arm interrupted my thoughts. I turned to see Abby watching me with a bemused smile on her face. Dressed in an old flannel shirt and jeans, her silver hair was still braided from the night before and draped over her shoulder in a thick coil. Green eyes sparkled as her smile widened.

"Don't worry so about your mother, dear. She's simply trying to help," she said in a voice that gently carried the rhythm of the valley.

Rolling my eyes, I exhaled slowly. "Read my mind, did you?"

She lifted one shoulder in a careless shrug. "It was hard not to," she said. "You were thinking so loud that I couldn't tune you out."

"Peachy," I replied with a snort. "Since most of the cousins have some kind of talent, is everyone going to be eavesdropping on my thoughts the entire visit?"

Abby chuckled. "That depends on you. They won't poke around in your head uninvited, but when someone's feelings are so close to the surface as yours are now, it's hard not to pick up on them. It's going to be up to you to keep your mind shielded."

"Great . . . well at least the gift passed over Mother."

She chuckled again. "Don't sell your mother short. She might not be psychic, but she's intuitive, and she can read you like a book."

Not what I wanted to hear. I kicked a small stone and sent it tumbling down the mountain. It bounced and clattered through the bushes, startling a bird resting there. His indignant cry of "Drink your teee" rang out over the valley.

"A towhee," Abby said with a wistful smile. "I haven't heard one of those for years."

Her eyes took on a faraway look.

"See that road that winds up the next mountain?" she asked, pointing to the distant slope. "It brought your grandfather to this valley. He came to do the surveying for the road." She waved a hand at a spot just below us. "Those bushes, where the towhee's hiding . . . they're wild blackberries. Every summer, my mother and I would hike up here and fill our baskets." Her smile deepened. "She made the best blackberry jam."

Just look at her, I thought. This visit is important to her, so quit it. Forget about spooky Great-Aunt Mary, your overbearing mother, and being surrounded by psychic cousins. Enjoy this visit, and enjoy spending time with her and Tink.

Throwing an arm around her shoulder, I gave her a quick squeeze. "Thanks for bringing me here, Abby."

"This was my special place," she said, leaning against me. "I always felt like the queen of the world, standing here looking down on the valley. It seemed like nothing bad could happen here," she murmured as memories seemed to roll over her, "not like—" She abruptly stopped.

I cocked my head and glanced over at her. "Huh?"

Straightening, she moved a step away from me. "Never mind." She turned and her green eyes narrowed. "I brought you up here for a reason . . . I have a few things that I need to discuss with you."

"Like what?"

"I think it's time you took my journals."

"What?" I exclaimed, taken completely off guard by her statement. "Why do I need your journals?"

A slight frown puckered Abby's forehead. "You know they're always passed down to the next generation. It's been done that way for over a hundred years." She took a deep breath and exhaled slowly. "And each new witch has added her magick to them."

"Sure, but why give them to me now? You're still writing your journals, aren't you?"

"Yes, and you need to start yours. If you had the journals that were passed on to me when Mother died, you'd have more of an opportunity to study what others have written. They might inspire you to begin telling your story."

I thought about the leather-bound notebook Abby had recently given me. I *had* started writing in it—I'd written about the day only a couple of months ago when the old Ophelia had been stripped away. Old fears, old doubts, had been torched as fire seemed to tear through my soul. It had been scary, yet exhilarating, and for the first time in my life I finally felt at peace with who and what I was. I had finally started to embrace my gift instead of fighting against it. *But* I didn't want to be responsible for the journals.

Abby sensed my reluctance and shrugged. "You're supposed to have them . . . you might as well take them now." She paused. "And while we're on the subject, there are other things that have been in the family—my mother's mortar and pestle; my grandmother's cast-iron kettle; a bag of crystals that once belonged to Flora—I want to make sure you have those someday, too."

"Why are you bringing this up now?"

"I don't want them to leave the family. They're possessions we've had for years," she said softly, "and they carry with them the energy of all those who've gone before . . . the hopes, the dreams . . . it's fitting that they should be yours, and after you, Tink's."

A tickle of fear shivered up my spine. "Abby, is there something you're not telling me?"

"No," she replied as a shadow of a smile played across her face. "It's just . . . we never talk about these things, and—"

"I don't like talking about this," I jumped in, cutting her off. "It makes it sound like you're not going to be around."

"Oh, my dear girl," she said, lifting a hand and tucking a stray strand of my brown hair behind my ear, "I'm not going to be here forever, and I worry about you . . . you've had such a hard time accepting your gift—"

"I've accepted it," I said, interrupting her again.

"I know, but you still have a lot to learn. The journals will help."

I shifted nervously. "Okay, so I'll take the journals, but why bring up the mortar and pestle, the cauldron?"

A shutter seemed to fall across Abby's eyes. "No reason." She turned her head away from me and stared out over the valley. "Returning to the mountain has caused a lot of memories to surface. I remember when my mother gave the journals to me and the talk we had. She passed a mantle on to me. Time's approaching for me to do the same."

As Abby talked, I studied her profile. When had those crow's-feet around her eyes deepened? And in the growing morning light, her hair seemed more white than silver. A realization hit me—Abby was getting older, just like everyone else. *No,* my mind screamed, refusing to accept what was before my eyes, *Abby's timeless.*

"I don't want any mantles. I still have a lot to learn, and I need you to teach me," I insisted.

"Ophelia," she said in a stern, strong voice, "don't let your fears blind you to the natural progression of life."

I crossed my arms over my chest. "I don't care," I said, knowing I sounded like a petulant child. "I don't want to talk about this now."

She sighed. "All right." Looking at me, she smiled. "We'll discuss it when we're back home." Tucking her arm through mine, she steered me back toward the path leading down the mountain. "Let's go help Aunt Dot with breakfast."

As I fell into step beside her, I felt the rightness of it all— me and Abby together—that was the way it should be, and that was the way I intended it to stay.

The aroma of fried ham and fresh coffee hit me as soon as we crossed the porch of the old farmhouse. The two fat, tabby cats lazing on the windowsills smelled it, too. As soon as they saw us, they jumped down from their perches, followed us to the door, and waited hopefully for it to open. What a couple of mooches, I thought, smiling down at them.

Much to the cats' dismay, I stopped at the door and saw Aunt Dot standing at the stove just as I'd imagined her, cooking. I watched as she grabbed a pot holder and used it to grasp the battered enamel coffeepot. With a sure hand that belied her ninety-one years, she poured a bit of its contents into the cast-iron skillet, stirring and scraping the pan as she did.

"Red-eye gravy," Abby whispered to me.

Hmm, ham drippings mixed with coffee. That should be an interesting taste combination.

Abby once again read my mind and gave me a poke in the ribs. "Shh, don't knock it until you've tried it. It's good. You can either pour it over a slice of ham or on your grits."

Grits? Another Southern dish I hadn't tried. Ground corn boiled until it reached the consistency of wallpaper paste. Yum, I thought sarcastically. I didn't know if I wanted to try them, either, but not eating what was served would be rude. I didn't want the Southern cousins to think I was some kind of uppity Yankee. I'd eat what was placed on the table and at least pretend to be thankful for it.

Tink stood next to Aunt Dot, chattering away as she slathered sweet-cream butter on a mound of toasted bread.

"How many different kinds of fairies are there, Aunt Dot?" she asked.

Fairies and Aunt Dot . . . go figure. I still doubted their existence in spite of Aunt Dot's insistence.

Abby made a move to open the screen door, but I stopped her. I wanted to listen in—one of my less attractive habits—on their conversation. I cocked my head.

"Ack, there are many, many different sort. And fairies are just like people—some are kind and helpful, but others want nothing to do with humans. You're wise to stay away from those." She paused to move the skillet to the back of the stove. "Some live in the hills, in caves; some live in trees."

Tink turned toward Aunt Dot and leaned against the counter. "Why haven't I ever seen one?" she exclaimed.

'Cause you're too young to drink elderberry wine, I snickered to myself, answering Tink's question. Aunt Dot's sightings always seemed to occur after she'd drank some of the lethal elderberry wine that she and Great-Aunt Mary bottled up every year. The one with the secret recipe containing moonshine. It was just another reason that I wasn't totally convinced that fairies existed.

Oh yeah, sure . . . I *had* seen those lights that seemed to follow Tink around on a midsummer's night, but they *could've* been really big lightning bugs.

Aunt Dot faced Tink and, raising her hand, laid it gently on the top of Tink's blond head, as if in a benediction. "Don't fret, Titania," she said, using Tink's real name. "Your mother had a reason for naming you after the Queen of the Fairies. You'll meet them when it's time." A smile brightened her wrinkled face. "Who knows? Maybe you'll see our Nisse this visit."

I shot a questioning glance at Abby.

"Scandinavian house fairy," she whispered. "He protects the homestead."

"I didn't last time," Tink grumbled, "and I sat up all night waiting. I even had a bowl of grits with butter and brown sugar for him."

"The bowl was empty the next morning, wasn't it?" Aunt Dot asked.

"Yes," Tink answered reluctantly.

Aunt Dot chuckled. "Ack, he's a clever one, our Nisse. He waited until you dozed off before gobbling it down, but don't worry, child. He'll remember your kindness." She picked up the platter of ham and made her way to the table. "If you two are done eavesdropping," she called out in a loud voice, "breakfast is ready."

Two

Abby and I crossed the kitchen like two little kids caught with their hands in the cookie jar, but Aunt Dot ignored our red faces and motioned us to the table.

"Have a seat. Mary will be out in a minute," she said, bustling over to the stove. "Her rheumatism's acting up, and—"

"Nonsense, Sister," announced a strong voice. "Nothing wrong with me. I just needed to work out a few kinks."

My head whipped toward the doorway. There she was . . . Great-Aunt Mary, sitting in the wheelchair she sometimes used to get around the house. Dressed in a cotton housedress similar to Aunt Dot's, and with old-fashioned hose rolled down to the top of her sturdy shoes, she sat as if a rod had been rammed down her back. No osteoporosis there. Her hooked cane lay across her lap, ready to snag any unsuspecting passerby with whom Great-Aunt Mary had decided she wanted to have a word. A smart kid quickly learned to stay out of reach—I'd been a smart kid. From behind her glasses, those pale blue eyes glanced at Abby before landing on me. Tilting her head back, her eyes raked me up and down.

"Ophelia," she finally said in a curt tone, "I see you haven't changed much."

"Ah, well," I stammered, "I—I did have a growth spurt. I'm taller since the last time you saw me."

"Stands to reason," she replied, breaking her stare as she grabbed one of the wheels of her chair and spun it toward the counter. "I haven't laid eyes on you since you were thirteen."

Moving to the table, I gripped the back of the closest ladder-back chairs. "Umm, you know how it is with teenagers—"

"Yes," she broke in, "never have time for their elders." Her face softened as her gaze landed on Tink. "Thank the stars you learned from *your* mistakes and are teaching this one some respect."

I clamped my mouth shut. Great. Now not only would I be receiving advice from my mother, but also my hundred-year-old spinster aunt.

As if I'd conjured her, the screen door suddenly slammed shut and my mother breezed into the room, with my father following behind. Even at this time of the morning her hair was perfect, her face made up, and her clothes were of the latest fashion . . . for Florida. Her bright clothing stood out in the rustic kitchen with its wood-burning stove, scarred oak table, and old plastered walls stained from years of wood smoke. She looked like she belonged in South Beach, not the Blue Ridge Mountains.

My father was a different story—he looked exactly as he should. A somewhat vague, retired professor who now spent his days playing golf in Palm Springs and putzing around with his favorite hobby, archeology. His face broke into a big smile when he spotted me.

"Ophelia," he cried, holding out his arms.

I released my stress-induced grip on the chair and ran to him. "Dad, gosh, it's good to see you," I replied as I received a bear hug.

Not letting go, he stepped back and sized me up. "You look well."

I nodded.

His eyes narrowed. "But there's something different about you," he continued in a cautious voice. "I can't quite put my finger on it, but—" He broke off and looked over my shoulder at my mother. "Maggie, don't you think there's something different about Ophelia?"

Uncomfortable with their scrutiny, I wiggled out of my dad's embrace and hugged my mother. "Hey, Mom."

After returning my hug, my mother held me at arm's length and studied me as intently as my father had. "Yes, I think you're right, Edward. What—"

"Mom, aren't you going to say hi to Tink?" I asked, cutting her off.

I felt a momentary pang of guilt, siccing them on Tink like that, but I didn't want to go into a long explanation about my epiphany, especially not in front of Great-Aunt Mary.

Tink didn't seem to mind me throwing her overanxious grandparents at her. She shyly stepped forward and allowed both of them to smother her. She took their murmurs of "My, look at how much she's grown since Christmas," and "Isn't she pretty?" in good stride. She even smiled when my mother started to give her advice on proper skin care. "Use sunscreen and moisturize, moisturize. Don't want wrinkles someday, do you?"

I saw Mother's eyes slide my way with that statement, but I ignored her.

I don't know how long the lecture would've continued— Mom was on a roll—but a loud "ahem" from Great-Aunt Mary interrupted her. Chagrined, both she and my father stepped over to Great-Aunt Mary and paid their respects to her and Aunt Dot.

Glancing at Abby, now sitting calmly at the table, I caught the twinkle in her eye as she watched Mother kiss up to the Aunts. *Yup, this was going to be some visit.* With a quick shake of my head, I joined her at the table.

My father detached himself from the group of women at the stove and crossed to Abby. Leaning down, he wrapped an arm around her shoulder and gave her a peck on the cheek.

"You look exceptionally lovely this morning, Abby," he said with a big grin.

She fluttered a hand in his direction. "Oh stop, Edward," she said in a tone that belied her words.

With a chuckle, my father pulled out the chair next to her and sat. "I've been reading about this area, and—"

"Edward," my mother said, placing a bowl of jam on the table, "they're not going to let you go digging things up around here." She turned accusingly toward me. "You went up the mountain this morning, didn't you?"

My eyes slid toward Abby then back to my mother. "Yes."

Crossing her arms over her chest, she stared down at me. "I would've liked to have gone with you."

"Maggie," Abby said, drawing her attention, "we've plenty of time in the coming days for all of us to go." She smiled gently at Mom. "I think it would be nice if Ophelia, Tink, and *you* all accompanied me up the mountain." Her smile widened as she laid a hand on my mother's wrist. "To have all my girls with me would be wonderful."

Placated, Mom uncrossed her arms. "Well, okay then."

Dad, ignoring the exchange between Mom and Abby, leaned forward and focused on Great-Aunt Mary. "Now, about this area . . . I've read several Native American tribes hunted this valley."

"Yes," Great-Aunt Mary said, positioning her chair at the head of the table. "This valley's provided sustenance for many over the years, and our family's respected that." She gave a quick nod as she ladled a spoonful of grits onto Tink's plate. "We've tried to be good stewards of the land. The family still holds—except for one—every acre my grandfather bought."

Abby stiffened slightly in her chair.

Glancing sideways, I saw she sat with her head bowed, staring at her plate. She'd laid down her fork and her hands were hidden beneath the table. I reached out and grasped one. It felt ice cold. "What's wrong?" I asked softly.

Her head shot up and her eyes went directly to Great-Aunt Mary. Their gazes locked and something unspoken passed between them.

Perplexed, I squeezed Abby's hand and repeated my question.

It broke the spell.

A forced smile played across her face while her eyes moved toward Tink. "Would you pass me the red-eye gravy, dear?"

Oh no you don't Abby, I thought, you're not sliding out of this one. I turned sideways, placed an arm on the back of my chair and studied her. "What's going—"

"Ophelia," Great-Aunt Mary said, cutting me off, "your grandmother said you've finally decided to get with the program."

Catching me off guard with her terminology, my brows wrinkled. "Huh?"

"You've decided to use your gifts, use your magick."

Everyone's attention now centered on me. I dropped my arm and shifted nervously. "Um, well, yeah, I guess—"

"You guess?" Great-Aunt Mary interrupted from between puckered lips while her eyes pinned me to my chair.

I stopped fidgeting and faced her. Squaring my shoulders, I met her stare with one of my own. "Yes," I replied in a strong voice, "I have."

She gave a snort, and I watched as her eyes traveled to a spot directly over my left shoulder.

A shiver shot up my spine.

Damn, she'd done it again!

"There's one last slice of ham, Ophelia," Aunt Dot said, holding the heavy platter in front of my face as we stacked the dirty dishes on the counter.

The meal had been wonderful—even the grits and the red-eye gravy—but I didn't think I'd ever be hungry again.

I held up my hands in a gesture of submission. "I can't, Aunt Dot," I exclaimed. "I'm stuffed. I'm going to have to hike up the mountain ten times to work off all this food."

"Oh, nonsense," Mom said as she dried one of the stone-ware plates. "If anything I think you've lost weight since Christmas."

"No, I haven't." I argued back. "I've—"

Great-Aunt Mary's voice suddenly rang out. "No, Edward, I don't think that would be a good idea."

Mom had Dad well-trained. After we'd finished eating, he tried to help the women carry the dishes to the sink, but he was shooed back to his seat at the table. Aunt Dot told him in no uncertain terms that in the mountains, the men don't wash dishes. *That* remark caused my mother's eyebrows to lift so high they disappeared beneath her razor-cut bangs. Given no choice, Dad stayed at the table quietly talking with Great-Aunt Mary. Only now the conversation had turned not so quiet. I sensed an argument coming.

"But I won't disturb anything," Dad insisted. "I simply want to take a look around."

Great-Aunt Mary spun away from the table with the bowl of jelly resting on her lap. "No," she insisted again, "you don't know these mountains. A man could get lost and wander for days—"

"I won't get lost."

"Humph," she said, grabbing a jar and scraping the jelly into it. Her pale eyes fastened on me. "Sure seems your family has a problem sticking their noses in where they don't belong."

"Ah . . . " I stammered, trying to think of a response.

Dad saved me the trouble. "I was told there's a line of burial mounds that run through this valley. I just want to take a look at them."

Great-Aunt Mary wheeled to face him. "Have you ever thought, Edward, that there are some things best left alone?"

"I'm not afraid of spirits," my dad said quietly.

Shaking a finger, her lips tightened. "Maybe you should be. There are things in this valley that a Yankee like you couldn't possibly understand."

Please give it up, Dad, I thought. You're not going to win an argument with her. But my dad was Danish, and Danes never give up.

"I may be a Yankee, but I've been a historian for forty years, Mary. I've been to many places considered haunted and never suffered any ill effects."

"Well, there's a first time for everything," Great-Aunt Mary scoffed.

"But—"

"Are these mounds along ley lines, Grandpa?" Tink suddenly piped in.

Great-Aunt Mary's features relaxed when she turned her attention to Tink. "What are those, child?"

"Oh," Tink replied, flapping a dish towel, "lines of energy running through the earth. I read about them on the Internet." Her lavender eyes sparkled. "They've even mapped them out and discovered sacred sites built right on top of them."

"Sacred sites?" I asked.

"Yeah . . . it's really cool . . . churches, burial mounds, standing stones—"

Next to me, I heard Abby's quick intake of breath. Looking at her, I saw her lips clenched so tight a white line formed around her mouth. Her eyes were focused on Great-Aunt Mary, and again something passed between them. Great-Aunt Mary gave a slight shake of her head, and Abby seemed to deflate. Puzzled, I moved toward her, but she quickly crossed to the table and started vigorously wiping the worn surface.

"What did you say they're called, child?" Great-Aunt Mary asked, ignoring Abby.

"Ley lines," Tink replied.

Folding her hands in her lap, Great-Aunt Mary smiled. "We don't use fancy words around here, but Pappy Jens always said this valley's full of magick. It's one of the reasons he chose this spot." Wheeling back to the table, she positioned her chair next to Dad. "We've lots of things planned for y'all, Edward," she said sternly. "You're not going to have time to go traipsing around the mountains."

Dad shifted uneasily in his chair. He immediately had my sympathy. Would Great-Aunt Mary intimidate him enough for him to give up his plans?

Nope. I knew my father, and just maybe I'd go with him on his little jaunt. The idea of thwarting Great-Aunt Mary had a certain amount of appeal.

Her eyes traveled around the room like a general observing his troops. "Now, y'all need to unpack," she said, waving her hand at Tink, Abby, and me. "We're having lunch at Cousin Lydia's."

I stifled a groan. I didn't want to be impolite, but I honestly didn't think I could cram one more morsel of food into my mouth. Maybe they'd let me take a nap instead, I thought hopefully. Nah. I could see by the expression on Great-Aunt Mary's face that she wouldn't tolerate any insubordination from the ranks.

Three

Abby and I trudged back to the small bedroom we were sharing. Tink was camped out in the finished attic where she had stayed during her last visit. She loved it up there. She said looking out over the valley from the dormer windows gave her time to think, but I imagined it would also be a good spot for her to hide away from adults.

Once in the back bedroom, Abby and I got busy unpacking. The room contained two twin beds with old-fashioned iron headboards. Thick feather beds had been placed carefully over ancient mattresses and metal bedsprings. Sheets and pillowcases, softened by a thousand washes, had welcomed me late last night. Under the sheets and covered with a hand-stitched quilt, I'd nestled down and dropped into oblivion immediately.

When I'd commented on my sound sleep, as I was dragged up the mountain, Abby informed me that my quilt could be thanked for my restful night. The bold blue and yellow rosettes pieced together with muslin, now aged to a pale ivory, were really hex signs. The rosette was the sign for good luck . . . blue the color of protection, and yellow the color of health.

I looked at the bed now and wished I could crawl back in.

Abby saw my wistful look and gave me a quick poke in the ribs.

"You'd best get started," she said, opening the door to the armoire, or chifforobe as she called it.

Instantly, the room filled with the acrid scent of moth balls. Wrinkling my nose, I crossed the room and removed a couple of the wooden hangers. Tossing them on the bed, I hauled out my suitcase and began unpacking.

"You need to talk your father out of snooping around," Abby suddenly said.

I stopped. "You've got to be kidding," I replied with a snort. "If Dad wants to look at those burial mounds, he will." I paused and picked up another T-shirt. "You know . . . I think I might go with him and see—"

Abby's hand shot out and grabbed my wrist. "You can't," she exclaimed.

"Why not?"

Letting go, she shrugged. "It's like she said, people get lost."

"Oh come on, Dad's been exploring for years. He knows what he's doing," I said, and plopped down on the bed next to Abby's carry-on bag.

She crossed to the chifforobe and placed the hung clothes on the wooden rod. "I'm afraid I must *insist* you don't go wandering off, Ophelia," she ordered in a hard voice.

Irritated, I grabbed Abby's carry-on and unzipped it. "Are you going to tell me what the big deal is?"

I saw her shoulders tighten.

"What do you mean?" she asked without turning around.

"Look, it doesn't take a psychic to know something's up with you and Great-Aunt Mary. I saw that look you gave her at breakfast." I stuck my hand inside the bag and felt a sheaf of papers lying on top. Grasping them, I began to draw them out when she glanced at me over her shoulder.

"No." Abby whirled and rushed over to the bed. Snatching the carry-on, she slung it to the floor. "I'll take care of that."

Fisting a hand on my hip, I stared at her. What in the hell was going on? First she freaked when Great-Aunt Mary mentioned how long the homestead had been in the family, then again when Tink talked about ley lines. She didn't want Dad meandering around the valley, and now she didn't want me messing with her carry-on. My radar was on full alert. I clasped my hands in my lap and focused on a spot on the far wall, emptying all thoughts from my brain. With one deep, long breath I tried to reach out to her with my mind.

"It won't work," she said, laying a hand on my shoulder and breaking my concentration. "I've had a lot more years to practice keeping my thoughts to myself than you."

"Ugh," I exclaimed, and threw myself against the headboard. "Why won't you tell me what's going on?"

"There's nothing to tell, my dear," she replied calmly. "You're imagining it."

"Bull," I shot back, wrapping my arms around me. "You've been uptight all morning. You know I could do a rune reading to figure this out."

"To do a reading about me, without my permission, would be intrusive." She shook her head. "You wouldn't do that."

"Then tell me, so I won't have to."

Abby crossed to the window, drew back the plain curtains and opened it. Standing there, she took a deep breath of the fresh air now blowing into the room and chasing away the smell of the moth balls.

"I'm sorry if I seem nervous . . . " Her voice trailed away. "I told you this morning that being here has brought back a lot of memories . . . " She paused again. "Sadly, not all are pleasant."

Drawing my legs beneath me, I shifted on the bed. For a moment the only sound in the room was the creaking of the bedsprings.

She moved away from the window and faced me. Leaning back against the wall, she sighed. "What happened was a long time ago. It's over and done." She smiled faintly. "There's no reason for you to be concerned."

Narrowing my eyes, I studied her. She looked like she was telling the truth, but Abby was not only good at hiding her thoughts, she was an expert at hiding her feelings.

I was still thinking about whether to believe her when I heard the noise. At first I thought it was the bedsprings, but it didn't creak, it rattled.

Maybe something had fallen out of Abby's bag when she grabbed it and the breeze filling the room had suddenly sent it rolling across the uneven floorboards?

I cocked my head to listen but heard nothing. Scooting forward, I made the bed creak again and heard the sound.

Rattle, rattle, rattle.

Getting to my knees, I peered over the edge of the bed, but saw nothing.

Rattle, rattle, rattle. This time the sound was followed by a hissing noise, like air slowly escaping a tire.

Confused, I raised my head and looked at Abby. Her face had lost all of its color, and with arms flat at her sides, she stood plastered against the wall. An expression of pure horror had turned her green eyes dark.

"Abby!" I shrieked and started to swing my legs to the floor.

"No!" She held up a hand, stopping me. "Don't move—s-s-snake." Her voice was a harsh whisper.

Cautiously peeking over the edge, I saw it. Its triangular head swayed back and forth from just under the hem of the bed skirt while its forked tongue flicked the air. Slowly, slowly, its thick, round body began to undulate out from underneath the bed . . . straight toward Abby.

I stifled the scream rising from deep inside.

Oh my God, oh my God—I had to find a weapon! Looking madly around, my eyes searched for something, anything, I could use to bash the snake. The clock? No. The lamp? No. And what if I threw something and missed? What if I just pissed it off instead of killing it? Would it launch itself at Abby?

A cold sweat broke out all over my body as I watched

the snake move closer and closer to Abby. I had to do something. Ripping off my shoe, I was getting ready to hurl myself toward the snake and clobber it with the shoe when the door flew open. Great-Aunt Mary wheeled swiftly into the room and with one quick motion scooped up the snake with the crook of her cane and flung it past Abby, out the open window.

Four

The shaking finally stopped. My hand didn't even tremble as I lifted the cup filled with lemon balm tea to my lips. The fragrance of lemons soothed my nerves, and the hot liquid eased my tight throat. Finally trusting myself not to burst into tears, I looked at each of the women in the room. Aunt Dot fussing over Abby; Abby still white and trembling; Tink, her lavender eyes wide; and Great-Aunt Mary, sitting at the head of the table, much as she had during breakfast. Thank goodness Mom and Dad had already returned to Cousin Lydia's. I couldn't handle my mother right now.

With a voice still thick from fear, I asked the obvious.

"Want to explain how that rattlesnake got inside?"

Aunt Dot ignored me and became suddenly obsessed with wiping down the already clean countertop.

I focused on Great-Aunt Mary.

She lifted a bony shoulder. "This house is old. It has a lot of chinks needing to be filled." She looked over her shoulder. "Sister, remind me to ask Duane to do some caulking."

"Great-Aunt Mary, it was a *big* snake. I don't see how it could've crawled through a crack." Setting my cup down, I leaned forward. "And most snakes avoid humans, so why was he in the house?"

She laid her folded hands on the table. "The nights are

getting colder . . . the snake must have been looking for a warm place. He probably crawled in sometime last night."

I choked on my tea. "He was underneath the bed all night?"

"Possibly."

Great. I'd had my last restful sleep here. I could see it now—I'd be straining all night, listening for another telltale rattle.

Great-Aunt Mary read my expression. "Don't fret, Ophelia. I'll make sure a snake never enters this house again," she said firmly.

I thought of the conversation I'd overheard between Aunt Dot and Tink. "How? Ask your Nisse to be a little more alert?"

I knew I sounded disrespectful, but at that point I didn't care. Abby could've been seriously injured and the idea made me angry.

"For a fairy whose job it is to protect, he didn't do a very good job, did he?"

Aunt Dot whirled away from the counter and rushed over to me. "Oh, Ophelia, you mustn't say that. You'll offend him."

Right now I was more worried about getting bit by a snake than dealing with a ticked-off fairy, but Aunt Dot looked so concerned that I decided I'd been mouthy enough for one day and kept silent.

"Sister will lay a spell," she said with a nod.

Abby glanced up at Aunt Dot, then at me. "I think it would be best if we didn't share what happened this morning with Maggie and Edward," she said, changing the subject.

No kidding. Mom would faint and Dad would want to spend the night guarding our door with a shotgun. Which—when I thought about it—didn't seem like a bad idea.

I was puzzled, though. Cocking my head, I studied everyone again. Abby was a psychic with the gift of foreseeing the future. Aunt Dot communed with the fairies. Great-Aunt Mary and Tink received messages from beyond the veil.

And me? I seemed to have a talent for finding things. I was in a house full of women who all possessed a sixth sense, and not one of us foresaw any danger. Why?

But before I could voice my question, Great-Aunt Mary pushed away from the table and headed for the kitchen doorway. "It's nearing lunchtime—we need to get ready to walk to Cousin Lydia's."

I rose swiftly to my feet. "You're kidding, right?" I asked.

Great-Aunt Mary spun around. "I never kid," she replied bluntly.

That one I believed.

"Great-Aunt Mary, we've had a shock, especially Abby. You can understand why we may not be feeling too social right at the moment, can't you?"

"No. If you let all of life's little bumps upset you, a body'd never get anything done."

With that remark, she headed out the door.

I looked at Aunt Dot in bewilderment. A rattlesnake one of life's little *bumps*?

With a light pat on my cheek, she smiled. "Get used to it, child."

Dad had come back from Cousin Lydia's to help escort Great-Aunt Mary and Aunt Dot. The wheelchair left at home, both aunts strolled sedately on either side of my father, the wheels of their walkers leaving thin tracks in the dusty road. Abby had positioned herself on the outside, next to Great-Aunt Mary. Her hand rested lightly on Great-Aunt Mary's arm as the little procession made their way toward Cousin Lydia's. Tink and I brought up the rear, and in our hands we carried Aunt Dot's contributions to the luncheon—two homemade apple pies fresh from the oven. Wrapped in dish towels, I could feel their warmth while the aroma of apples and cinnamon followed us like a cloud.

"Hey," Tink said abruptly. "I've got a question."

"Okay, shoot," I replied, getting a tighter grip on the pie.

"Great-Aunt Mary and Aunt Dot are sisters . . . why don't we call Aunt Dot 'Great-Aunt Dot'?"

I gave a soft chuckle as I watched my elderly aunts toddle along head of us. "When I was your age, I asked Abby the same thing." Stealing a glance at Tink, I gave her a wide smile. "Aunt Dot doesn't like to be called a 'great-aunt.' She said it made her sound too old."

Tink's brows knitted in a frown. "But she's only nine years younger than Great-Aunt Mary."

"I know." Lifting a shoulder, I shrugged. "But that's the way it's always been. On the other hand, I think Great-Aunt Mary relishes her title of 'great-aunt.'"

"She's kind of formidable, isn't she?"

I snorted. "That's a nice way to put it," I said with a shake of my head. "You should've seen her go after that snake. I didn't know a woman her age could move that fast."

Tink glanced over at me, her eyes suddenly full of concern. "That must have been really scary. Are you okay?"

"Yeah," I replied, hooking my free hand through her arm, "but I'm worried about Abby. Do you think she's acting strange?"

Tink tilted her head and pursed her lips. "She didn't have much to say about the snake, but maybe she's been a little nervous."

"Did you notice her reaction when you mentioned ley lines?" I stared at Abby's straight back. "What do you know about them?"

"Not much," Tink replied, flipping her long hair over one shoulder. "They're lines of energy running through the earth. Some guy back in the 1920s mapped them out in Great Britain. He noticed that a lot of prehistoric sites, like Stonehenge and Avebury, were aligned with each other." She glanced at me, her eyes shining with excitement. "Here's the really cool thing, though. Wherever two lines intersect, there's a lot of poltergeist activity and UFO sightings."

"Do you really believe that stuff?" I scoffed.

She giggled and rolled her eyes. "Jeez, Ophelia. I'm a medium and my family is a bunch of witches. Why wouldn't I?"

I laughed. She had a point. In spite of the setting, we weren't exactly the Waltons.

When we arrived at Cousin Lydia's, the scene was a repeat of breakfast multiplied. Wide planks set on sawhorses and covered with checked tablecloths lined her yard. Ham, fried chicken, meat loaf, buttermilk biscuits, corn bread, bread and butter pickles, black-eyed peas, calico beans baked in a syrupy sauce, and more pies and cakes than I could count, bowed the tops of the makeshift tables. The air filled with the smell of home cooking, and my stomach growled in response.

So much for never wanting to eat again.

Women, in plain dresses or in cotton T-shirts and jeans hustled back and forth from the house to the tables, their hands laden with more food. A few of them stood at the tables, removing plastic wrap and aluminum foil while they shooed away marauding insects. Men, dressed in jeans, rough-spun shirts, ball caps, and work boots, sat in lawn chairs scattered about the yard, swapping tales and watching their womenfolk work. Occasionally one would rise and help fetch a heavy iron pot or a basket loaded with food.

As Tink and I added our offering, I noticed the women eyeing each new entry into the "who could cook the most" contest that seemed to be going on. It was as if they were gauging how their donations stacked up to everyone else's. I saw more than one eyebrow lift when a young woman, no more than eighteen, placed a bag of Doritos next to the pea salad. After she'd walked away, one of the women nudged the woman standing next to her.

"That Ruthie," she said, nodding toward the retreating girl, "I guess a new bride doesn't have much time for cookin'."

The group tittered in response.

Turning away from the table, I observed Great-Aunt Mary. Someone had placed a comfortable armchair from inside the house beneath one of the spreading elm trees, and she sat like a queen on a throne receiving the homage of various relatives.

Suddenly, out of the corner of my eye, I spied Aunt Dot, with a light of determination shining on her face, bearing down on me. I looked around for a place to hide but was too late. She grabbed my arm and pulled me from group to group. I heard so many names that my mind went into overload—I'd never be able to remember so and so, a cousin three times removed who married a great-great-great-niece of so and so on the Chisholm side.

A family tree? Dang, it was more like some kind of a vine meandering off in a dozen different directions. I couldn't keep it all straight. Not that I had to—it seemed my reputation preceded me, thanks no doubt to Aunt Dot. Instead of talking about how we were all related, the cousins were more interested in murder and mayhem.

"My land, did you really find a basement full of dead bodies?" one cousin queried.

"Um, yeah—"

"Did it stink?" a young man asked.

"Ah—"

"Getting shot? Does it hurt?" another piped in.

"Yes," I exclaimed.

"How many times you been kidnapped?"

"More than I care to be," I fired back.

I shot Aunt Dot a dirty look during my interrogation, but she was oblivious. She stood there, her wrinkled face wreathed in smiles, like she'd brought home a trophy.

Finally, my rescue arrived in the form of a blonde, about my height, with a soft southern voice and eyes that shifted in color as quickly as a cloud drifting across the moon.

She drew me over to the end of one table. "Here, darlin'," she said, pressing a glass filled with cold amber liquid into my hand. "It's sweet tea. You must be parched after answerin' all those questions."

I nodded and took a big gulp.

Holding out her hand, she smiled. "I'm Lydia Wiley, by the way. I'd try and explain how we're related, but I imagine you've heard enough of that for one day."

Returning her smile, I took her hand. I felt it instantly—a wave of warm, green, healing light wash over me. Closing my eyes for a second, I allowed myself to enjoy the sense of peace emanating from her.

"You're a healer, aren't you?" I asked as I let my eyes drift open.

Lydia's hand released mine and went to the medallion she wore around her neck. A rectangle of beaten silver with three swirls was engraved on its polished surface.

"Yes, mostly midwifing, treating colicky babies, colds, that sort of thing." She eyed young Ruthie, standing obediently at an older woman's side. "I expect I'll be attending that one," she said with a nod in Ruthie's direction.

I looked at Ruthie's flat stomach. "She's pregnant?"

Lydia bobbed her head and gave me a sly glance. "She is, but she doesn't realize it yet. About six weeks along, I think." She waved a hand toward the woman next to Ruthie. "Her mama-in-law is going to be thrilled. She's had 'grandma fever' for a long time."

"Lydia, do you mind if I ask you a personal question?" I asked with hesitation.

"Go right ahead, sweetie."

"Does it bother you knowing things about the people around you?"

Her chameleon eyes shifted from green to blue as they traveled from cousin to cousin. "Some. When I lay hands on a body, and I know the sickness is too deep." Her voice dropped low. "When I know not even a doctor with his city ways can help, it fills me with a bone deep weariness." She faced me. "But Great-Aunt Mary's helped me learn to live with it over the years."

I was shocked. "Great-Aunt Mary's helped?"

Lydia laughed. "Yes, darlin', I know. She's a persnickety one, isn't she? But she's done many kindnesses for the people of these mountains, even ones that don't hold with our ways." She paused and her eyes darkened. "I heard you had a run-in with a snake?"

"How did you know? Did you sense it?"

"There's other ways to learn things, other than tapping into somebody's mind," she replied, leaning close. "It's called good, ol'-fashioned gossip."

"Gossip, huh?"

"You bet," she answered with a chuckle. "Word around here travels faster than a grass fire in a high wind."

Huh, sounded like Summerset.

Taking Lydia's arm, I drew her away from the table. She was obviously very talented, maybe she could give me insight into why Abby was acting strangely.

"Lydia, I have another question for you," I began earnestly. "Since we've arrived, Abby hasn't been herself. I was wondering . . ."

A shutter seemed to fall across Lydia's pleasant face and her eyes turned a cloudy gray. "Honey, you won't be doing your grandmother any favors by digging up the past."

Five

The rest of the day passed uneventfully. The cousins seemed to accept their Northern relatives and to forgive us for the fact that, except for Abby, we hadn't been born and raised in the South. Their curiosity finally trickled off. I kept stealing glances Abby's way, but she appeared relaxed and happy to connect with family she hadn't seen in years.

Cousin Lydia's remark gnawed at me for the rest of the afternoon, though. What did these people know that I didn't? Looking at their faces, I debated about dropping my mental shield and doing a little probing. See what I might sense. But I couldn't do it. As Abby always pointed out, tiptoeing through someone's head wasn't nice. So as the sun made its arc across the valley, I smiled and tried to ignore the questions lurking in the corners of my brain.

When the shadows had grown and chased away the afternoon warmth, Great-Aunt Mary rose, grasped her walker, and announced it was time to go home. Abby, Tink, and I offered to stay and help Cousin Lydia clean up, but she pooh-poohed us away with a "Y'all must be tired."

Our little group trooped home the way we'd come—our hands heavy with foil-wrapped leftovers. Once at the house, we stored them in the already brimming refrigerator and the five of us settled down in the living room. Great-Aunt Mary picked up her crocheting, flicked on the TV, and the room filled with the sound of Clint Eastwood's distinctive snarl. With a contented sigh from both of them, the Aunts leaned back to watch *Dirty Harry* while their needles clicked a steady rhythm.

Ignoring the action on the screen, my eyes traveled around the room. This household was such a contradiction . . . two elderly women living alone, following the ways of those who'd gone before. They cooked on a wood-burning stove, preserved their own food, and used kerosene lamps, yet watched satellite TV. It was a homey scene. Tink sat at Great-Aunt Mary's feet, leaning back against her chair, as intent on *Dirty Harry* as the Aunts. Abby rested in an armchair across the room, slightly removed from the group, studying the sheaf of papers that I'd noticed in her carry-on. With her reading glasses perched on the end of her nose, every so often she'd frown and scribble in the margin. Were they new pages for her journal? She caught me watching her and a faint smile tugged at her lips before she returned to her papers.

Resting my head on the back of the couch, I closed my eyes and let the noise carry me away.

In the dream, I felt an awareness of coming home centered deep inside me as I moved effortlessly through the woods. The feeling hummed through my whole body, down my thighs, my legs, into my arms, and out my fingertips. If I could have seen myself, I knew that I'd be glowing with the intensity of what I felt. I didn't know where I was going, but like iron drawn to a magnet, I was pulled to a spot at the far end of the valley. Emerging from the trees, I saw it—a glade at the base of the mountain.

Water cascaded down the slope and into a crystal clear pool. Beneath its surface, fish darted, their scales catching the fading light in flashes of blue and green. Dragonflies with wings spun of gold and silver darted through the air.

And around the pool were flowers—hundreds of flowers. Foxglove, black-eyed Susans, wild lilacs, grew in profusion, and their light, airy scent washed over me.

Across the clearing stood a circle of seven red stones that seemed to glow with a light of their own. The slabs rose out of the ground like standing sentinels, with heavy lintels joining one to the other. It reminded me of a small Stonehenge. From the center of the circle came the lilting voice of a woman singing an old folk song.

I drifted closer.

She sat, with her legs tucked under her, on a blanket spread out on the grass. Her shining cap of mahogany hair blocked her features as her head dipped to stare at the small child curled up on the blanket. As she sang, she stroked the little girl's hair . . . hair the same shade as hers. From the corner of the blanket an old dog sprawled, watching her. He, too, listened to the young woman's song.

The scene was so lovely, so calm, that I longed to be a part of it. With a desire so sharp it hurt, I wanted nothing more than to curl up on the blanket and let the young woman's song wash over me, too. I moved across the threshold of the circle.

I felt as if I'd been hit with a bolt of electricity. The glade disappeared. I was on my feet, staring wildly around Great-Aunt Mary's living room. The sound of the woman's song had vanished, replaced by squealing tires and gunshots reverberating from the TV.

"Land sakes, child," Aunt Dot cried over the noise as Abby and Tink rushed to my side.

Suddenly the only sound I heard was the pounding of blood in my ears. My vision blurred.

Abby's voice penetrated the fog. "Ophelia, look at me," she commanded.

I fought to focus on her face wavering before mine. Finally the beating in my ears receded and my eyes cleared. Taking a deep breath, I sank to the couch.

"Wow," I hissed.

Abby and Tink sat on either side of me, and as I inhaled deeply again, Abby stroked my hair, in much the same way the woman in the glade had caressed the child.

"Did you have a bad dream?" she asked.

Pressing my fingertips to my forehead, I shook my head. "No, it was a terrific dream, until I crossed into the circle," I muttered.

Abby looked concerned. "What circle?"

"The stone circle . . . " I paused, trying to recall all the details. "A woman and a child . . . a yellow dog."

Feeling the weight of everyone's eyes upon me, I dropped my hands. The light from the now silent TV flickered wildly on all their faces. Great-Aunt Mary sat rigidly in her chair, the remote grasped tightly in her hand, while Aunt Dot stared at me with concern written on her face. I glanced at Tink. Her eyes were troubled. I gave her a tiny grin and the look faded.

And Abby? She sat ramrod straight with her hands gripped tightly in her lap, no longer looking at me.

"Abby?" I began, with my voice full of questions.

"It's bedtime," Great-Aunt Mary announced, cutting me off. "Ophelia, you obviously ate too much rich food today. I suggest you not eat so much tomorrow."

I almost laughed. Since she'd been one of the ones shoving food at me all day, I found her remark ironic.

Abby immediately rose and crossed the room to help Great-Aunt Mary to her feet. I watched as Great-Aunt Mary laid a hand on Abby's cheek and the tension seemed to ooze out of Abby.

Taking her walker from Abby, she turned, and with Aunt Dot right behind her, both sisters toddled out of the room and down the hall to their respective bedrooms.

"Abby—" I began again after they'd left.

"Oh my, all this fresh mountain air has made me tired, too," she interrupted, giving a wide stretch. "I think I'll head off to bed." She pivoted and gave me a big smile.

I eyed her skeptically. "Aren't you worried about more snakes?"

"Don't be silly," she replied with a dismissive wave of her hand. "Another snake wouldn't dare enter this house." She looked at Tink. "What about you, dear? Are you going to bed?"

Tink rose and shoved her hands in her pockets. "Not to sleep. I think I'll go up to the attic and read." She glanced over her shoulder at me. "Are you going to be okay?"

Crossing to her, I threw my arms around her shoulders and gave her a big hug and a peck on the cheek. "I'm fine. Great-Aunt Mary was probably right . . . too much food." I gave her a playful swat on her bottom. "Don't stay up too late reading."

With a grin, she skipped away from me. "I won't," she called out as she headed up the stairs.

I followed Abby back to the bedroom and watched as she gathered her nightgown and robe. Leaning against the doorjamb, I crossed my arms and waited for her to turn around.

"What?" she said.

"I'm not stupid," I replied cryptically.

"Of course you aren't, dear. You're a very bright woman," she said as she moved to go around me.

Reaching out, I tugged on her sleeve, stopping her. "If you're not going to explain what's going on, I'll find out for myself," I threatened.

Abby's face lost some of its color, and I felt a pang of guilt.

"Just leave it alone," she said in a quiet voice as she twisted out of my grasp and headed toward the bathroom.

Frustrated, I crossed the room and sat down hard on the bed. Remembering the snake, I yanked my legs underneath me and scrubbed my face in my hands as I thought about Cousin Lydia's warning. I'd never do anything to hurt Abby, and my questioning was definitely making her uncomfortable. Everyone had a right to their secrets, didn't they? And evidently Abby had a few of her own.

I dropped my hands and stared off into space, thinking.

Maybe her discomfort had something to do with the circumstances of her parents' marriage? During Aunt Dot's visit to Iowa, I'd learned that Annie, Abby's mother, had forced her father to let her marry Robert Campbell by getting pregnant. There was a lot of censure attached to that back in the thirties, and Abby hadn't appreciated Aunt Dot letting *that* skeleton out of the closet.

That had to be what was making her uncomfortable, I thought, standing. She was afraid Aunt Dot would start telling tales again.

Satisfied that I'd solved the riddle, I moved to the dresser and pulled open a drawer to grab a pair of sweatpants and a T-shirt.

"Damn it," I cried as I rummaged through my clothes.

I couldn't believe my eyes . . . every T-shirt, every stitch of underwear, had been turned wrong side out and tied into knots.

Six

"Would you look at this mess?" I exclaimed, grabbing one of the T-shirts and pulling at the knot.

"What is it?" Abby, now dressed in her nightgown, stood in the doorway, her long silver hair half braided for the night.

"Someone was here while we were gone."

She crossed the room to my side. "Impossible."

"Oh, yeah?" I replied sarcastically, and held up one of the shirts. "Then explain this?"

Her eyes widened in surprise. "Your clothes are all in knots."

"No kidding. And unless there's something about Great-Aunt Mary that we don't know about, someone—"

Aunt Dot, appearing in the doorway, interrupted me. She entered the room and came to stand next to Abby. "Is something wrong, child?"

Silently, I held up another knotted T-shirt.

Her face blanched. "Oh my," she exclaimed. "I knew you'd offended him."

"Who?" I asked, throwing the T-shirt down in disgust. "I've been here less than twenty-four hours. Even for me, that's not enough time to tick someone off."

"Our Nisse," she whispered. "He heard what you said."

"Huh?"

A stubborn look settled on Aunt Dot's face. "You accused him of failing to protect the house."

"Oh, for Pete's sake," I cried, rolling my eyes. "I don't believe this is the work of some silly little fairy. Don't you think it's possible someone slipped in while we were gone? The house wasn't locked, was it?"

"Of course not," she huffed, "we never lock the doors."

"Well then." I looked down at my tangled clothes. "Obviously someone's been here. Any suspects?"

Abby's eyes darted toward Aunt Dot, but she missed Abby's look. Instead, she picked up one of the shirts and began untying the knot.

"Ack . . . " She paused, looking at the shirt thoughtfully. "Maybelle's youngest, Caleb, does have a peculiar sense of humor. He might have thought it funny to play a little joke on y'all."

I didn't know which idea I liked better—an offended Nisse or a fourth cousin ten times removed rummaging through my underwear. Neither scenario brought much comfort.

Crossing to my bed, I grabbed the quilt and a pillow then tucked my sweatpants and T-shirt under my arm. I headed for the door.

"Where are you going?" Abby asked as I brushed past her.

"I'm sleeping on the couch."

"You can't," Aunt Dot said, following me from the room. "That old davenport's lumpier than day old oatmeal. You won't sleep."

"Don't care," I called over my shoulder. "If I'm on the couch, it's going to be harder for someone to slip into the house undetected." I stopped and turned around. "And Aunt Dot, do you think you could at least lock the doors?"

"Well . . . I don't know . . . " She cast a nervous glance at Abby, still standing in the doorway to the bedroom. "I suppose maybe we'd better."

I marched down the hallway, and, after turning on the small lamp located on the end table, dumped the bedding onto the couch. Picking up my night clothes, I went to the bathroom and changed. Not trusting Aunt Dot to lock up, I checked all the windows and doors in the main part of the house to make sure they were secure. Satisfied, I crossed to the kitchen, my bare feet slapping on the hardwood floor.

Hanging on the wall, next to the wood-burning stove, was a nice heavy poker.

Grabbing it, I returned to my makeshift bed and plopped down. With a quick look around the softly lit room, I turned off the light and pulled the quilt up to my chin.

"All righty, then," I murmured to myself as I cradled the poker to my chest. "Just let anyone try and sneak in *now.*"

Little fingers of energy pricked at the edges of my mind, beckoning me to leave my dreamless sleep behind. As my eyes slowly opened to a room soft with shadows, I realized what had pulled me awake.

Magick. It lurked in those shadows, drifting around me in currents that caused my senses to tingle. The last remnants of sleep fled. A low voice came from the kitchen, muttering words I couldn't quite make out. I scooted to the edge of the couch and peeked around the corner of its overstuffed arm.

Aunt Dot stood by the table facing a young woman. Dressed in a frayed bathrobe, the mellow light of a kerosene lamp turned Aunt Dot's hair into a blue halo. Whispering softly, she moved an object held in her hand deliberately over the young woman's body. I watched while she traced the girl's head, neck, shoulders, and each arm. Stopping for a moment, she shuffled behind the girl and repeated the process down the girl's back. When she reached the base of the girl's spine, she grasped a chair, and with a small groan, lowered herself to her knees. She then moved the object down the girl's legs—all the time continuing her whispers. When she'd finished, the young woman turned and helped Aunt Dot to her feet. In silence, Aunt Dot pressed the object into her waiting hands.

The magick around me spiked and I shivered.

She left the girl standing at the table and hobbled over to the Hoosier cupboard. Opening a drawer, she removed a square of black material and spread it out carefully on the counter's surface. Next she lifted two glass jars down from the shelves and unscrewed the metal lids. Instantly, the air seemed to fill with the scent of herbs. Dipping into each jar, she gently placed a small amount of each one in the center of the material. She finished the process by sprinkling the concoction with black pepper. After drawing the corners together, she wrapped a thin strand of black yarn around the top, tying it off into a little bag. She bowed her head.

With a whoosh, I felt the magick gathered in the room rush toward her. Swaying, she raised her head and tilted it back, as if she were absorbing all that energy and forcing it into the small black pouch.

Slowly, the magick eased to a trickle, then nothing. Satisfied, Aunt Dot turned and crossed to the young woman, now sitting at the table.

"Here," she said, offering the pouch to the girl, "wear this next to your heart."

A look of apprehension flitted across her face. "Should I put it on a string around my neck?"

Aunt Dot cackled. "Ack, no," she exclaimed. "Your mother will skin you if she catches you wearing a conjure bag."

"What should I do?" she asked.

"Stuff it in your bra," Aunt Dot replied in an even voice. "Put it on the left side."

The young woman bobbed her head, and I heard the rustle of clothing.

"What do I do with the egg?"

"On your way home, smash it in the center of the cross-roads." Aunt Dot wagged her finger in the young woman's face. "And don't look back . . . keep walking."

The girl nodded as she rose to her feet. "I really appreciate this, Miss Dot." She shuffled her feet. "Don't know when I can pay you."

Aunt Dot laid a hand on the girl's shoulder. "Don't worry about it, child."

"Maybe I can bring you and Miss Mary a bag of nutmeats?" she asked with a hopeful note in her voice. "There's a mess of black walnuts on the ridge."

"That'd be fine," Aunt Dot replied gently, dropping her hand.

The girl dipped her head. "I don't know what I was thinking."

In the dim light, I saw Aunt Dot's lips tighten. "You've lived in these mountains long enough to know she's one to avoid."

"I know," she said with a lift of her chin, "but I wanted Billy to notice me so bad." She ended with a plaintive note in her voice. "It seemed the only way."

"Love spells backfire."

The girl gave a snort. "Don't I know it. Now I can't shuck him. Follows me around all the time with big moony eyes." Her shoulders shivered. "It gives me the creeps . . ." Her voice trailed away as she stared off into space. "I begged her to undo the spell, but first she just laughed at me, then she got mad. Ever since, I've felt like there's a black cloud following me around, just like Billy." She shook her head. "It's more than a body can handle."

Aunt Dot took the girl's arm and began to lead her to the door. "This won't end Billy's infatuation, but if you do what I've told you, it will get rid of the hex."

The girl pulled up short. "But what do I do about Billy?"

"That is a problem. You'd best just stay away from him until her spell tires out."

"Then I can't go nowhere," she whined with a stamp of her foot. "I'll have to stay home with Ma all the time."

"I'm afraid, child," Aunt Dot said in a kind voice, "that's the price you'll pay for trying to control another person with magick."

"It don't seem right," she replied.

"Neither is stealing a person's free will," Aunt Dot answered, tugging her toward the door. "Don't fret . . . her magick's weak . . . it'll wear off. I just hope you've learned something."

"I have—I surely have," the young woman cried as she opened the door. "I'm staying away from Billy *and* that witch!"

Hearing the door slam, I ducked my head back and quickly shut my eyes as the shadows crossed the room. Carrying the lamp, Aunt Dot was headed back to her bedroom, and I didn't want her to know I'd witnessed her performing magick. Once I knew it was safe, I opened my eyes and stared at the ceiling.

All my life, Abby had told me stories of the mountain and the women who'd lived here. I knew all about my great-grandmother, Annie, and what an amazing healer she'd been. I knew about Flora and her ability to call the weather, Aunt Dot with her fairies and potions, Great-Aunt Mary and her spirits. But never once had Abby mentioned a witch in our family handing out love spells and manipulating others, a practice definitely against our family's code of behavior.

Why?

Seven

The next morning after breakfast dishes were finished, I stole out onto the back porch. The two tabby cats watched me with narrowed eyes from the porch swing as if they were trying to figure out whether I was good for a hand-out. Seeing that I held nothing in my hands, they curled their tails around their fluffy bodies as their eyes slowly closed.

I turned away from the cats and looked out over the valley. I went over the past twenty-four hours—snakes, angry fairies, and midnight visitors . . . I thought my life in Iowa was weird. Who would've expected this peaceful valley to contain so much drama? I didn't know how two little old ladies, living alone, stood the excitement.

The sound of a high-pitched giggle broke into my thoughts. Tink and Dad were prowling around underneath the old willow tree that grew by the barn. They walked slowly in circles, heads bent while they kicked the leaves at their feet. Every so often one would crouch and examine the ground. Maybe Dad was giving Tink some pointers on how he went about finding arrowheads? Intending to join them, I took one step toward the edge of the porch when the screen door slammed. I pivoted toward the sound.

"Ophelia," my mother called, "where are you going?"

"I thought I'd go see what Dad and Tink are doing," I said

with a wave toward the barn. Glancing back, I saw that Tink and Dad had disappeared. Shrugging, I turned toward my mother. "Forget it. They're gone."

Mom crossed to the porch swing and, after shooing away one of the cats, sat. Patting the weathered boards, she looked up and smiled. "Why don't you come sit with me? I'd like to talk to you."

Oh, goody. Parenting advice. I stifled my groan and joined her on the swing.

A thin plume of steam rose from the heavy cup Mom held in her hand, and for a moment we just sat there, slowly swinging back and forth and enjoying the brisk mountain air.

"Mother and the Aunts are going visiting this morning," she said, breaking the silence. "Are you joining them?"

"No. I thought I'd hang out here. It's been an exciting twenty-four hours and I'm a little overwhelmed right now. I need some time by myself."

"Well, if you change your mind, Lydia and I are going to the General Store this afternoon."

"Maybe," I replied, without making a commitment.

"I heard about what happened to your clothes," she said abruptly.

Mother surprised me. She didn't want to pass out advice after all. Nope, she wanted to talk about fairies.

My mouth twisted in a wry grin as I shook my head. "Aunt Dot's Nisse."

With a smile, she nodded. "You don't believe in them?"

"No," I replied with a quick glance over my shoulder. "Do you?"

She didn't answer immediately. Taking a sip of her coffee, her eyes roamed the yard. "I don't deny that anything is possible," she finally said. "Not possessing a gift myself, all my life I've tried to understand Mother's talents . . ." She paused while she focused on me. ". . . and yours. Finally, I gave up. My approach is just to ignore this family's peculiarities."

"What about Dad? How did he feel marrying into a family of witches?" I asked.

Mom's expression tightened. "He obviously handled it better than Andrew," she replied, referring to my own ill-fated engagement so many years ago. Her face softened. "No, your father has always been a remarkable man. One of the things that drew me to him was his curiosity, his sense of wonder. It's what makes him such a good historian and a good man." She gave a slight lift of her shoulder. "Finding out that magick does exist and that there's more to life than what we see has always delighted him."

"Did he ever meet Abby's mother, Grandma Annie?"

"No, she passed away when I was eighteen." Mom warmed her hands on her cup. "Grandma Annie was wonderful. I loved coming here when I was a kid," she murmured. "She made the best biscuits and gravy." A small smile played across her face. "I can still see her standing at the stove, stirring the gravy and humming."

"Did you visit often?"

"We did when Grandma was alive, but the visits were shorter and more sporadic after she died. Mother adored her, and I think it was hard for her to come back without Grandma here."

"Abby talks about her a lot . . . they must've been very close," I commented.

"They were. I only heard harsh words pass between them once."

"Really? When?"

"It was on one of our last visits. Mother wanted Grandma Annie to move to Iowa and live with us. When she refused, they got into it."

"Grandma Annie won?"

"Yes. I remember her saying that no matter what the future held, she was born in the mountains and she'd die in the mountains." Mom gave a small grin. "It's one of the few times I've seen anyone get the best of Mother."

"Abby never mentioned how Grandma Annie died."

"I know . . . she never talks about it." She turned on the swing and faced me. "I don't know if Grandma saw her own death or what, but one day she just took to her bed. A week later, she was gone."

"That's it?"

She nodded. "Mother was so upset when we came back for the funeral—"

"I'm sure she was grieving," I interrupted.

"It was more than simple grief." Mom blew on her coffee and took another drink. "It was as if she carried this black rage inside, waiting to be unleashed. Everyone could sense it, even me."

"But Abby's always had great control over her emotions," I interjected.

"Not this time. She finally blew up at Great-Aunt Mary."

"You're kidding?" I couldn't imagine anyone, even Abby, ever taking on Great-Aunt Mary. "Do you know what the fight was about?"

"Not really. It happened the night after Grandma's funeral. I was in bed, in the attic where Tink's sleeping now, and they were in the kitchen." Mom tugged on her bottom lip before she continued. A frown drew her brows together. "I heard their voices through the floor, but I couldn't make out everything they were saying. I was too scared to even sneak over to the grate and eavesdrop."

"So you don't know what the argument was about?"

"Not really. From the snippets I heard, it seemed that Mother wanted to do something, and Great-Aunt Mary didn't approve."

"But you don't know what it was?"

She shook her head. "No. I did ask Mother about it the next morning, but she told me in no uncertain terms to drop it, so I did." Mom sighed. "We left a couple of days later and the incident was forgotten."

"It never came up again?"

"No."

"Has she ever mentioned anyone in the family doing love spells?"

Mom's eyes flew to my face. "What?" she asked in a shocked voice.

I explained the scene I'd witnessed last night in the kitchen. When I was finished, Mom chuckled.

"A 'back door Betty.'"

"Huh?" I asked, perplexed.

"'Back door Betty's and Bobby's.' That's what the Aunts call them. They're folks from around here who say they don't believe in magick, yet when they're in a pickle, they don't have a problem asking one of the Aunts or cousins for help . . . " Mom paused as she pushed the swing slowly with her foot. " . . . just as long as their *neighbors* don't find out they're going to the witch woman."

"They sneak over in the middle of the night—"

"And rap at the back door," Mom said, finishing my sentence. "Hence 'back door Betty or Bobby.' Then in a couple of days there'll be some kind of payment, again left in the middle of the night, by the back door."

"I heard the girl say something about a bag of nutmeats," I replied, remembering what I'd heard.

"Right. People around here don't have a lot of cash, so they pay any way they can—a cord of wood, a dozen eggs, vegetables from their gardens, whatever they think the witch can use." Mom's face grew serious. "Evidently this girl thought she was hexed?"

"Um-hmm," I said slowly. "She'd asked for a love spell then changed her mind when it didn't work out like she'd thought it would—"

"'Be careful what you wish for,'" Mom muttered.

"Exactly. I guess her lack of gratitude made the witch angry—" I broke off, remembering what Aunt Dot had told the girl about the unnamed witch's magick. "Do you think one of the cousins has gone against the family's tradition?"

Mom shook her head swiftly. "Absolutely not. Everyone shares Mother's attitude . . . you don't mess with a person's free will. And," she said stridently, "I've never heard of any-one in the family putting a curse on someone."

"Yeah, but what if one of them tried?" I asked persistently.

Mom shifted on the swing and looked at me, one eyebrow raised. "Do you really think Great-Aunt Mary would allow that?"

"No," I replied, my tone short. "So if Aunt Dot wasn't talking about one of the cousins, it means there are other witches in these mountains."

"That would be my assumption."

"Have you ever heard stories about *another* family practicing magick?"

"No."

I leaned toward her. "Wouldn't it be interesting to know if there is?"

My mother smiled.

Eight

I forced myself to relax and enjoy the afternoon. Abby and the Aunts were still out visiting, and Tink and Dad were off to who knows where. I sat on the porch swing once again, dressed in comfy sweatpants, my old University of Iowa sweatshirt, and tennis shoes, debating whether to read the latest Mary Wine romance or Angie Fox's demon slayer, both buried in my carry-on. Hmm, hot sex or hot adventure? Maybe neither and a nap instead. I'd almost made up my mind when a Chevy SUV came rambling up the back road in a cloud of dust and stopped.

Cousin Lydia.

The car door slammed and she walked to the front of the SUV. Shading her eyes, she called out, "Y'all come with us, darlin'. We're headed down to the General Store."

I searched for an excuse not to go but came up empty.

"Okay," I replied with some reluctance. "Give me a chance to change."

I ran in the house and back to the bedroom. After changing into jeans and a decent T-shirt, I flew into the bathroom. As I twisted my hair and anchored it in place with a clip, I took a quick peek at myself in the mirror. I really should slap on some makeup, I suppose, I thought. Nah . . . it's not like anyone around here knows me. Satisfied I looked okay—maybe not great, but okay—I joined Mom and Lydia.

As we bumped along the mountain road, I considered asking Cousin Lydia about other witches living in the area, but decided against it. I'd leave it to Mom to ferret out the information. She could be far more subtle than I.

Twenty minutes later Cousin Lydia pulled to a stop in front of Abernathy's General Store. Three other buildings sat at the little crossroads, a post office, Maybelle's Beauty Shop, and a Shell gas station. Food, gas, beauty supplies, and their mail—the crossroads was a one stop shop. And from the beat-up pickups and SUVs gathered in the parking lots, I could see many of the mountain's residents did just that.

Abernathy's was housed in a wooden building, and its weathered boards looked like they'd received their last coat of paint about twenty years ago. Wide steps led to a broad porch littered with rustic chairs and benches. Several elderly men dressed in bib overalls had gathered there, and as I exited Lydia's SUV, I couldn't help smiling to myself. It's the same no matter where you go. Back home we referred to old men like the ones swapping tales on the porch as the "Liars' Club." Without even listening to them, I knew they were exchanging gossip and trying to top each other with stories of what was happening in the valley. And in each telling, the rumor would be exaggerated until one couldn't recognize the original story.

Shaking my head, I followed Mom and Lydia through the glass door and into the store. Instantly, the sweet smell of feed and the aroma of herbicide mixed with wood smoke hit me. A Ben Franklin stove sat in the middle of the large room, dividing the store into two parts. On the right, housewares and canned food lined the high shelves. On the left, farm and gardening supplies. Wooden barrels filled with peanuts and root vegetables sat on the floor next to a long counter stretching the length of the building. Near the antique cash register, similar to the one Abby used in her greenhouse, sat large glass jars with pickled pigs' feet and hard-boiled eggs swimming in brine.

Several women dressed in jeans, with baskets on their arms, milled up and down the long counter, visiting as they looked over the wares. Another woman stood in front of the bread rack, squeezing loaves of bread as she tried to find the freshest one. Toward the back, two women fingered the bolts of bright cotton print, plain muslin, and polyester.

Cousin Lydia led us up to the counter. "Miz Abernathy, I'd like you to meet my cousins from up North," she said to the stick thin woman standing behind the counter.

The woman settled her thick glasses on her nose and looked us up and down.

"This is Mrs. Margaret Mary Jensen, Abby's girl, and her daughter Ophelia," Lydia said pleasantly.

Mrs. Abernathy focused on me. "Not married, are you," she stated.

"Ah, no ma'am," I mumbled, surprised at her forthrightness.

"Following in the footsteps of your Great-Aunt Mary, heh?"

My surprise turned to shock. I was nothing like Great-Aunt Mary. Great-Aunt Mary was spooky and struck fear into the hearts of small children. That was not *me*. Shooting a stricken look at Cousin Lydia, I silently pleaded for her help.

Chuckling, she took a step closer to me. "Why Miz Abernathy, things are different now days, especially up North. Women don't marry so young." She turned and gave me a big smile. "And besides, Ophelia isn't on the shelf yet."

Mrs. Abernathy switched tactics and turned her attention to my mother. "Miz Jensen, is your mother visiting, too?"

"Of course," Mom replied in an easy voice. "We're all here to celebrate Great-Aunt Mary's birthday. Why do you ask?"

Mrs. Abernathy crossed her arms over her thin chest. "I'm surprised your mother came, that's all."

Mom's face tightened. "And why is that?"

Mrs. Abernathy's eyes darted to Cousin Lydia then back to Mom. "Well, after Miz Annie died, your mother never seemed to have much use for family ties."

Uh-oh, I sensed a battle brewing as Mom's shoulders went back and I could almost see her hackles rise.

"Excuse me for contradicting you, Mrs. Abernathy," Mom said with bite in her tone. "Family's always been important to my mother and—"

The tinkling of the bell over the door interrupted her as Mrs. Abernathy's attention shifted to the person standing in the doorway. Her face washed white, and to my ears, it seemed the chattering in the store suddenly stopped.

"You'll excuse me," she said quickly, "Janice needs my help with the material."

With that she hustled down to the end of the counter and the women looking over the bolts of fabric, leaving Cousin Lydia, Mom, and me standing alone.

In fact, everyone seemed to withdraw from us.

Confused, I turned to the woman still standing by the door. Tall, thin, and about my age, her dark brown hair framed a face with prominent cheekbones—she was pretty in an exotic way. Our eyes met and hers flamed with anger as a sneer curled her lips.

What's up with her? I thought, my eyebrows knitting together. I'd never seen her before in my life, so why was she pissed off at me?

Cousin Lydia, tugging on my arm, broke into my thoughts.

"Come on, let's go," she hissed at me.

Before I could reply, a man strode up to the woman.

"Sharon Doran, you can tell that no good uncle of yours I don't appreciate him cheating me," the man spat out at her.

As he spoke, I felt the room swamp with tension. The woman switched her attention from me to the man standing at her side.

"I don't know what you mean, Oscar." Her voice had a dangerous edge.

"That cow he delivered yesterday. It wasn't the one I bought—he pulled a switch on me." His face turned an angry red. "And if he don't make it right, I'll call the law."

She turned halfway until she faced the man. Taking one step, she got in his face. "I don't think you want to do that," she threatened.

The man deflated before my eyes. Lowering his head, he muttered something but was too far away for me to make out his words. He dodged around her and stumbled out the door.

As he did, a slow smile spread across the woman's face.

She looked at me again, and the next thing I knew, she headed straight for me.

Cousin Lydia gave my arm another tug, but I shook her off. Holding my ground, I intended to find out what this woman wanted with me.

She marched up to me, but before she could speak, Cousin Lydia stepped between us.

"Sharon, there's no need—" she started to say, but the woman cut her off.

"Stay out of this, Lydia," she barked, stepping around her. "You." She jabbed a finger at me. "You tell your doddering old aunt to stay out of my business."

I guess I knew who the rival witch was now.

Drawing myself to all of my five-foot-four height, I stared at her. *"Who are you?"*

She tossed her head and let out a raw laugh. "Stick around these mountains long enough and you'll find out."

Immediately, I sensed my mother moving to my side.

"Young woman—" she began, her voice dripping ice.

When this Sharon focused her attention on my mother, her eyes narrowed. "And *you* tell your murdering mother to get the hell out of here, or she'll finally pay for what she did."

Did she say "murdering"?

My mouth dropped open, but before I could snap it shut, Cousin Lydia grabbed my arm and my mother's and pulled us toward the door.

"She called Abby—" I gasped as Lydia hauled us out of the store.

"Never mind," Lydia interrupted. "Everyone knows the Dorans are all crazy."

She hustled us out the door and into the bright sunshine. Squinting against the sudden light, I looked around and tried to gather my thoughts. As I did, I spotted a group of men gathered by one of the old pickups bearing a Confederate flag. There was something familiar about one of the men . . . something about the way he carelessly stood talking with the other men . . . about the way he wore his hair tied back in a ponytail.

Oh my God, it couldn't be.

I pulled away from Lydia and took one step toward him.

He turned and, seeing me, a look of total shock crossed his face. Recovering himself, he gave his head a slight shake and pivoted, putting his back toward me.

I spun around, and muttering a line from *Casablanca*, joined Mom and Lydia waiting for me by the SUV.

"What did you say?" Mom asked.

"'Of all the gin joints, in all the towns'—" I started to repeat the line then stopped. "Oh never mind, Mom, you wouldn't believe me if I told you."

Glancing over my shoulder one last time, I saw Sharon Doran exit the store. She strolled over to the group of men, and my mouth fell open once again as she possessively took the arm of the man I'd been staring at. Then he looked down at her and smiled a smile he'd once given to me, and I felt a pang of jealousy slam my heart.

With a shake of my head, I climbed into the backseat of Lydia's SUV, and as we drove away, the crazy woman's accusations were forgotten and only one thought bounced around in my head . . .

What in the hell was Cobra doing in these mountains?

Nine

The drive back to the house began in silence. I sat in the backseat, trying to get over the shock at finding Cobra, aka Ethan Clement, DEA agent, in the mountains of North Carolina. And not just any mountains, *my* mountains.

The last time I'd run into Ethan had been when he helped rescue Tink from the clutches of two kidnappers. I knew, since that time, he'd kept tabs on me via information from our sheriff, Bill Wilson. In way of explanation, Ethan had said he wanted to make sure I didn't fall off my broom. Ha ha, quite a wit, that Ethan. But in spite of his teasing ways and unpredictability, I couldn't help liking him.

"Humph." I gave a soft snort. "Let's be honest, Jensen—it goes a bit beyond liking," I muttered to myself.

And it did. I found Ethan very attractive, and obviously so did Sharon Doran. Who wouldn't? Tall, with a broad chest and lean hips, he wore his jeans very well. And then his eyes . . . gunmetal gray, cold as an ice storm at times, yet they could flare with a heat that could hit like a fist in the gut.

My thoughts brought me back to Sharon Doran. Based on what she said about keeping Aunt Dot out of her business, she had to be the witch handing out love spells, and it was obvious that she hated my family, Abby in particular. Why? Was it that she saw our family as "business competitors"?

And why had Abby never mentioned her or the Dorans in all her tales about the mountains? I didn't buy Cousin Lydia's explanation that the Dorans were crazy. The kind of hatred I felt rolling off that woman had to have a reason. My curiosity got the best of me.

Leaning forward, I framed how I would begin my interrogation, but Mom beat me to it.

"Who is Sharon Doran?" she asked suddenly.

Cousin Lydia kept her eyes on the road, but squirmed uneasily. "The Dorans are a shiftless lot," she replied tightly. "You'd best stay away from them."

Her eyes met mine in the rearview mirror and she quickly looked away.

"That doesn't tell me why she hates us," I said carefully.

"The Dorans hate everyone."

I shook my head. "Sorry, Lydia, that doesn't cut it. She's a witch, and not a very ethical one at that."

From my perch in the backseat, I heard Cousin Lydia's sharp intake of breath.

"How do you know that?" she asked softly.

I quickly related last night's events, and by the time I'd finished, I felt her vibrating with indignation.

"Cecilia Kavanagh." She gave a long sigh. "Foolish, foolish girl. She's been after Billy Parnell since she was fourteen—"

"Not anymore," I interjected. "Things didn't quite work out like she'd expected."

"Humph, they never do." Lydia's hands gripped the steering wheel. "If her mother doesn't pull in the reins on that one, there's sure to be trouble ahead."

I laid a hand on her shoulder, giving her a start. "I need to know about the Dorans, Lydia."

Cousin Lydia abruptly slowed the vehicle and pulled onto the grassy shoulder. Putting the SUV in park, she turned off the motor and faced me. An air of sadness seemed to settle over her.

"I can't tell you much more than you already know. Sharon's a witch, and you're right, not a very honest one. Everyone in the valley is scared of her . . . anyone who crosses her seems to have nothing but trouble afterward."

I scooted forward. "Have the Dorans always lived in the valley?"

"No, they came to these parts right after the war. Sharon's grandparents, that is." Lydia's eyes narrowed. "Her grandmother was just like her—meaner than a hornet. I heard the only one old Granny Doran never intimidated was Annie."

"Abby's mother?"

Lydia nodded. "I guess it was quite a battle between the two of them, then something happened around the time Sharon's grandfather died . . . late forties, I think." She lifted a shoulder. "After his death some kind of truce was reached. Ever since, the Dorans stay on their side of the valley and we stay on ours."

"What caused them to quit fighting?" Mom asked.

"I don't know . . . no one ever talks about it. The only ones left who know what really happened are Great-Aunt Mary and Aunt Dot—"

"And Abby," I cut in. "She'd have been in her late teens by then."

Desperate eyes darted to mine. "Aunt Dot's done nothing but brag about how good you are at finding the truth, Ophelia, but please," she pleaded, "let whatever happened stay buried."

"But what if that Sharon tries to cause us trouble?" I huffed. "I don't like her threatening Abby."

"She can't hurt her—Great-Aunt Mary will protect her," Lydia insisted.

"Great-Aunt Mary is a century old."

"Stay away from the Dorans." Lydia laid a hand on my wrist. "Please. I see only tragedy coming from poking into the past."

"You see, or you *see*?"

"You know what I mean," she said in a stern voice. "My talent lies in healing, but lately I've been having dreams."

Mom shifted to face her. "What kind of dreams?"

Lydia drew a deep breath and let it out slowly. "Bad ones . . . " She hesitated. "I see death."

"Whose?" Mom asked, leaning forward.

"I don't know," she replied, her voice weary. "I've tried to interpret them, but clairvoyance isn't my gift."

Disgusted, I shoved back in my seat. Great here we go again, I thought. Lydia was just like Abby. Vague, misty imaginings that tell you nothing concrete. For the millionth time I wished this psychic stuff was a little more specific.

I stared out the window as Lydia started the SUV and pulled back onto the gravel road. This was a novel situation for me. I knew Lydia had great talent—I felt it from the moment I'd met her—but the only other gifted person I'd ever been around was Abby. I'd learned to have total faith in her, even when her hunches were undefined. Could I put my trust in Lydia's gift as well?

I didn't know. Her words conflicted with what I sensed. A niggling sense of danger nagged at me from deep inside, and no matter what Cousin Lydia wanted, the past wasn't going to stay buried.

What should I do? Listen to Lydia's instincts? Or my own?

Based on Lydia's advice, Mom and I agreed to say nothing of our run-in with Sharon Doran. It was the right decision. Abby appeared happy and relaxed during our early supper, and even Great-Aunt Mary seemed chipper. I didn't want to spoil the mood by bringing up the Doran family. But if I seemed quiet, no one noticed.

After supper something else flickered on the edge of my radar. Dad and Tink had wandered off again. They were up to something . . . I knew it . . . but I didn't have time to worry about it now. My mind was still locked on the incident with Sharon and our conversation with Lydia.

I needed time to myself.

Grabbing my sweatshirt, I made an excuse about needing a walk and took off up the path to Abby's favorite spot. It was still early enough in the day that I could do what I needed to do and make it back to the house before dark.

I had my runes.

Reaching the outcrop of rock overlooking the valley, I didn't take time to enjoy the scenery. Instead, I pulled out my runes, a linen square, my abalone shell, and a ball of sage. Placing the sage in the shell, I lit it and let the smoke cleanse and clear my mind. I reached down and picked up the worn leather pouch holding my runes.

Ever since the night Abby had given me the runes, I'd felt their energy, but today they were electric. The pouch that I held in my hand seemed to almost quiver. Red river rock, they were from this mountain and valley. Carved by my great-great-grandmother, it was almost as if they knew they were home.

Carefully, I framed my question: Should I try to uncover the past?

I slowly pulled open the pouch, and as I'd done so many times, slipped my hand inside, expecting to feel the cool smooth stones.

Heat burned at my fingertips and a shock shot up my arm, making all my nerves tingle. With a yelp, I quickly withdrew my hand.

"What's going on?" I muttered, staring at the bag lying in my lap.

Maybe I wasn't ready. I tilted my head back and watched white clouds drift across the sky. Focusing on them, I let the smoke from the sage fill my senses and, closing my eyes, blanked everything out except my question.

Again I asked: Should I try and uncover the past?

From deep within I felt the power of the mountain gather and grow inside me. I became one with the earth and sky.

My fingers twitched and every nerve in my body seemed on alert. Eyes still closed, I let my fingers slide back into the pouch.

Someone touched my shoulder.

I yelled and shot to my feet, dropping the bag. The outcrop was slick, and in my haste I was dangerously close to the edge.

With a scream, I felt myself sliding into nothingness.

Ten

Abruptly, strong arms grabbed me from behind and hauled me away from the edge. Limp with relief, I tried to pry the arms away from around my waist, but they only tightened. No longer afraid of falling, I *was* suddenly afraid of whoever held me.

Why didn't they release me?

I struggled and fought their grasp. Finally, the heel of my hiking boot connected with a shin.

"Ouch!"

The arms fell away and I spun around to confront my rescuer.

"Damn it, Ophelia, you could be a little more grateful," Ethan said, rubbing his shin. "If I hadn't caught you, you'd have tumbled down the mountain."

Fisting my hand on my hip, I glared at him. "If you hadn't snuck up and startled me, I wouldn't have been so close to the edge."

"I called your name," he said accusingly.

"I didn't hear you. I was busy," I shot back as I marched over to where the runes lay.

Ethan's eyes traveled to the linen square and the abalone shell. "So I see." His eyebrow arched. "I won't ask what you were doing . . . I don't want to know."

"It's none of your business anyway," I grumped back at

him. Shoving everything in my pockets, I looked back at him. "What are you doing here?"

I watched as his eyes scanned the mountain and valley. "I don't like talking out in the open. There's a safer place not far from here," he said with a jerk of his head. "Follow me."

Regardless of whatever Ethan might be involved in now, I trusted him, so I did as he said and trudged down the trail leading away from the outcrop. When the path narrowed, Ethan stopped. He grabbed a pile of brush lying against the side of the mountain and began moving it to the side.

The mouth of a small cave soon appeared.

With a flourish, he motioned me inside and I took one step forward.

Cold dank air from the cave eddied around me. Hesitating, I peered into its darkness. "Are there bats in here?" I asked with trepidation.

"Wait." Ethan stepped around me and entered the cave. A second later I saw the flicker of a lighter and the darkness vanished as he lit an old lantern. Placing it on a rock, he pulled me into the cave and rearranged the brush so it was blocking the entrance.

My eyes scanned the small cave. Rolled blankets lay piled in the corner, and a small fire pit had been dug out in the center. A stack of wood sat next to it. He even had canned goods lined up against one jagged wall.

"Cozy little place you have here, Ethan," I said sarcastically, shooting him a look over my shoulder.

"Home away from home," he said with a chuckle. "I see you haven't lost your sense of humor, Jensen."

"I haven't lost anything," I replied abruptly. "What in the devil are you doing here?"

"Isn't it obvious?" He fingered his ponytail. "I'm on assignment." Moving to the center of the cave, he stopped in front of me. "I could ask you the same question, but I already know that answer, so I'll ask another," he said, cocking his head. "What did you do to Sharon Doran today?"

My eyes widened. "Me?" I pointed to my chest. "Why do you assume that *I* did anything?"

He gave a low laugh. "Something must've happened inside that store. She was spitting venom all the way home." His smile faded. "She really hates you, Jensen. You'd better watch your back."

"I've already figured that one out," I said, sinking down onto a large boulder.

His face lost its amusement. "I'm not kidding around, Jensen—the Dorans aren't nice people—"

"So I've heard," I said, breaking in.

"You need to stay away from them," he continued.

I thought about Cousin Lydia's warning. "I've been told that one, too."

A look of exasperation crossed his face. "Then for once in your life . . . listen."

"I'd like to," I replied, scrubbing my face with my hands. "This trip was supposed to be a pleasant little family vacation, but then I run into a stranger—Sharon—and she starts threatening my family." Squaring my shoulders, I dropped my hands and looked at Ethan with determination. "I have to protect them."

With a sigh, he sank down on the boulder next to me. "Do you know why Sharon hates your family?"

"It seems there's bad blood between her family and mine . . . a feud that's lasted fifty years or so," I said wearily.

"Do you know what started it?" he asked.

"No. The only ones who know are Great-Aunt Mary—"

"I've heard about her," he interrupted. "Is she really as scary as they say?"

"She can be." I turned my head to look at him. "She's a medium, you know, and she has this habit of looking past you. Like she sees something you don't." I sighed. "It can be very disconcerting."

He chuckled again. "I can imagine."

"But back to this feud . . . Abby and Aunt Dot—" I broke off as a thought popped into my head. "Aunt Dot? What if

you run into her? I wouldn't trust her not to give you away
. . . she wouldn't mean to, but—"

A sudden brush of his hand on my knee stopped me.
"Don't worry about it, Jensen. I spotted her one day coming
out of the beauty shop." He kicked a small stone by his foot.
"I couldn't believe it. Running into your relatives in a back-
water like this." He smiled. "Who'da thunk it?"

"I know," I said with a nod.

A spark of fear ignited. "I didn't give you away, did I?"

"No, they were too busy cutting a deal to notice you."
Ethan rubbed his thighs against the cold seeping from the
rough walls of the cave. "But to be on the safe side, I'm staying away from Abernathy's. I don't want to run into Tink or
Abby."

Leaning sideways, I nudged him with my shoulder. "I
take it the Dorans are into selling drugs."

Another grin tugged at the corner of his lips. "You know
I can't tell you that."

"Are you in a lot of danger?" I asked in a hushed voice.

"Well, there are a lot of places in these mountains to stuff
a body, and—"

"That's not funny," I exclaimed, not letting him finish.

Ethan faced me and his cool gray eyes warmed. "If I
didn't know better, Jensen, I'd think you cared."

I dropped my chin, breaking his stare. "I owe you, you
helped me find Tink—" The words came out in a rush.
"—and even though your humor leaves something to be de-
sired, you're not a bad sort of a fellow."

His strong fingers gently squeezed my knee, but there
was nothing gentle in my reaction. A charge shot through
me, and the chill in the cave disappeared.

Not wanting him to see my reaction, I scooted over a bit
to put some space between us.

Ethan dropped his hand and the temperature in the cave
fell.

"I'll be okay," he said, slapping his thighs and standing.
Holding out a hand, he helped me to my feet. "You'd better

head back. It's going to be dark soon, and these trails can be tricky at night."

Together we walked to the cave's entrance, and after blowing out the lantern, Ethan moved the brush aside. We stepped out into the gathering twilight.

"Can you find your way back?" he asked. "If not, I'll—"

Knowing what he was going to say, I held up a hand to stop him. "No, I don't want to take the chance of someone seeing us together." I gave him a big smile. "I'm psychic, remember? I ought to be able to find my way home."

I turned and took one step. His hand shot out, stopping me. He pulled me around to face him.

"Wait." With his hand still on my arm, he stared into my eyes and his face lost all its humor.

Again I felt the jolt of attraction.

"I've had to spend time with Sharon, Ophelia, and I'm not kidding, she's dangerous. Be careful," he warned.

I nodded, breaking the connection. Pivoting, and with a wave over my shoulder, I left Ethan standing at the mouth of the cave and began my trek down the mountain.

One thought kept me company on the way home . . . just *how much* time did Ethan spend with Sharon?

The next morning I put all thoughts of Ethan aside as I stood on the porch finishing my coffee. I was more concerned about the reaction I'd had to the runes. Or should I say their reaction to me? Ever since Abby had given them to me, I'd relied on them to help me. Their answers were often confusing, but eventually they'd always sent me in the right direction. They were my safety net. What if I found I could no longer work with them? How would I interpret my hunches without them?

And then there was Abby—I depended on her guidance, too. It would be so simple to ask her about the past, but Lydia had said I wouldn't be doing Abby any favors by digging around in events that occurred over fifty years ago. Did I dare ignore her warning and ask anyway? After all, I barely knew Lydia.

No, I thought with a shake of my head. I could tell that whatever was eating at Abby, she didn't want to talk about it. And my grandmother was a stubborn woman. If she decided I didn't need to know, no power on earth would persuade her to tell me. I'd have as much luck questioning Great-Aunt Mary. But just the thought of that gave me the chills.

Nope, I was truly on my own this time. No runes, no Abby—I had no choice but to rely on my gift to guide my actions. I could only pray that I had enough confidence to put my trust in it.

Turning to join the Aunts and Abby, who were still in the house, I noticed Dad and Tink scoot around the corner of the barn. What were those two doing? Okay, maybe that was at least one mystery I could solve.

I set my cup on the porch rail and hurried toward the barn, but when I rounded the corner, they'd disappeared. Shoving my hands in the pockets of my sweatshirt, I scanned the woods to the north. There . . . I caught a glimpse of Tink's red jacket moving through the trees and rushed after them.

They were so intent on what they were doing that they didn't hear me barreling through the fallen leaves . . . until I stepped on a fallen branch. They whirled at the sound of the wood breaking.

Guilt was written on both of their faces.

Tink held a forked stick in her hands, and seeing me, she quickly stuck it behind her back. Dad didn't have a stick. No, he gripped a piece of paper.

I didn't know why he had the paper, but I knew why Tink had the forked stick. Dowsing.

Crossing my arms, I eyed the both of them. "What are you doing?"

"Ah, ah . . . " Tink shot Dad a furtive look.

"Ahem." Dad cleared his throat and walked toward me,

leaving Tink standing there with her hands still behind her back.

"Ophelia, we're conducting research," he said in his best "Dad" voice.

"What kind of research?"

"Umm, well." He shuffled the leaves at his feet. "We're following ley lines. Tink's tracing them with the dowsing rod."

"Yeah," Tink piped in as she took her place next to Dad and held out the forked stick. "It's willow, and I made it just like Abby taught me." Her lavender eyes shone with excitement. "It's so cool, Ophelia. We're following the lines to burial mounds." She glanced at Dad and smiled. "Grandpa bought this really neat map and—"

I fastened a look on my father. "Let me see that map," I said, holding out my hand.

Reluctantly, he passed it to me.

"Oh, Dad," I muttered as I studied the paper in my hand.

I didn't know much about maps, but I knew enough to know someone had ripped it out of a plat directory—I recognized the county roads and landmarks. It was covered with big, black X's.

"So X marks the spot, is that it?" I asked with a tinge of sarcasm.

Tink and Dad both happily nodded.

"Where did you get this?"

"I bought it from one of the cousins on Sunday," he replied defensively.

Rolling my eyes, I sighed and handed the paper back to him. "You've been skinned."

"No, I haven't," he insisted. "He assured me each mark denotes an ancient burial mound. We're going to prove that they were all built along the ley lines."

"Have you checked out this burial mound here?" I asked, pointing to an X in the center of the map.

"Ah, no. We started at this point," he replied as he placed a finger on an X in the corner.

"Really?" I turned and started back the way I'd come. "You should've started with the center one," I called back over my shoulder.

"Why?" he hollered after me.

I pivoted and narrowed my eyes at him. "It's the Aunts' house."

Dad's groan echoed through the woods.

Eleven

Snakes under the bed, runes that didn't work, rival witches, feuds, threats, and now Dad and Tink wandering around looking for burial mounds—and all I'd been worried about was Mother's unsolicited advice. Ha! This vacation was turning out to be more than I'd expected.

Maybe a brisk walk would clear my head, so after leaving Tink and Dad, I veered off through the woods until I came to the gravel road and followed it up the valley.

The only thing missing was Lady, my dog. We'd taken many walks such as this back home in Iowa, and I wished for her company now. But she was safe at home, and along with Queenie, our cat, and T.P., Tink's dog, staying with Darci.

"And no doubt getting spoiled," I muttered to myself.

Thinking of Darci, my assistant/best friend/partner in crime, I suddenly laughed, startling a blue jay. Boy, oh boy, would she like to be here now. A valley full of witches was right up her alley. And running into Ethan again? Wow, she'd love that. I bent down and picked up a long stick. No, the way this visit was going, Darci would only cause more problems. With her blond hair and great figure, these country boys would be wearing a path to the Aunts' house. I had enough to handle without Darci breaking hearts right and left. In a way, I was relieved her college classes kept her from inviting herself along, but it would be nice to talk to her right now. I could use an ally.

Putting thoughts of home away, I continued down the road. Run-down trailers with old cars sitting on blocks were interspersed with neat two-story farmhouses. In a few places long lanes wound away from the road and the only indication of a house nearby was a thin plume of smoke rising above the trees.

I didn't know how many of these farmsteads belonged to relatives, but I recognized several of the last names on the mailboxes. Old Jens had been ahead of his time—instead of leaving all his property to his two sons, his daughters had inherited equally with their brothers. As a result, the names of the family holding the land had changed as his female descendants married. Wiley, Murray, Maclean, and Drummond were all last names of various cousins.

Stopping, I leaned against a fence rail and watched two yearling horses frolic in the pasture beyond. It really was a beautiful, peaceful place. At least at first. The longer I stayed, the more I learned about the hidden currents running beneath the placid surface of this community.

Evidently the Dorans were one of those ripples, and a big one at that. What could've happened to cause a fifty-year-old feud? Had they moved into these mountains and tried to usurp my family's position as the local wise women? Was it some kind of a witch war? If that were the case, why hadn't Abby ever mentioned it? She loved telling stories about her childhood in the mountains and about her mother. And a tale about Annie facing off with another witch would've been a good one. Knowing Abby, I couldn't believe that she wouldn't have used such a story, if for no other reason than to teach me the difference between using magick for good or for ill.

The whole thing baffled me.

I pushed away from the fence and continued down the road. I'd just passed another mailbox, one with no name, sitting at the end of a lane when I felt it . . . a spark of magick. Shaking my head, I took another step. What did I expect? With this many witches living in such close proximity to one another, it was a wonder that the valley didn't glow at night.

Wait, I thought, slowing my steps and turning around to face the mailbox. Something was off. Working magick carries with it the signature of the witch that created it, and this was wrong . . . sloppy. As if someone had scrawled big black letters over a clean white sheet of paper. The spell felt muddied, dirty.

I retraced my steps back to the mailbox and caught the faint scent of something rotten. Squatting, I poked at the weeds growing around the post with my stick until I found it.

A spoiled potato. Beneath the red ants crawling all over its surface, I saw brown, squishy spots. I wrinkled my nose in distaste. Yuck. Poking it again, I noticed something odd about its shape. It had been peeled and it wasn't round like a normal potato. No, it looked like it had been carved into a shape . . . a human shape.

I flipped it over with the stick. A large rusty nail protruded from the figure's stomach.

My own stomach twisted at the sight. A poppet. Someone had made an effigy of the person living there, stabbed it with the nail, then left it to rot in the sun. Not good, not good at all, and in spite of the warm sun beating down on me, I felt a chill.

Dropping the stick, I stood and peered up the lane. All I saw was the bumper of an old pickup sitting under a tree. Was the person who lived here home?

Suddenly, the tree's branches rustled, and lifting my head, I saw a red-tailed hawk staring across the distance at me.

Dang it—it had to be a hawk. I seemed to have an affinity with them—Abby had called them my animal guides, and said to pay attention whenever I saw one.

"Okay, okay," I muttered as his amber eyes seemed to call to me.

I trudged up the lane.

Rounding the corner, the first thing I saw was a big black dog sleeping on the porch of the old house, in front of the door. Well that settled that—I was not going to the door with the dog there. I made a move to turn and the dog lifted its head. Two brown eyes stared at me, and lips curled back to reveal strong white teeth.

Not wanting to challenge the dog, I averted my eyes while I thought about my dilemma.

What do you do now, Jensen? If you run, the dog will chase you.

But the dog settled it for me. From the corner of my eye, I saw him stand, stretch, and softly pad off the porch. And trot straight toward me.

Angling my body toward the house, I stood as quietly as I could, considering that the desire for flight raged through me. Still not meeting the dog's stare, I waited.

He approached with his ears back and his tail up. Stopping a couple of feet from me, he lifted his head and sniffed the air before moving closer. Finally, he halted at my feet.

Sweat formed on my upper lip and I fought the need to wipe it away. Any sudden movement now could result in a serious bite. Keeping my breathing steady, I felt the dog's snuffles as he moved his nose up and down my pant leg, and I prayed that the next thing wouldn't be his teeth.

Finally he finished, and with a soft *wuff,* walked away from me over to a tree. Plopping down, he calmly laid his head on his paws and closed his eyes.

I wiped the sweat from my lip as I turned toward the house. Slowly crossing the yard, I kept glancing over my shoulder to make sure the dog didn't change his mind. Once at the steps, I gave the dog one last look then climbed to the porch.

Paint peeled from the front door and nearby sat an empty dish and a pan filled with dirty water. Dead flies floated on the surface.

With a look at the dog, now sleeping on his side, I nudged the bowl with my foot. Poor thing. I wondered when he'd last had food and clean water.

Frowning, I rapped on the door.

No one answered.

I knocked louder and called out. "Is anyone home?"

Still no answer.

Ah well, I thought with a shrug, I tried.

As I pivoted and took a step away from the door, the window to my left caught my attention. The shades were up and curtains were pulled back.

Hmm, if I walked over to it, I thought, I could see inside. Then I'd know if anyone was home. But what if they were and they caught me peeking in their window? Regardless of my family connections, I was an outsider, and folks around here were leery of strangers. I didn't want to find myself looking down the barrel of a shotgun. I moved toward the steps, then stopped.

There it was again . . . the same prickle of magick I'd felt at the mailbox, only stronger, nastier. I'd been too worried about the dog to sense it earlier. Glancing over my shoulder at the tree, I looked for the hawk. He'd disappeared.

Not a good sign.

With resignation, I stepped over to the window and looked in. The shock sent me reeling off the edge of the porch. I righted myself before hitting the hard dirt.

The dog rolled over, raising his head, and stared at me again.

Easy, Jensen, easy. I forced myself to walk with slow steps as I passed in front of him.

Shaking by the time I reached the end of the lane, I whipped out my cell phone and with trembling fingers punched 911.

The screen read: NO SERVICE.

I tore down the road and ran to the next house. I pounded on the door until a red-faced woman wearing an old-fashioned apron answered. As she opened the door, I caught the aroma of fresh baked bread. My stomach knotted.

"Can I help you?" she asked, her voice wary.

"Y-Y-Your neighbor," I stuttered.

Her face relaxed and she opened the door wider. "Why you're Lydia Wiley's Yankee cousin, aren't you?"

"Yes." I took a deep breath and pointed over my shoulder. "Your neighbor—"

"Oscar?" she asked, taking my arm and drawing me inside. "Is something wrong?"

"He's dead," I blurted out.

Lydia found me sitting at the woman's table trying to drink the sweet tea that she'd forced on me. She gave the woman, a Mrs. Gordon, a quick nod before striding over and pulling out a chair.

Sitting, she took my hand in hers and leaned forward. "How are you?"

"Was I right?" I asked, ignoring her question. "Is he dead?"

"Yes," she replied softly.

"Did you call the sheriff?"

"Yes, I left him at Oscar's."

Oscar? I'd heard the name from Mrs. Gordon, but I'd been too unnerved for it to register. Now I got it as the image of the man who'd had a confrontation with Sharon Doran flashed through my mind. I stole a look at Mrs. Gordon, busy at the stove but with her head slightly cocked in our direction. I lowered my voice.

"He's the one who threatened to turn in the Dorans, isn't he?" I asked.

Lydia hesitated. "Yes," she finally answered.

Suddenly the kitchen seemed too small. I rose and murmured my thanks to Mrs. Gordon before I fled out the door, leaving Lydia to explain the strange ways of her Northern relatives.

Meanwhile, outside, I grasped the porch railing and took a deep cleansing breath of the mountain air. Lydia had said anyone who crossed the Dorans met with misfortune, and poor Oscar certainly had. She'd also talked about sensing death, and the conversation was right after we'd witnessed his run-in with Sharon Doran. Was it his death she'd felt?

Before I had time to pursue that line of thought, the screen door banged and Lydia joined me on the porch. Together, we walked to her SUV in silence.

After we both buckled up, she leaned forward and was about to turn the key when I reached out and touched her hand, stopping her.

My throat tightened and I swallowed hard. "Did you see the poppet?"

"Yes." Her jaw clenched as she started the engine. With a quick glance at the side mirror, she cranked the wheel and headed the vehicle down the lane.

"Sharon?"

She nodded, not looking at me. "Another death to lay at her door," she whispered softly.

"What?" I sat back in my seat and crossed my arms over my chest. "You can't believe she hexed him dead with a poppet made out of potato?"

"I've seen stranger things happen in these mountains."

"Oh come on—magick can't kill," I scoffed.

Lydia's hands tightened on the wheel. "Tell that to Oscar." She shot me a sideways glance. "You've never seen a hex work?"

"No, I've read about them in the journals. And Abby's talked about what can happen if magick is used in a negative way." Sitting forward, I turned toward her. "Don't you have to believe in the witch's power in order for it to hurt you?"

"Oh, people around here believe in Sharon's power, all right," she said in a firm voice.

"But I heard Aunt Dot say her magick was weak," I insisted.

"All I know is what I've seen . . . Oscar insulted her, she cursed him, now he's dead."

The ramifications of Lydia's remarks hit me hard. Sharon had not only threatened Oscar that day at Abernathy's, but also Abby. Was her magick really that strong? Strong enough to harm Abby? I felt beads of cold sweat gather on my upper lip. Wiping it away, I turned and stared at the passing homesteads as thoughts raced around in my head.

And in the distance, the church bells began to toll.

Twelve

News of Oscar's death spread quickly throughout the valley, and when Abby heard the story, her reaction surprised me. Instead of asking questions, a look of great sadness seemed to come over her and she quietly left the room. Aunt Dot and Great-Aunt Mary hadn't much to say about it either. Was it because of the connection to the Dorans? Given Oscar's confrontation with Sharon, everyone in the valley suspected that she'd cast a spell against him, but no one came out and said it. They were all afraid.

But no one knew about the poppet. Lydia had recommended that we leave that part out. She'd gone back later and taken care of it by burying it under an oak tree to end the magick. She'd also adopted the big black dog . . . Jasper.

Now, two days later, I found myself standing in a sea of black and over an open grave as I watched them lower Oscar Nelson's coffin into the ground. Not imagining that I'd be attending a funeral, I hadn't brought what the Aunts' considered appropriate clothes for the occasion, so I wore a borrowed dress of Lydia's. Abby stood next to me, wearing a distinctly old-fashioned dress of Great-Aunt Mary's. Mom, however, had used the event to buy another little black dress to add to her overflowing closet. At least I hadn't had to worry about rounding up something for Tink. Given her sensitivity to cemeteries, we'd all agreed it would be best if she stayed at the house with Dad.

I tried to weasel out of the funeral, but it didn't work. The Aunts had let me skate the night before when they hadn't forced me to attend the wake. Thank goodness. I'd watched them toddle out of the house with Lydia, their arms laden with baskets of food—rolls, ham, salads, and two pies—all gifts for Oscar's grieving family. When they arrived home, they couldn't quit going on about how *natural* Oscar looked. How a dead person looked *natural* was beyond me, but I nodded politely.

Earlier, when we entered the church, I'd heard a few whispers as we passed by. I didn't know if the attendees were gossiping about Yankee relatives or the fact that I'd been the one to discover the body, but I ignored the whispers and focused on Abby.

All during the lengthy service, she'd been unusually pale and her face looked pinched. I couldn't understand why. Had Oscar been one of her childhood friends? Maybe her first boyfriend? I tried asking her about it, but she blew me off. And now all I wanted to do was get through the rest of the day.

This old cemetery had been in existence for years, and I knew the family burial plot was somewhere nestled among the pines. The only one missing was Robert—he'd never left France. And from where I stood, I could pick out the writing on many of the weathered stones. "My beloved wife" followed by the year 1868. A lamb or a praying angel with the date of birth and date of death too close together. Children who'd never made it past their fifth birthdays.

My attention was suddenly caught by an old woman standing at the back of the crowd on the other side of the open grave. She was dressed in a faded black coat, but around the bottom of the coat dangled a swath of bright fuchsia. Not exactly the somber black that all the other women wore. Her shoulders were hunched forward with age, and she had wisps of gray hair hanging from beneath her hat. A hat that may have been the rage in 1942, but now looked old and battered. A black veil hid her features, yet I could feel her eyes appraising me. With a slight nod of acknowledgment, she took a step back and disappeared behind the man standing to her left.

Puzzled, I leaned close to Abby and was about to point out the strange old lady when I heard Oscar's coffin bump the hard ground. Looking across the grave, I watched as a man stepped away from the group standing next to the gaping hole. He picked up a handful of dirt, and walking slowly up to the open grave, cast it in.

I heard it thud and scatter as it hit the lid.

It was the signal to leave, and as everyone turned, a sudden hush fell over the crowd. Next to me, Abby gasped.

Sharon Doran stood a short distance away, holding a bunch of fall flowers, next a stone with "Doran" carved in bold lettering.

The hush turned to an indignant buzz while the mourners scurried by her, their faces averted. Every so often someone would cast a glance over their shoulder, as if to make sure Sharon didn't follow them.

Taking Abby's arm, I escorted her over the rough ground on the way to Lydia's waiting SUV. We'd almost made it when Sharon stepped directly in front of us.

"You're the one," she said with a nasty sneer as she pointed to Abby. "I never have gotten a good look at you."

I wasn't going to stand for this. "I'll meet you at the car," I said as I blocked Sharon.

When Abby was a few yards away, I focused my attention back on Sharon. "It appears you aren't welcome here," I stated, referring to the sideways looks she was getting from the retreating group.

She lightly stroked the petals of the flowers she held. "I'm just here to put flowers on my granny's grave," she said in all innocence.

Yeah, right.

"Well, you're timing stinks." I made a move to pass her, but she sidestepped in front of me.

"I told you to leave, but you're not listening." She jerked her head toward Oscar's still open grave. "I hope you remember this."

I took a step forward. "Are you threatening me?"

She arched an eyebrow as she carelessly lifted a shoulder.

Narrowing my eyes, I crossed my arms. "I suggest you back off. I've heard the stories . . . you've got everyone around here scared." I dropped my arms. "But I'm not one of them."

As I said it, I felt the power jolt through me, fueled by my anger. I tamped it down. This was not the place for a showdown.

Turning on my heel, I looked over my shoulder at her as I walked away. "You can take your little bag of tricks and stuff it."

Back at Oscar's the first thing I noticed were women going around the room, uncovering mirrors draped with black cloths, and starting clocks.

"What are they doing?" I asked as Aunt Dot shoved a plate of food in my hands.

"Ack, the mirrors stay covered until the body's taken off for burial."

"Why?"

She made a tsking sound as if everyone should know the answer to that question. "If a body sees themselves in a house shared by the recently departed, they'll be the next to die."

"Same thing with the clocks?"

"No," she said slowly. "It's done out of respect for the deceased. Lydia took care of it while she was waiting for the sheriff." Her voice carried a little note of reproach.

I guess I should've gone in when I found the body and stopped them.

With a shake of my head, I began to cross the room to where Abby sat on a chair against the wall, paler now than she'd been at the funeral. As I passed a couple of women, I caught a snatch of their conversation.

"Did you see her, bold as brass standing there?" one of them asked in a shocked voice.

Were they talking about Sharon?

I dawdled by pretending to admire the group of photographs laid out on the table near them. I wanted to hear what they had to say.

"Yes," the other hissed. "And did you notice Granny Doran's grave? Not a blade of grass growing—nothing but weeds."

"Humph, as evil as she was, there'll never be nothin' but."

Okay, if you're bad, grass won't grow over your grave . . . got it.

Out of the corner of my eye I saw one of the women glance my way. Turning her head, she leaned in closer to her companion.

I strained to hear her whisper.

"And now, with Abigail here." She raised her eyebrows and gave her friend a knowing look.

The other woman nodded her head slowly. "Nothing but trouble," she said sadly.

Trouble for whom?

After the funeral, my curiosity ran high, but I tried ignoring it by taking long walks and reading. I also kept my senses on the alert for any bad magick headed our way. I still didn't know if I believed a witch could kill with spells, but I had no intention of finding out. Hopefully, by showing Sharon at the cemetery that I wouldn't be bullied, she'd leave us alone. And as long as she didn't try any of her tricks on us, I'd follow Lydia's advice and stay away from her.

It was after one of those walks that I arrived back at the

house to find Great-Aunt Mary sitting on the porch in one of the ancient rocking chairs. Her crochet hook flashed in the sunlight, keeping pace with the even back and forth sway of her chair.

My heart did a slow slide to the pit of my stomach. So far on this trip, I'd managed to not be alone with her, and I would've preferred to keep it that way. My eyes searched the yard for a sign of Abby or Aunt Dot, but I didn't find them. I had no choice—the only way into the house was past Great-Aunt Mary. With heavy feet, I crossed the yard and climbed the steps to the porch.

"Been out for a walk?" she asked, not raising her head from her work.

"Ah," I mumbled as I slipped by her, "yeah."

Almost to the door, I thought. One more second and I'd be inside, away from her. My hand reached for the handle of the screen.

"Sit a spell," she suddenly commanded.

I yanked my hand back, and with reluctance took a place in the rocker next to her.

"What are you making?" I asked, watching her hook catch the dark purple yarn and turn it into an ever growing chain.

"An afghan for Tink," she replied, her face softening as she said Tink's name. "You've quite a girl there."

Oh, my gosh, Great-Aunt Mary said something nice to me. "I know," I answered, trying not to sound boastful. "Tink is a treasure. Adopting her was one of the best things I've ever done."

Great-Aunt Mary lifted her head, her pale blue eyes focusing on a spot near the corner of the barn. A wistful look stole across her wrinkled face as her hands stilled and the rocker stopped.

"I've often wondered—" She shook her head, cutting herself off. "I've seen a lot of trouble in my century of living, and I've known too much about the private lives of folks around here . . ." Her voice dropped and I had to sit forward to catch her words. "It's made me never regret not marrying, but I do miss children," she said almost to herself.

Frowning, her rocking resumed at a quickened pace and her hook darted around the yarn.

"Not that I didn't have my chances at marrying, mind you," she continued in a strong voice. "Joseph Carmicheal courted me something fierce. Could've had him if I'd wanted," she finished with a sniff.

Did I dare ask why she hadn't wanted him? But before I could, she continued.

"He got tired of waiting around for me to make up my mind. Got himself married to a gal over by Asheville, had a passel of kids, and went to an early grave, leaving his widow to fend for herself." Her head wobbled from side to side as her hook flew faster. "And with all those children . . . just as well I didn't marry him."

The way she sat, her spine straight and her mouth in a thin line, said she spoke the truth, but I sensed something deeper. A feeling of opportunities missed, of joy not experienced, lurked in the corner of her heart. A corner that she never revealed to anyone. I felt I should say something comforting to her, but she was such a hard woman that I didn't think my sympathy would be appreciated. She wouldn't want to know that I saw the chink in her armor.

I said nothing and an uncomfortable silence lengthened.

Great-Aunt Mary shifted in her seat, and as she did, I could feel her draw the shell back around her once again.

"Humph," she abruptly said, breaking the silence, "I heard you had words with Sharon Doran, not once but twice."

"Lydia told you?"

Her eyes fastened on me. "I don't need to rely on others." She shifted her attention to the far mountain and her hook paused. "Restless spirits roam these hills."

I waited for her to explain.

"That girl's granny's one of them," she said, focusing on her crocheting again.

All my good intentions about ignoring the Dorans went

out the window as my curiosity reared its little head. Okay, Jensen, here's your chance—she was the one who mentioned them—ask a few questions.

I sat forward. "Has the grandmother been gone long?" I asked, easing into the subject.

"No," she replied. "She recently crossed over. Or at least that's what she should've done," she finished cryptically.

Mean old Granny Doran haunted the mountains, huh? Peachy. What was supposed to be a family reunion was turning into something entirely different. Now I could add a nasty ghost to my list of concerns. Just how many more Dorans did I have to worry about?

"Are the Dorans a big family?"

"Big enough," she snorted. "They started with the three boys. Only one left is the eldest—Zachary—a more deceitful man than him never drew breath." She gave her head a slight shake. "The middle one was killed in a bar fight down in Knoxville, and the youngest—Sharon's daddy—was killed along with his wife, in a car accident. Drunk driving."

"That's a lot of tragedy for one family."

Her eyes swung in my direction. "I'm not saying they deserved an early death, but all three of those boys were wild and wicked."

The image of Sharon staking a claim on Ethan sprung to mind. Were there other Doran women waiting to pounce on him? "What about their daughters? Are they wild and wicked, too?"

"Sharon's the only girl child in the family." Great-Aunt Mary snickered. "She's cut a wide swath through this valley, that's for certain, and wicked?" She paused and her eyes narrowed. "Someday her deeds will come home to roost."

Might as well lay it out on table, I thought. "I know she's a witch, Great-Aunt Mary. I saw how everyone acted at the cemetery. They all think she caused Oscar Nelson's death."

"Ha, Oscar's had a stomach ailment for years. He died of a hemorrhage and that's the truth," she huffed. "Her a witch?" Great-Aunt Mary's lips twisted in a sneer. "She thinks she understands magick, but she doesn't. She uses it for her own selfish reasons. She's hoodwinked everyone in this valley."

"How?"

Great-Aunt Mary placed her crocheting in her lap. "All her worthless cousins and her uncle thinks her spells protect them . . . they can do anything they want and nothing will touch them," she said without really answering my question. "Time's a-comin' when it's going to fall down around their ears."

Again I thought of Ethan and his undercover assignment. Did Great-Aunt Mary "see" Ethan as the instrument of justice that would bring the Dorans down? Should I ask her? Could I ask her without giving Ethan away?

"Ah," I stammered, "I have a question—"

Her cackle cut me off. "You're full of questions, girl, but you won't get any more answers from me."

Her smug attitude irritated me.

"I can find out on my own, you know," I blustered. "You have your ways and I have mine."

She cackled again as she gathered up her yarn. "No, you don't. When you were a girl, maybe," she said, shoving the yarn and pieces of Tink's afghan in a bag lying next to her chair. "You've ignored your talent too long for it to be of much good."

I jerked forward, insulted by her remark. "You're wrong," I insisted.

"I'm not," she argued back. "I told your grandmother years ago to get a handle on you, but she ignored me. Now it's too late. You'll never be what you were meant to be, more's the pity." She rose slowly to her feet and gave me a hard look. "You've let the family down."

I shot up. "I have not—you just wait and see." The words flew out of my mouth. "If that woman tries any of her hocus pocus on us," I jabbed a finger at my chest, "I'll put a stop to it."

She shook her head in disgust. "You're no match for the

likes of her, even if her magick is weak. I'll do it. I've been protecting this family more years than you've been alive."

"You didn't keep the snake—"

I cut myself off. *How could I be so stupid?*

"Sharon," I hissed, glaring at her. "She—"

Great-Aunt Mary straightened her shoulders and met my stare with one of her own. "You just settle down." Her eyes were blue steel. "I made a mistake . . . I underestimated how sneaky she is. It won't happen again."

Thirteen

For the rest of the day my conversation with Great-Aunt Mary echoed in my head like an irritating song. No matter how hard I tried focusing on something else, there it was, repeating itself over and over again.

She's wrong, I insisted silently. *Every day I feel my gift growing stronger. It's not too late. It can't be.*

Finally, after supper, I'd had enough. Great-Aunt Mary might have intended to protect the family, but I had a few ideas of my own. While she showed Tink how to crochet, and Abby and Aunt Dot watched yet another cop show, I excused myself and headed outside. By now it was too dark to climb the mountain. I grabbed the kerosene lantern hanging on a hook by the back door and, after lighting it, made my way across the yard to the barn. I thought I would find what I needed there. Holding the lantern high, I grasped the battered door and shoved.

Creaking, it swung open on its rusty hinges. I stepped inside.

A warm circle of light surrounded me, but past the bright edges, the sound of sudden scurrying came from the dark corners. Peering into the blackness, I held the lantern higher and tried to make my circle larger. I didn't need some stray mouse running up my pant leg. *Whew.* I breathed a sigh of relief—not a mouse. A mother cat with three kittens watched me cautiously from a hay bale in the corner. And right next to her—along the back wall—was an old workbench.

Crossing to it, I dug around until I found a dusty coffee can full of six penny nails. I selected one whose point was still sharp. Next I grabbed a piece of the lath that the Aunts used for kindling. Snapping it in two, I laid half of it on the bench and walked to the center of the barn. With a sigh, I eased myself down and crossed my legs.

It only took a moment to lay out my supplies—the lath, the six penny nail, my abalone shell, and a ball of sage. As I'd done on the mountain, I lit the sage, only this time instead of inhaling its purifying smoke, I passed the lath back and forth through the fumes. When I was finished, I picked up the nail. Carefully, I began etching the first rune.

"Algiz," I whispered softly, and imagined any harm cast this way vanishing like a mist in the face of its powerful protection.

"Nauthiz." Saying the name of the next rune, I carved it beside Algiz. As I did, I focused my desire to keep my family safe onto the long scratches I made into the lath.

Lifting the lath, I gently blew away the shavings before moving to the next rune.

"Kenaz." The image of a fire burning brightly in the hearth appeared in my mind. I saw its warmth move slowly through the house until the entire building was wrapped in a protective glow.

"Berkano." Pictures of my family flitted through my mind. Tink, Abby, Aunt Dot, Lydia, even Great-Aunt Mary. I saw Algiz standing before them like a shield.

Taking a deep breath, I began to carefully form the next rune. This was an important one—it focused the power of the runescript onto one specific person. Only Laguz would be appropriate. The symbol of a woman with extraordinary gifts . . . Abby. She seemed to be at the center of whatever was happening right now.

Satisfied I had it right, I made the sixth rune—Eihwaz, a rune that turned tragedy into triumph. The evil I sensed gathering around Abby would dissipate and only good would remain.

And last but not least, I formed the final rune: Inguz, the symbol of a successful conclusion. It sealed the power of the previous six runes.

Holding the lath close to the lantern, I looked over each rune, seven in all. The number seven itself was magickal. It, too, would lend its power to my carvings. Lifting the lantern chimney, I stuck each end of the lath into the fire, charring them and containing the magick now permeating the small piece of wood.

After clearing my space, I cast the ashes in the air with a sigh of thankfulness and returned the sage to the earth. I rose to my feet and wrapped the runescript in a clean white cloth. Sticking it and my shell back in my pocket, I picked up the lantern and headed out of the barn.

As I crossed the yard back to the house, a small smile twitched at the corner of my mouth and I patted my pocket. Once this was under Abby's mattress, she'd be safe.

I stopped and stared across the valley. My smile faded as I thought of Sharon, and anger pricked at me.

Mess with us, will you?

Even though I'd been the last one in bed, I still couldn't sleep. I lay there in the darkness, staring at the ceiling and listening to Abby's soft snores. Happy with myself, I snuggled down in bed. She was safe . . . I knew it. But what about the windows and doors? Had I checked them?

With a small groan, I threw my legs over the side of the bed and quietly padded out of the room. Halfway down the hall, I noticed a light coming from the living room. Great, another "back door Betty"? Peeking around the corner, I saw Aunt Dot, alone, sitting in her recliner, reading a book.

"Hey there," I said in a loud whisper as I entered the room. "You couldn't sleep either?"

With a smile, she placed her book facedown in her lap

and smiled. "Part of getting old, child. Your inside clock goes haywire."

Walking to the couch, I sat and curled my legs underneath me. I eyed Aunt Dot speculatively. I'd done what I could to protect Abby, but I still wanted to know what happened to start this blood feud. And Aunt Dot *was* chatty. During her visit to Iowa she'd let several family skeletons out the closet, much to Abby's dismay. Wonder if I could pry out a few more?

"I told Sharon Doran to back off," I said abruptly.

Aunt Dot pushed the footstool of the recliner down and sat forward. "I know . . . everyone at Oscar's was whispering about her showing up at the cemetery," she said unhappily. "It was a sorry day when the Dorans came to these mountains."

"It was right after the war, wasn't it?"

With a shake of her head, she leaned back in her chair. "I don't like thinking about it."

Dang. Aunt Dot was as stubborn as Abby. Evidently this late night tête-à-tête wasn't going to give me the information I wanted unless I came up with another plan. I fought the desire to suddenly snap my fingers—I had it—elderberry wine. The Aunts bottled their wine containing a secret ingredient every summer. And the secret? A goodly dose of moonshine. I didn't know who provided them with the white lightning, nor did I want to. I did know that the stuff was potent.

I squirmed a little as I thought of a way to encourage my elderly great-aunt to drink alcohol in the middle of the night. But what could it hurt?

I gave a big fake sigh. "Boy, I sure wish I had something to make me relax."

Aunt Dot, placing her book on the floor, rose quickly to her feet and barreled toward the kitchen. "Warm milk. I'll make you a glass right now."

Scrambling to my feet, I rushed after her. "Gee, Aunt Dot, you'll need to fire up the stove. It's late. I don't want you to go to all that trouble."

"Ack, no trouble," she said over her shoulder.

"I have a better idea . . . " I paused. "Remember when you were in Iowa? I had the best night's sleep after drinking some of that terrific wine," I finished wistfully.

"The elderberry?"

"Yes," I sighed.

Okay, so I'd slept hard that night because I was tanked to the gills—Aunt Dot hadn't shared her secret with me yet—I didn't know I was drinking a hundred proof moonshine. As a result, I'd had the mother of all hangovers.

Aunt Dot looked at me with hesitation. "But it's not Saturday," she said. "We only have wine time on Saturday night."

Okay . . . I'd try a different tack.

"Wine is really good for you, you know," I said in a reasonable voice. "It's full of antioxidants."

"Anti what's-a-dants?"

"They keep your body going," I said with a chuckle.

"Oh."

Moving to stand next to her, I laid a hand on her shoulder. "Never mind, Aunt Dot." I opened the cupboard and removed two small glasses. "I think a little glass of wine would be good for us, don't you?"

A sly look crossed her face. "Sister wouldn't approve."

I returned her look with one of my own. "Neither would Abby, but they're both asleep, aren't they?" I asked with a wink.

She gave a soft cackle. "They won't know, will they?"

"I won't tell if you don't," I replied, grinning.

While I carried the glasses back to the table, she opened the cupboard next to the sink and took down a half bottle of wine. Placing it on the table, she took the chair next to me.

I pulled the cork and poured us both a glass, with a little more in Aunt Dot's than in mine.

"Skol," I said, lifting my glass to hers.

"Skol," she replied, and took a big swallow.

As I sipped mine, I noticed a bowl sitting in the corner by the warm stove. Smiling, I jerked my head toward it.

"Trying to placate your Nisse, Aunt Dot?"

A small frown flitted across her face. "Every night I've put out a fresh bowl of grits, and every morning it's still there untouched." She glanced over her shoulder at the bowl then back at me. "He's really angry, and I'm beginning to think he won't show himself until you're gone, Ophelia."

Aunt Dot really believed in this house fairy thing. I might not care about the feelings of something I wasn't convinced even existed, but I did care about her. I reached across the table and laid my hand on hers. "I'm sorry if I made him mad."

"Ack," she replied with a shake of her head. "They're peculiar creatures, easily offended. It could be he's just moved out to the barn for now. I'll coax him back to the house once it's just Sister and I again."

Taking another sip of wine, I tried to decide the best way to pump Aunt Dot for information. Start slow and don't blow this, Jensen, I thought as the sweet liquid slid down my throat.

"Abby's mom and dad sure had a great love story," I started out, keeping an eye on her reaction.

She shook her head quickly. "Abby doesn't like me talking about it."

I gave her a playful nudge. "But Abby isn't here, is she? After all, Robert and Annie are my great-grandparents. Shouldn't I know about them?"

"Well then," she answered, her eyes shining as she took a healthy drink of the wine. "Robert Campbell carried a torch for our Annie from the moment he laid eyes on her."

"Did Annie feel the same way?"

"Ack, no." Her face softened with memories. "Annie was beautiful. Her hair was her glory, though . . . dark auburn it was . . . and shone so bright in the sun." She smiled broadly. "All the boys would hang around her like bees to a flower."

"Why did she fall for Robert?" I asked.

Aunt Dot winked as she tapped her forehead with one finger. "Your great-grandfather was a wily one. He kept his feelings a secret and ignored her. Annie didn't like that."

I laughed softly. "He was a challenge, huh?"

"Yes he was," she answered with a nod. "It wasn't until the pie auction at a barn raising—"

I held up a hand, stopping her. "Pie auction?"

"All the single women make pies to be auctioned, and the young men bid on them. The one who bids the highest gets to sit and have pie with the girl who baked it."

"I see." I took a small sip of wine. "Did Annie's bring the most?"

She laughed. "Not that night. Robert had paid all his friends not to bid." Her eyes twinkled as she poured herself more wine. "One of her rivals' pies went the highest. It was a good lesson for my sister to learn. She'd started to take those around her for granted." Chuckling again, she shook her head. "I thought Annie would kill Robert when she learned the truth, but by then she was in love with him, so she forgave him. All their married life they joked about how much that pie had really cost him."

"Your dad didn't approve of the marriage, Robert being a Campbell and all, did he?"

"No, he did not. He never forgave the Campbells for joining the English at Culloden." Her voice became firm. "If Robert hadn't kidnapped Annie—"

"Whoa," I broke in, shocked. "He kidnapped her?"

"Oh," she said with a wave of her hand, "Annie went willingly. That kind of thing happened all the time back then. When the family wouldn't approve of a marriage, the young couple would take off and hide out in the mountains for a few weeks, living off the land and running from the families. Then when the couple returned, the family had to accept the marriage, because . . . well, you know."

"What happened if they got caught?"

"Depended on the family." She drank the rest of her wine and poured another. "There were stories of some young men mysteriously disappearing."

"They were murdered?"

She shrugged. "Pa wouldn't have killed Robert, but no doubt in my mind he would've given him a beating if he'd caught him."

"Robert took quite a risk."

"Yes he did, but I know they had help." She glanced over her shoulder and her voice dropped. "Sister snuck food to their hideout, but she'd never admit it."

Surprised, my eyes widened. "I didn't think Great-Aunt Mary was a romantic."

"Annie was Sister's real live baby doll," Aunt Dot said with a smile. "She would've done anything for her."

"And Abby was the result of the kidnapping," I said softly.

A hot blush spread up Aunt Dot's neck and she nervously sipped at her wine. "Yes."

I reached over and patted her hand. "I don't care when Abby was conceived. I think Annie and Robert's love story is really cool."

"But it ended too soon," she said in a voice tinged with sadness. "When Robert didn't come home from the war, Annie moved back here with Abby."

She brought up the war . . . this was my chance.

"Wasn't that about the same time the Dorans came to the mountains?" I asked, keeping my voice even.

"N—" She stopped short. "Ack, I don't remember."

"Gee," I said, refilling her glass. "I could've sworn that was what Lydia said."

With a sigh, she lifted her glass. "It was after the war." After taking a drink, she placed it on the table and folded her hands. "Old Granny Doran was in the family way with their youngest. That boy must've been only about two when a fever took the old man."

"Was Granny Doran a witch like Sharon?"

I saw Aunt Dot's hands tighten, and her eyes darted from side to side.

"It's not right to speak of the dead."

Her remark took me off guard. We'd just spent the last twenty minutes talking about Annie and Robert. Why not Granny Doran?

"Great-Aunt Mary told me her spirit didn't cross over."

"Sister told you about Granny Doran?"

Well, sort of, but I wanted Aunt Dot to think that I knew more than I did.

"Yes," I replied in a confident voice.

"Humpf," Aunt Dot said, picking up her glass. "It doesn't surprise me that woman haunts these hills." She took a drink. "She always had more confidence in her gifts than she ought to."

"What do you mean?"

"She wasn't much of a witch, and neither is her grand-daughter," she huffed. "Causes more trouble than good. It was the old man who had the real power."

"He was a witch?"

"Not a witch. The seventh son of a seventh son." Aunt Dot drained her glass and rose to her feet. Removing the bottle, she crossed the kitchen and put it away. "And he was just as evil as his wife and granddaughter. Heaven only knows what would've happened to folks around here if Annie would've let him bully her into giving them Abby."

Grabbing the glasses, I hurried over to join her at the counter. "Wait a second . . . they wanted to take Abby?"

She gave a disgusted nod. "He knew the gift ran strong in our family, especially in Abby." Her lip curled. "Pah," she spit out, "since Annie had no man to provide for her and Abby, he thought he could hound her into agreeing." A fierce light shone in her eyes. "But he didn't know my sister."

I clutched the sleeve of her robe. "Is that what started the feud?"

She shook off my arm and turned toward the living room. "I don't like talking about that time. I'm going to bed."

"Wait!" I cried, rushing after her. "Abby's never mentioned a word of this."

"She wouldn't," Aunt Dot replied softly. Lifting a hand, she stroked my cheek. "Don't worry about it, child. It all happened so long ago. He's dead, his wicked wife's dead. The only one left who can cause any trouble is that Sharon. And she's no match for Sister."

As I watched Aunt Dot toddle off to bed, I hoped she was right.

Fourteen

"This is weird," I mumbled to myself in my sleep. I knew I was dreaming but what I saw in my mind didn't have the misty, vague feeling that most dreams do. It felt real.

I stood in the corner of an old cabin, just out of the circle of light coming from a single bulb hanging in the center of the room. Flyspecked wallpaper covered the walls of the kitchen, and the smell of stale cigarettes mingled with the sour aroma of unwashed bodies. Ugh. A group of men sat gathered around the kitchen table. Shadows played across their faces as the poor excuse for a light fixture swung slowly on its frayed cord. And even in my dream, I felt the tension surrounding them.

The man at the head of the table spoke in a low, insistent voice. I strained to hear his words, but the loud ticking of a clock muffled them. He wore a work shirt darkened with sweat, and his hands, lying in front of him on the table, were grimy. Brown eyes in a face shaded with a grizzled beard darted to each man as he spoke. They stopped when they landed on the man to his right. Ethan.

At the unkempt man's words, Ethan sat back in his chair and propped one arm across the back. He opened his mouth to speak but was interrupted when a woman suddenly stepped into the light and wrapped her arms around his shoulders. With her long brown hair hiding her face, she bent and whispered in his ear. He nodded once and rose.

Taking his arm, Sharon Doran led him from the room. As they left, low chuckles and lewd looks from the remaining men followed them.

They stepped out the kitchen door and into a warm summer's night. A full moon lit their way while hand in hand they crossed the porch and walked into the woods.

Wake up, wake up, cried a voice inside my head, but my eyes felt glued shut. And without a will of my own, I felt myself being pulled along behind them.

They walked through the woods as a gentle breeze rustled the tall grass at their feet. They finally came to a stop at a glade, and in the dream, I sensed something familiar about this place. It was the clearing with the standing stones.

But it had changed. The wildflowers were gone, and in their place tall thistles grew. The water that had cascaded into the pool had dried to a trickle, and the pool itself had turned a dark, slimy green. And the stones? No warm glow surrounded them now. They looked flat and lifeless, their rough surface twined with kudzu.

My hands clenched into tight fists and a great sadness filled me. Something had taken this once peaceful spot and turned it harsh and ugly. I wanted to warn Ethan. He needed to leave this place, but I was only a silent witness to the scene that I knew was about to play out.

I watched as Sharon dropped Ethan's hand and danced away from him to the center of the stone circle. In the moonlight, she laughed and spun in a wide arc, her arms outstretched. Stopping, she faced him and a seductive smile spread across her face. Lifting a hand, she slowly undid the first button on her shirt. Then she moved to the next . . . and the next, her eyes never leaving Ethan and her smile never changing.

Like a man possessed, Ethan suddenly crossed the distance between them with long strides and gathered her in his arms. Her triumphant laugh rang through the glade as he pressed his lips to the side of her neck.

I could almost hear her purr.

Oh my god, I thought, covering my eyes with my hands. I don't want to see this.

I bolted upright, scanning the room. My heart raced and a thin sheen of sweat covered my forehead. Wiping it away, I looked at the bed next to mine and saw Abby's still form. I inhaled deeply, then let it out slowly.

"Well, that answered a question," I whispered in the darkness while a profound feeling of disappointment settled in my still racing heart. "Ethan and Sharon are lovers."

The visit was turning out to be more than I expected. Thanks to my dream, I'd lost all respect for someone that I'd begun to care about; I'd learned that an old secret continued to haunt our family; and the mountains weren't as peaceful and idyllic as I remembered from my childhood. I felt like an actor, dropped in the middle of some Greek tragedy without knowing my lines.

I just wanted to go home.

Everyone seemed to pick up on my mood and cut me a wide berth, including my mother. I caught their long looks and the head shakes. Even Dad and Tink stopped their whispering in the corner and cast a sideways glance in my direction. Finally, as I was helping put away the breakfast dishes, Tink sidled up to me.

"Are you going shopping with Grandma in Asheville today?" she asked me.

"I'm not really into shopping today," I replied as a little voice inside my head said, *Are you ever?*

Lavender eyes studied my face closely. "You want to hang out with me and Grandpa?"

Throwing an arm around her shoulder, I forced a smile. "Thanks, but I think I'll stay here, maybe read a little."

"Are you okay?"

"Yes," I lied.

She leaned closer and her voice dropped to a whisper. "Grandpa and I want to show you something."

"Another map?" I asked, giving her a playful squeeze.

She shot a look over her shoulder at Dad as he strolled out the kitchen door. "No, Grandpa threw it away." Tipping her head toward mine, her face grew serious. "It's really important."

Concern sparked. What had those two been doing? "Okay," I replied, wiping my hands on a dish towel. "Let's go."

I followed Tink out the door and across the yard. Turning the corner of the barn, I saw Dad waiting for us. Tink walked up to him and he handed her two el-shaped pieces of wire.

She grasped the short end of the L in each hand and pointed them straight out in front of her. Immediately the wires crossed, forming an X.

Dowsing rods. A vision of another one of the cousins bilking Dad out of more money flashed in my head. "Where did you get those?" I asked suspiciously.

"Grandpa made them for me." Her eyes sparkled. "Aren't they cool? They work a lot better than the willow ones I made at home."

She took a step away, and I watched the rods move back to their original position in her hands. Sidestepping to her left, the rods crossed again.

"See?" she said with a triumphant look over her shoulder.

I came up to her and placed a hand on her arm. "You found your ley lines?"

"Yeah," she answered with a quick nod, and stuck the rods in her back pocket. Grabbing my arm, she pulled me after her as she skipped away from the barn. "Come on, wait until you see what we found."

Glancing back at Dad, I gave him a skeptical look. He answered me with a huge smile.

With a shake of my head, I let Tink drag me off into the woods.

It was a beautiful morning. Blue jays called from the tree-tops as squirrels skittered through the branches. Ahead, I thought I caught a glimpse of a white-tailed deer bounding through the dry leaves.

I felt the remnants of my dream fade. So what if Ethan was a sleeze? Yeah, he'd come to the rescue when Tink had been kidnapped and I'd always be grateful, but there'd never been any romantic attachment. We were only friends, or had been. At the moment, I didn't know if I even wanted to be friends with a guy who'd sleep around, even if it was part of his cover.

When we stepped into a small clearing, I felt the prickle of awareness creep up my spine. The woods became very silent and a weight pressed down on me. I skidded to a halt.

"I don't think this is a good idea." I turned toward Tink and saw the concern I felt mirrored on her face.

"I know . . . I feel it, too." She pulled on my arm. "But it's just in this one spot." Pointing to the trees ahead, she took a couple of steps. "The feeling goes away when you reach the edge of the clearing."

Reluctantly, I followed her. She was right—once we stepped back into the woods, the feeling vanished as quickly as it had come. The timber was still quiet, but the oppressiveness was gone. Now all I felt was a sense of calm, a sense of reverence.

Dropping my arm, Tink bounded ahead. "There," she cried, twirling around to face me. "Do you see it?"

"See what?" I asked. "All I see are more trees and a small hill."

Dad stepped next to me. "It's not a hill, Ophelia. It's a burial mound," he said in a hushed voice.

I squinted at the supposed burial mound. Thin saplings grew across the crest and dry leaves caught in dead vegetation covered its sides. Looked like a hill to me.

Dad saw the skepticism on my face and stuck his hand in his pocket. Withdrawing it, he held out his hand, palm up. Lying in its center was a small red stone, and carved on it were three swirls, just like the ones on Cousin Lydia's amulet. Tink ran over to join us.

"Isn't it awesome?" she asked excitedly.

My eyes flew wide. "Dad, you're going to be in such trouble—"

He held up his other hand, cutting me off. "I haven't been excavating the burial mound," he insisted. "I found this over there, by the base of that tree. At first I thought it was a rock, but when I brushed the dirt away, I saw the carvings."

"What is it?"

He traced the swirls with a finger. "I don't know . . . " Pausing, he eyed me with speculation. "Could you touch it and—"

I quickly took two steps back, holding up my hands. "No way. There's been enough freaky stuff going on around here without me picking up on something from a dead civilization."

"What kind of 'freaky stuff'?" he asked, cocking his head.

"Never mind." I stuck both hands in my pockets. "I'm not touching it." I peered at the stone. "If that is a burial mound and the stone is part of the grave goods, how did it get over by the tree?"

His eyes narrowed. "On the far side of the mound there are signs of digging—amateur artifact hunters, I presume." He shook his head in disgust. "They've ruined so many sites with their blundering." Sighing, he continued, "I suspect one of them dropped it."

"Do you know how old it might be?" I asked.

He slipped the carving back into his pocket and looked toward the mound. "It's hard to say without sending it to a lab, but my guess would be it's from the Mississippian culture."

"And how long ago was that?"

"Roughly 900 to 1700 A.D."

"Wow." A thought occurred to me. "I don't think Great-

Aunt Mary would approve of you pulling in a team of archaeologists to find out."

He laid a hand on my shoulder. "I have no intention of launching a dig. Tink and I are only trying to prove her ley line theory."

"That the lines connect these sites?"

"That's right."

"Have you—" I stopped and looked at Tink as a fear sprang to mind. "Tink, do you think it's a good idea for you to be wandering around burial mounds?"

The vision of some ancient American spirit taking a liking to Tink and attaching itself to her flipped through my head.

She giggled softly. "It's okay. I've kept my shield up like Great-Aunt Mary taught me and not tried to reach anyone."

"Okay, but has *anyone* tried to reach you?" I asked, not satisfied with her answer.

"No," she replied with a roll of her eyes. "Quit worrying . . . I haven't even seen any shadows flitting over the mound."

I let out a sigh. "Good," I replied sternly, "keep it that way."

On our way back, I felt the same unease as we stepped into the clearing. Tink had removed her dowsing rods from her pocket and was watching them cross and uncross in front of her. When we reached the center of the clearing, the points went crazy and began to pull to her left. Without thinking, she veered off, following them.

"Tink, no," I cried out, watching her move farther and farther away from us as she concentrated on the thin metal wires.

Dad spun and ran after her. One second he was running, the next he lay facedown on the ground.

"Dad!" I hollered, rushing to him.

Hearing my cry, Tink spun and raced toward Dad's prone figure. "Grandpa!"

Together we rolled him onto his back.

"What happened?" Tink asked, her eyes clouded in fear.

But before I could answer, Dad groaned and his eyelids fluttered open. "Damn it . . . I stepped in a hole."

"Look at me," I commanded as I stared into his pupils. I breathed a sigh of relief—they weren't dilated. Grasping his upper arm, I helped him to a sitting position. "Can you stand?"

"Of course I can stand," he replied in an irritable voice as he tried to move to his knees. He fell back on his butt and looked at me. "My right foot . . . I think I broke it. Your mother's going to kill me," he exclaimed.

Fifteen

While Tink ran for help, I stayed with Dad and waited for the cavalry to arrive. It did in the form of Lydia and two strapping male cousins.

Flushed and out of breath, Lydia knelt next to Dad and extended her hands, palms down, over his head. Never touching him, she slowly moved them downward. Her eyelids closed and the air around us thrummed with a clear green vibration.

The compression that I'd felt earlier emanating from this spot lifted, banished by Lydia's healing energy.

When she reached his right foot, she opened her eyes and removed his boot. The foot inflated like a balloon. Quickly, Lydia laid one hand on the top of his foot and the other on his arch. The swelling stopped and the tissue actually began to shrink back to its normal size.

After a moment, she sighed and sat back on her heels. "That should help," she said with a nervous glance to the edge of the clearing. "Thank goodness it's not broken."

"It's not?" I asked, surprised.

Lydia stood as the cousins moved to Dad's side and pulled him upright. "No." Her forehead wrinkled and she rubbed at the creases. "It's a bad sprain." Moving her hand from her forehead, she placed it on Dad's shoulder. "You're not going to be wandering around for the next couple of days,

Edward," she said in a soothing voice. "You need to keep that foot elevated and wrapped in ice."

Dad grimaced.

"Don't worry, Grandpa," Tink said, skipping up next to one of the cousins who supported Dad's weight. "I'll take care of you."

Relieved that his injury wasn't more serious, I found myself suppressing a smile at Tink's statement. Dad hated being fussed over as much as he hated inactivity. And with all the women in the household, he could look forward to being cosseted within an inch of his life.

The Aunts and Abby would force him to drink nasty herbal concoctions to speed the healing, and Mom would alternate between lecturing him for tramping around the woods and bossing him. He wouldn't be able to twitch without one of them getting on him like flies on stink.

Nope, it wasn't going to be pretty, I thought as our little group made our way across the clearing and headed for home. We'd gone a short distance when Lydia placed her hand on my arm, stopping me.

"What were you doing in the clearing?" she asked abruptly.

"Nothing," I answered as I watched Dad, Tink, and the cousins pull ahead of us. "They wanted to show me a burial mound." Cocking my head, I looked at her. "Did you know it was there?"

"Yes," she replied with hesitation. "There are several around here, but Great-Aunt Mary doesn't cotton to anyone snooping around them."

"Is that why the clearing feels so ominous? Did she cast a spell to keep people away?"

Lydia rubbed her forehead before speaking. "No, she hasn't been out here in years . . . no one in the family has."

"Why?"

She dropped her hand and focused on my face. "It's not a good place. The Dorans own land just on the other side." Turning, she started to move away.

My hand shot out and grabbed her sleeve. "I thought the family owned all the land in this section?"

"We do," she answered, shrugging out of my grasp, "except for that one little parcel."

Before I could open my mouth, she hurried to catch up with the others, leaving me with unanswered questions.

Once we arrived at Cousin Lydia's, no mention was made of the clearing and the Dorans. Lydia bustled about getting Dad settled on the couch with his foot propped high on feather pillows. After wrapping it with an ice pack, she hurried off to the kitchen to prepare an herbal drink, while Tink and I pulled up two chairs and kept Dad company.

The corners of his mouth turned downward. "I'm not going to like whatever it is she's brewing, am I?" he asked with resignation.

Thinking back to all the junk Abby had poured down my throat over the years, I shook my head. "No, probably not."

"That's what—"

The front door flying open cut off his words as Aunt Dot charged into the room, her cane thumping the hardwood floor of Lydia's living room.

"What happened?" she asked, her old eyes scanning the room with a squint.

A chagrined look crossed Dad's face before he answered. "I stepped in a hole and twisted my foot. Lydia said it's just a sprain."

Aunt Dot hobbled over, and I quickly stood, giving her my chair. Propping her hands on the top of her cane, she studied Dad. "Where?"

"The clearing north of the house," he replied as Lydia handed him a cup of foul smelling liquid.

Aunt Dot's attention immediately shifted to Lydia, and my radar went on full alert as I felt them both tense. This family had a secret, and whatever it was, it was a whopper. The whole situation was making me perturbed, but before I had a chance to pursue that thought, the door popped open again. Mom and Abby stood in the doorway, their arms loaded with shopping bags, grins on their faces.

Their grins died when they saw Dad lying on the couch with his foot raised. Dropping the bags by the door, they both hurried over to the couch.

"Edward," Mom gasped. "You're hurt!"

Reaching out, he took her hand. "Now, now, Maggie, I'm all right. I blundered into a hole and sprained my foot."

Mom's eyes narrowed as she stared down at him. "What were you doing?"

Dad, circled by five women and a girl, all staring at him, shifted uncomfortably on the couch as Tink rushed to his defense.

"We're tracing ley lines, Grandma," she interjected.

Mom's attention turned to Tink. "Ley lines?"

"Yeah." Her blond ponytail bounced as she nodded enthusiastically. "I'm using dowsing rods, and I found lines that run from the barn up the valley. And guess what?"

Dad gave his head a small shake, but Tink missed it.

"We found a burial mound . . . isn't that awesome?"

Abby's face drained of color while her eyes fastened on Lydia. "Where? Where did Edward fall?"

Lydia licked her lips nervously. "The clearing," she replied softly.

Abby gasped and her eyes filled with tears. "The past . . . I can't escape it, can I?" she asked with finality.

Lydia took a step toward her. "Abby—"

But before anyone could stop her, she spun and fled out the door.

I went from perturbed to pissed off. Shoving my hands on my hips, my eyes raked over Aunt Dot and Lydia.

Their shoulders slumped.

"I want to know what happened . . . now!" I exclaimed.

Straightening, they exchanged a look and their expressions hardened with stubbornness.

"I told you I don't know," Lydia muttered, brushing past me as she headed for the kitchen.

Aunt Dot rose and hobbled after her. "I don't remember," she called over her shoulder.

"Bullshit," I muttered to myself. Noticing Tink's wide-eyed look, I turned to Mom for help.

She shook her head and placed a hand on my arm. "Let it go, dear. Your father's okay." She let out a long breath. "In a few more days, this celebration will be over and we can go home. Everything will go back to normal."

I had a feeling it wasn't going to be that easy. I'd seen the haunted look on Abby's face. I pivoted and ran out the door to find her, but she'd disappeared. Pausing, I chewed on my lip while I thought about what I should do next. There was only one answer: Great-Aunt Mary. She wouldn't feign ignorance as Aunt Dot had . . . she might tell me where to go, but she wouldn't pretend she couldn't remember. All I needed to do was persuade her.

I gave a snort. Right. I was so good at diplomacy. It wouldn't matter . . . soft words wouldn't work with Great-Aunt Mary. With that woman, a frontal attack was the best approach. Gearing myself for the confrontation, I marched down the road back to the Aunts.

Entering the house, the first thing I saw was Great-Aunt Mary and Abby sitting at the kitchen table. Abby was crying softly while Great-Aunt Mary made comforting sounds.

I felt a tinge of hesitation at the idea of intruding, but quickly tamped it down. I needed answers.

"What's going on?" I asked, taking an offensive stance.

Both heads whirled in my direction.

"You," Great-Aunt Mary said, jabbing an arthritic finger in my direction. "You stay out of it, girl. All your snooping around is bringing nothing but trouble, and I for one—"

Abby clutched Great-Aunt Mary's other hand, interrupting her. "That's not fair. Ophelia has nothing to do with this. It happened long before she was born."

Great-Aunt Mary's eyes shifted to Abby and her face softened. "You've babied her all of her life," she insisted. "Even though she was one of the chosen, she didn't want it, and you let her have her way." Her attention flew back to me and her eyes narrowed. "Now she thinks she can barge in here and do whatever she wants."

Abby pulled her hand away, drawing Great-Aunt Mary's focus back to her. She rose. "That's not true. Ophelia isn't to blame—I am," she said, wiping away her tears. "And it's time the price was paid."

Great-Aunt Mary pulled herself upright and squared her shoulders. Anger simmered on her face. "The price was paid."

"Not really," Abby murmured as she turned, then walked quietly back to our bedroom.

After she vanished down the hallway, Great-Aunt Mary fixed her anger on me, still standing in the doorway.

"Are you happy now?" she spat out at me. "You had to poke the hornets' nest, didn't you?"

Shock at her unfairness stiffened my spine, and I glared back at her. "I haven't done anything," I cried. "Dad and Tink were the ones rambling around in the woods, not me."

She pointed a knobby finger my way again. "You're the one asking all the questions, getting into a fight with Sharon Doran—"

"Hold it," I said, cutting her off. "*I* did not get in a fight with Sharon Doran. She was the one who approached me." Crossing my arms, I continued to glare at her. "And as far as asking questions? Sorry, but when someone threatens me and my family, I like to know the reason why."

Spinning on my heel, I slammed the door behind me and took off across the yard. I should go back and comfort Abby, I thought. She'd seemed so defeated. But I couldn't stand the idea of being in the same house as that old dragon. I'd go back and talk with Abby once I calmed down.

I kicked at the leaves as I marched along. Indignation at Great-Aunt Mary's accusations boiled through me. The only thing I was guilty of was trying to protect Abby, and to do that I needed to know why the Dorans hated us. But no one was talking, the runes weren't working, and my dreams weren't much help either. I felt like I was shooting in the dark. I knew the enemy, but not why she was the enemy. It was frustrating the hell out of me. Before I knew it, I was at the edge of the clearing where Dad had fallen.

I stopped, and once again the leaden atmosphere of the place weighed down on me. Bowing my head, I took a deep breath and imagined a golden bubble surrounding me. A bubble so thick that nothing could penetrate it. The weight lifted, and I took a tentative step toward where Dad had gone down. Then another, and another, until finally I stood over the spot.

Squatting, I examined the ground. Yup, a gopher hole. Dad had stepped in it in his haste to catch up with Tink. I raised my head and looked at the ring of trees surrounding the clearing. Tink's dowsing rods had acted crazy right about here and started steering her toward the other side of the clearing and the trees. What lay on the other side? Doran land.

I stood and walked slowly toward the woods. It was odd . . . I didn't grow up in these mountains, but I had in Iowa. People back home were as tied to the earth as these folks in the mountains. I understood how they felt. Land was precious, almost a sacred trust to those who owned it, and it wasn't parted with willingly in most cases. So why did my family sell a piece of it to the Dorans? A family that they hated? It didn't make sense.

Stopping at the edge of the clearing, I bowed my head and let my eyes close. Again I imagined my golden bubble.

I opened my eyes and confidently stepped into the woods and onto Doran land.

Sixteen

My shield held, but the weight of whatever lurked in the woods pressed down on me. My steps slowed and my feet felt heavy, as if I were slogging through snow. And quiet, the woods were so very quiet . . . muted and still . . . not even the leaves rustled. Silent as a cemetery. And just as dead.

A trickle of fear eased down my back and every nerve jangled. I should go back, but I felt driven forward. Then I stepped out of the trees. My stomach twisted.

I stood in the clearing from my dreams, and as in my second dream, when Sharon had seduced Ethan, it was vile. A trickle of dark water ran down moss covered stones into the stagnant pool where dead leaves floated on its surface. Weeds grew everywhere. In the distance the standing stones, once proud and glowing with an inner light, were being smothered by the clinging kudzu and turned into nothing more than green mounds. Only a glimmer of red stone peeked out here and there from beneath the thick leaves.

Staring at the stones, my throat suddenly clenched as if the kudzu held me in its suffocating grip, too. Unable to bear the choking sensation, I strode over to the stones and began ripping away the woody vines. I stopped.

Lightly stroking the exposed stone, I felt a hint of recognition as a picture of Dad's carved rock flashed in my mind.

The same ancient people who'd built the burial mound had created this circle.

With a sense of urgency, I pulled and snapped the kudzu. More and more of the red stone began to show, while the ground at my feet became littered with broken vines and twigs. And as I did, it seemed the stone beneath my hands flickered with life. Exhilarated, I worked faster until finally a large section was free.

Sweating and with fingers stained green, I took a deep breath and laid my forehead against the cleared stone.

An old familiar jolt arced through my body, paralyzing me, while the images formed.

A girl . . . no, a young woman waltzed through the standing stones, gathering wildflowers. Wearing a simple cotton dress, her features were muted by shadows, but her long auburn hair still glistened in the dappled light. Auburn hair? What had Aunt Dot said about auburn hair? Annie . . . Annie had auburn hair. Were these images of my great-grandmother?

A small smile formed on my lips as I watched her in my mind and the connection I felt with her grew. I sensed her joy, her happiness, but the feeling abruptly fled. She wasn't alone . . . others waited and watched beyond the circle of stones . . . two men, one young, one old, spied on her from the shadows.

The old one wore a slouched hat low over his eyes, but he resembled the grizzled man who'd appeared in my second dream. Hiding behind one of the stones, he lifted a hand and pointed to the far side of the clearing. The younger man nodded and silently moved in that direction. The old man went the opposite way.

I knew what they were doing. They were circling around the young woman, intent on trapping her. I watched in horror while, using the stones as cover, they crept around the outside of the circle and blocked her escape.

Lifting a hand, the old man signaled and together they rushed her. The young man grabbed her and threw her to the ground, trampling her basket.

Her scream echoed again and again.

I felt their hands on her, pinning her to the hard earth. I felt her head snap from side to side as she fought them. I felt her hands striking out at them. I heard the ripping of material. I heard her cries. A harsh wind blew over them as thunder shook the air and the earth rocked and the pellets of rain beat down on her.

Helpless to stop the vision of something that happened so many years ago, a sickness boiled in my stomach. My cry joined hers as a crack of lightning shot out of the sky, striking a tree and setting it ablaze.

Suddenly, the scene in my head vanished like a candle extinguished and another voice reverberated in the clearing.

"What in the hell is wrong with you?"

I opened my eyes to find myself staring into gray ones filled with concern.

Ethan stood in front of me with his hands on my shoulders. My fists lay curled on his chest. Confused and shaken, my eyes flew around the clearing. When had he appeared? I'd been alone when the vision overtook me . . . I thought. Had I been held so fast by the past that his presence hadn't penetrated my consciousness? Had he witnessed me having a vision?

No, no, I couldn't handle this, handle him, right now. I took a stumbling step backward, turned and ran.

My feet flew across the hard ground, across the clearing. Away, I had to get away from that place. I heard heavy footsteps closing in behind me. As I reached the edge of the woods, hands on my shoulders spun me around, and I would've fallen had they not caught me, holding me tight.

I struggled, but the fight went out of me as wracking sobs shook my body.

Ethan continued to silently hold me until I couldn't cry anymore. Spent, I gave a feeble push and he released me. I sank to the ground and covered my face with my hands.

In an instant I felt him next to me. Gently pulling my

hands away, he took a canteen from his belt and poured water over them.

"You've really skinned up your hands," he said, removing a handkerchief from his pocket and wiping the abrasions. "What happened and why were you beating the crap out of that rock?"

Taking the cloth, I took over drying my hands. "I don't want to talk about it."

"I think you need to," he persisted. "Look, I don't pretend to understand this psychic stuff, but you weren't 'here,' Ophelia. And whatever you saw really upset you." Sitting back in the grass, he watched me carefully. "I heard yelling . . . and when I got to the clearing, I saw you pounding against that stone." He shook his head. "When I tried to stop you, you started pounding on me."

Glancing at his chest, I saw little smears of red against the blue of his shirt. Blood . . . my blood from the scratches on the side of my hands.

"Sorry," I mumbled, mopping my face with a clean corner of the handkerchief. "I didn't mean to hurt you."

"You didn't," he replied softly, "but you sure scared me. I didn't know if you were going to snap out of it."

I drew my legs up to my chest and rested my chin on my knees. "I'm fine."

"You don't look it," he stated.

Letting out a shaky breath, I stared back toward the clearing. "The stone circle? It's a crime scene from a long time ago."

The cop in him came to the surface. "How long?" he asked.

Trying to do some swift calculations, I came up with an answer. "Over seventy years," I replied in a flat voice.

He lightly touched my shoulder and I shied away. Dropping his hand, he leaned forward. "If it's an old murder, there's no statute of limitations," he said quietly.

I knew Ethan was trying to comfort me, make me feel better. And I appreciated he wasn't questioning what I might have seen. He knew I'd witnessed a crime from a time long gone.

But the vision hadn't been of a murder. I knew I'd been witnessing a rape.

Refusing to answer his questions, I left Ethan standing at the edge of the woods and began my trek back to the Aunts. I tried to set aside the sickness I felt and reason out what I'd seen.

Based on the way she was dressed, the incident had happened decades ago. I'd felt a kinship with her. She had beautiful dark red hair. It had to be Annie.

For the past few days I'd poked and prodded, wanting to learn the reason for the long-standing feud with the Dorans. Now I knew. They'd attacked my great-grandmother, and I regretted that I'd ever sought the truth. Ignorance would have been better.

But I couldn't help wondering. The attack explained the grudge my family held against them—right now I felt my own hostility simmering deep inside—but why did they hate *us*? And how did they come to own that section of land?

Times were different back then. Sympathies didn't always lie with the victim, and even though I knew Annie had done nothing to provoke the attack, there might have been those who'd seen it differently. Had the family deeded the land to them as a bribe? As a payment to keep their mouths shut and not risk the ruin of Annie's reputation? Why hadn't Annie's father simply meted out his own rough justice to the men who'd hurt his daughter? And had the attack happened before or after Annie's marriage to Robert?

What if it occurred before the marriage? What if . . . ?

My knees began shaking and I stumbled to the nearest tree for support. Bile rose in my throat.

"Don't go there, Jensen," I whispered, swallowing hard.

My hand clutched at the tree, its rough bark cutting into the scratches on my palm. I hated that place, hated what had happened there. I'd like nothing better than to grab a torch and set fire to the whole clearing. Burn away the evil with cleansing flames.

But no . . . I couldn't do that. The best I could do was make it through the rest of this visit, counting the days until we could all go home and leave the ugliness behind.

"Whatever happened among those standing stones was a long time ago," I said aloud as I stepped away from the tree. "Leave it buried."

Lydia had been right. I should've listened.

I walked into the house to find Aunt Dot preparing an early supper. She took one look at my face and rushed over to me.

"Land sakes, child, what happened to you?" She grabbed my hands and held them out in front of me, looking them over. "You're covered with scratches." Leading me to the table, she sat me down then crossed to the cupboard. She took a crock from the shelf, returned, and after cleaning my hands with a damp cloth, began to slather salve on my abrasions.

"What happened?" she repeated.

"Nothing, I stumbled and fell into some thistles," I lied.

"Humph," she snorted, "seems to be a lot of falling going on around here all of a sudden."

"Where's Great-Aunt Mary and Abby?" I asked, changing the subject.

"Sister's resting before supper, and Abby isn't feeling well—"

"She's sick?" I jerked my hands back, cutting her off.

"Just a touch of the flu," she assured me. "Tea and a little toast will set her right."

I quickly rose. "She's in bed?"

Aunt Dot nodded.

"I'll go back and check on her."

I left Aunt Dot sitting at the table and hurried back to the bedroom. Pausing at the door, I saw Abby's still form lying on the bed next to mine. The shades had been drawn, casting the room in gloom. Crossing to the bed, I laid a hand on her forehead to check her temperature.

Her eyes popped open and she smiled.

"I'm sorry," I said. "I didn't mean to disturb you."

She scooted up in the bed and patted the space next to her. "You haven't. I wasn't asleep."

"Aunt Dot said you have the flu?" I asked, sitting on the edge of the bed.

She flapped her hand, dismissing my concern. "No, I think I'm simply tired. This trip has been more of a strain than I'd anticipated."

Part of me wanted to ask her what she meant, but I remembered the resolution I'd made in the woods—to leave the past buried. Instead I grinned and took her hand in mine. "It will be over soon, and then we can go home and life will be back to normal."

A slight smile lifted the corner of her mouth. "I hope you're right."

"I am. We can go back to all the teenage drama, Tink's puppy shredding toilet paper, and hearing more than we need to know about Darci's love life," I joked.

Abby chuckled. "It sounds good, doesn't it?"

"Oh yeah," I answered with a vigorous nod.

Her face grew serious in the faint light. "I'm sorry this trip hasn't been what you expected."

"Hey, it hasn't been bad," I said with forced brightness. "Great-Aunt Mary's only given me the heebie-jeebies once."

She frowned. "That's not what I meant." Pausing, she drew a hand across her forehead. "First, you find Oscar Nelson dead—"

"Abby," I interrupted her with a nudge. "It's not the first time I've found a body. I seem to have a talent for it."

"Then your father's hurt," she continued, ignoring me. "I'd hoped there wouldn't be trouble."

I needed to get her mind on something else. "Tell me about your dad," I said abruptly.

Her eyes widened in surprise. "Why do you want to know about Daddy?"

I shrugged. "You never say much about him . . . what was he like?"

"He was a wonderful man," she said wistfully. "He and Mother were so in love." Her fingers picked absentmindedly at the quilt. "Mother's heart never mended after she lost him."

"Do you have any photographs of him? I don't think I've ever seen one."

She folded her hands and sighed. "A few. We didn't have much money back then to have our pictures taken, but there is one of him in his uniform." Her eyes grew misty. "I've never thought much about photos. All I have to do is look at your mother and I see him."

"Really?" I felt a weight lift from my heart. "Mom looks like your dad?"

"The spitting image . . . down to the strawberry mole she has on her shoulder. Daddy had one just like it."

"Why didn't anyone ever mention this?"

"I don't know . . . is it important to you?"

"Ah, well . . . " I stumbled around for an answer. I didn't know if Abby knew what had happened to her mother, and if she didn't, I certainly didn't want to be the one to tell her. I didn't want to tell her that for an instant I'd questioned her paternity. There . . . I admitted to myself what I'd feared in the clearing, and I felt lighter for it. Especially since I knew my fears had been unfounded.

"It's just . . . well . . . it's nice to know that part of him is still here."

"Exactly," she said with a broad smile. "I think it every time I look at your mother." Her smile faded. "So much would've been different if he hadn't have died in the war," she said sadly as she laid her head back on the pillow. "I'm sorry, dear, but suddenly I'm really tired."

I popped to my feet. "I'll leave you alone now. You rest, okay?" Bending down, I gave her a quick kiss on the top of her head.

"I will," she said softly as I turned to leave.

Pausing at the door, I looked back at Abby. The sooner this visit was over, the better.

Seventeen

I clung to my resolution to let the past stay buried, but the next morning a restless feeling dogged me. Abby had missed breakfast, and in spite of her reassurances that her illness was nothing more that a slight case of the flu, I was worried. I'd wanted to spend the morning with her, but she insisted that all she needed was rest.

Translation . . . I can't sleep with you hovering over me.

Reluctantly I left her alone and moseyed out to the kitchen. Now the only ones left in the house were me, Aunt Dot, and Great-Aunt Mary—Tink had spent the night at Lydia's, and was no doubt smothering Dad with attention. Being on my own with the Aunts wasn't an easy situation. I didn't mind spending time with Aunt Dot, but all during breakfast Great-Aunt Mary's blue eyes shot daggers in my direction, as if I were somehow responsible for Abby's illness, Dad's accident, and any other problems that had reared their nasty heads during our visit. Conversation was stilted, and it made poor Aunt Dot so anxious that she almost burnt the biscuits. As soon as we finished eating, I grabbed Ethan's now clean, dry handkerchief and bolted.

As I hiked up to his hideaway, I thought about Great-Aunt Mary. Her comments over the past few days grated on me. She obviously thought I was spoiled—as an only child, it was a litany I'd heard most of my life—that I'd wasted my talents, that I'd betrayed my heritage.

Humph, she could think what she wanted. In a few days we'd be gone, and I wouldn't have to deal with her judgmental attitude. I couldn't wait.

I fingered Ethan's handkerchief as I walked along, and my thoughts switched to him. What a mixed bag those were. On one level, I couldn't seem to help being attracted to him, and not just physically, but emotionally, too. His acceptance of my gift was rare. The few men that I'd allowed into my life were either freaked by the whole thing or wanted to use me for their own reasons. Ethan didn't fall into either category. He seemed to accept me for what I was. He'd listened to me when no one else would, and as a result we'd found Tink.

But on the other hand, when I'd first met him, he was playing the role of a big, bad, biker. And, along with everyone else in town, I'd bought into it. Now he was just as convincing as a good ol' boy selling drugs. So who was he really? Was he a hero or a villain?

With a frown, I shoved the cloth into my pocket. It didn't make a difference. Whatever I might have felt for him, or had hoped to feel, was impossible now. His affair with Sharon had killed it.

Just as well, I argued with myself. I had a full life . . . I didn't need romance to make it complete.

But every now and then, when I saw happy couples, I couldn't help thinking . . .

"Oh drop it," I told myself, "look at the Aunts—they're happy."

I skidded to a halt, flashing back to the regret I'd sensed in Great-Aunt Mary. I wouldn't exactly call her happy. Is that what I might become someday? Aloof, scary, and except for an extended family, alone? At one point in my life that picture would've appealed to me, but now it didn't. I didn't want to spend my life holding everyone at arm's length.

I'd been so intent on my thoughts that I'd marched right

by the entrance to Ethan's hideaway. Shoving them away, I turned and retraced my steps until I found the cave. I squatted down and shoved the cloth deep into the branches that hid the entrance. I didn't want any white flapping material to draw anyone's attention to this spot. Standing, I turned to find the path blocked by Ethan.

"You've taken to wandering these mountains quite a bit, haven't you, Jensen?" he asked with a grin tugging at the corner of his mouth.

At a loss what to say, I stared past him, down the mountain. "Ah, I'm returning your handkerchief."

He chuckled. "That's okay—you could've kept it."

"No, I don't like keeping personal items," I said as I moved to step around him.

A touch on my arm brought me up short.

"I thought about you all night." His grin vanished. "Are you feeling better today?"

"I'm fine," I said sharply.

"Do you want to explain what happened?"

Sidling away, I refused to meet his eyes. "I don't want to talk about it."

And I meant it. I didn't want to think about the standing stones. As far as I was concerned, the Dorans were welcome to that cursed piece of land.

His hand stopped me again. "It might help if you talked it out."

"I don't need to talk it out. I need to get back to the house." I looked pointedly down at his hand still on my arm.

His hand fell to his side. "Look, if you're embarrassed about what happened in the clearing—"

"I'm not embarrassed," I insisted hotly. Actually I was—I must have looked like a wild woman, pounding on that stone then on him—but I didn't intend to admit it.

Cocking his head, his gray eyes roamed my face. "I'd really like to help you, Ophelia," he said softly.

This man would not quit badgering me. "I don't need help," I insisted, shoving my hands on my hips.

He took a step forward and his voice took a hard edge. "What happened to get you so pissed off?"

"Nothing," I declared, dropping my hands and taking a step back. "I just don't appreciate being interrogated."

"Ha!" He gave a rough bark of laughter. "That's funny coming from you. I've seen you in action, remember? You drilled that poor guy—"

I stood tall while I glared at him. "I thought he had a hand in Tink's kidnapping."

"And as I recall, you were ready to shake the truth out of him." His lips curled in a wry grin as he took another step closer. "Would it help if I tried that? Then would you tell me what has you is such a twist?"

Refusing to let him intimidate me, I held my ground. "I think you have more than enough problems without worrying about me."

"Jeez, Jensen," he said, his gray eyes suddenly warming. "I can't seem to help myself. There's just something about you that makes me want to play the white knight."

"Well, go play somewhere else," I shot back. "I don't need to be rescued."

"Maybe not, but I think you do need an ally," he said, looking me up and down. "Your family has been stonewalling you."

"How do you know?"

He shrugged. "I've heard talk."

"What kind of talk?"

He gave another shrug and said nothing.

I studied him carefully as my emotions waged a war inside my head. Which was he, hero or villain? I couldn't decide.

Ethan *had* helped me when I needed it most, even risked his career by doing so. It was tempting, oh it was tempting, to pour out all my thoughts and worries to him. I knew from our shared history that he was a good listener. Maybe he was right—I did need to talk it out. Maybe it would help me shake the twitchy feeling I'd had all morning. He'd been with the Dorans for months . . . that Zachary Doran was scum wouldn't come as any surprise. He could warn me if Sharon had any other tricks up her sleeve.

I pulled myself up short. Sharon and my dream. Ethan was literally sleeping with the enemy. No way could I trust him, and it made me angry.

"You can't help me. It might blow your cover." I spun away from him and started down the path. "And I wouldn't want to make your girlfriend jealous," I called back as a parting shot.

Ethan caught up with me in two long strides, and grabbing my elbow, spun me around.

"Wait a minute," he exclaimed. "What girlfriend?"

"Let's put it this way—I didn't realize just how *far* undercover you were!" I snapped.

His forehead wrinkled in a frown. "What in the hell are you talking about?"

"Sharon. Are you going to close the case before or after she expects you to marry her?"

His frown fell away while his eyebrows shot up. "Marry her?" he sputtered. "Are you nuts?"

"No, I'm not nuts, and I'm not stupid," I replied, crossing my arms over my chest.

"You're sure as the devil confused." He shook his head in dismay. "And now you're confusing me."

He certainly looked confused. He looked like he didn't have a clue what I was talking about. But I wasn't going to let him con me.

"Listen, slick, you'd better be careful," I said, jabbing a finger at him. "Remember, people in these mountains are famous for shotgun weddings."

He shook his head as if he were trying to clear it. "The would-be bride has to be preg— Ha!" he scoffed. "You have to have sex with someone first."

Arching an eyebrow, I stared at him without comment.

His jaw fell. Snapping it shut, he glowered at me. "You think I'm sleeping with Sharon Doran?"

"Aren't you?"

"Hell no," he proclaimed.

"Liar," I shot back. "I saw you."

Lowering his head, he shook it back and forth slowly. "You have fallen off your broom, haven't you . . . and it addled your brain. You can't see something that hasn't happened."

"But . . . " I hesitated. His sincerity took me off guard. "I had a dream. Sharon seduced you—"

"Not in this lifetime." He took a step closer. "The dream was wrong," he insisted.

Tugging on my lip, I tried to recall the dream. "It felt true." Turning my back to him, I stared down the mountain. The cabin, the men gathered around the table . . . the rustle of leaves broke into my thoughts and I felt Ethan standing close. This time I didn't move away.

"Have you ever been mistaken?" he asked quietly.

"Umm . . . occasionally." Turning, I cocked my head and studied him. He looked so earnest. "But it's because I've read the signs wrong. And this dream was pretty explicit. I saw you with her . . . she led you to the glade . . . the full moon . . . the summer breeze . . . you—"

He held up his hands, stopping me. "I don't want to hear the rest." He shuddered. "I don't care what the dream showed. I've never had sex with Sharon, and trust me, I've worked very hard to make sure I *never* do."

"But I saw the way she latched onto you that day at Abernathy's. Like she owned you."

A faint blush appeared on his cheeks. "Maybe in her dreams, but not in reality," he answered firmly.

In her dreams? A flash of inspiration hit me. "How long have you been here?"

"A couple of months?"

"You weren't here this summer?"

"No."

A huge sense of relief filled me. The scene I'd witnessed had taken place in the summer, not the fall. It wasn't of the past, but of the future. Or at least it was what Sharon had *planned* for the future. And sometimes the future could be changed. Ethan was a hero after all.

He caught my shifting emotions. "What?" he asked with a perplexed look.

How did I explain? I had to warn him what Sharon was trying to do without sounding crazy.

I scuffed the ground with the toe of my boot. "Let me ask you a few questions . . . are you missing any underwear?"

"Huh?" His voice sounded incredulous.

Well, so much for not sounding crazy.

Sighing, I looked at him. "Underwear . . . has she offered to do your laundry?"

"Yes."

"Did you let her?"

"Yes," he grudgingly replied.

"Was any of your underwear missing when she gave them back to you?"

"I don't know," he grumbled. "I don't count them."

"Has she ever offered you something to drink then drank out of the same cup or glass?"

He shifted uncomfortably. "A couple of times."

I snapped my fingers, remembering something from one of the old journals. "You haven't seen any skull-shaped candles lying around, have you?"

Ethan's eyes flared in surprise. "My God, no!"

"Does she have a picture of you?"

He gave his head a vehement shake. "Absolutely not. In my line of work, we avoid cameras."

"Has she ever given you a piece of candy?"

"How did you know?" he asked in amazement. "Yesterday . . . a piece of peppermint . . . I don't like peppermint, so I spit it out when her back was turned."

"Good for you," I said with a nod.

Pulling his hands through his hair, he stared at me in frustration. "You are the most—" He cut himself off. Dropping his hands, he continued, "Why all the questions?"

Pleased with myself, I gave him a cheeky grin. "Isn't it obvious?"

"No."

"She's trying to cast a love spell on you."

"With candy?"

I nodded. "Yeah, the woman, or the man, rubs it on the bottom of their foot then gives it to the object of their affection. It's supposed to make that person follow them."

"She touched her foot with that . . . and I . . . I put it in—" His face blanched and I thought he'd gag.

"Yeah, good thing you spit it out," I replied in a cheery voice.

With a shake of his head, he sighed deeply as the color came back into his cheeks. "Do the spells work?"

"I'm told they can," I replied, thinking of Aunt Dot's "back door Betty." "I don't know for sure. I've never tried it."

"Would you?" he asked, eyeing me speculatively. "Try one, I mean?"

"No, of course not. They're unethical."

A strange look crossed his face, but I ignored it.

"You need to be careful," I lectured, shaking a finger at him. "Keep track of your laundry and don't let her get her hands on it. Don't accept anything from her. Hide your hairbrush."

His face told me he took me seriously. "Is there any way that I can protect myself?" he said as he pointed at the chain around my neck. "You wear an amulet."

I thought about the runescript that I'd made for Abby. I could make one for Ethan, a sort of antilove spell.

"Yes, but I have to think about what would work." I shook my head. "You can't let Sharon see it. She'd know right away what it was and it might blow your cover."

Shoving his hands in his pockets, he chewed on his lip for a moment. "This assignment's been a mess from the get-go." He frowned, then rolled his shoulders as if trying to cast off one of Sharon's spells. "I'd better get back to the Dorans before someone comes looking for me." He laid a hand on my arm. "You'll be okay walking back?"

I nodded. "I'll make something for you and leave it in the cave. It'll be a piece of wood with carvings on it. Keep it with you where Sharon can't find it."

Giving me a squeeze, he smiled. "Thanks. I've got faith in you, Jensen."

With a wink, he turned and headed off into the woods.

Eighteen

On the way back to the house I stopped at the outcrop of rock overlooking the valley, Abby's favorite spot. Taking a deep breath, I let it out slowly. I was relieved that Ethan wasn't a creep with no morals, and his faith in me gave my heart a sorely needed lift. But I was worried, too. He balanced on a thin wire, keeping Sharon at a distance, yet still maintaining his cover. I'd do whatever I could to help him.

What? Whatever I made had to be small, small enough for Ethan to carry with him without being obvious. I couldn't carve a script as long in length as I had for Abby. Three would work, but which ones?

The first that sprang to mind was Thurisaz. A strong masculine rune, it represented thorns, brambles, a force of both protection and destruction. I saw Ethan surrounded by a ring of thorny bushes, being held safe in its center.

Ha, I snorted to myself, let Sharon's puny magick try and get past that one.

Next, I'd use Tiwaz. It was the rune symbolizing the old Norse god, Tyr. Noble in spirit, Tyr had sacrificed his right hand to save mankind. It also represented bravery and justice. And given his line of work, I'd say it fit Ethan perfectly.

I'd end the script with Thurisaz again, to seal my intent and further reinforce the protective circle around him. Yeah, justice guarded by a girdle of thorns . . . I liked that. It felt right.

My decision made, I turned and started to leave when I spied something out of the corner of my eye. Walking over to it, I squatted down. It was a pile of fine ash.

Had Abby been there, casting some kind of spell?

Poking the ash with one finger, I felt an object buried beneath the fine gray powder. I brushed the top layer away.

A crude clay figure lay in the center of the pile, its body covered with grime. With an increasing sense of alarm, I picked up the figure and wiped away the dirt from its face. Two bright emerald chips of glass glinted from the center . . . like eyes . . . like Abby's green eyes.

I shot to my feet and kicked the pile away, sending the ashes over the edge of the rocks.

"That bitch!" I hissed, clenching the poppet in my fist. Spinning on my heel, I took off in the opposite direction from the Aunts' house. I didn't know for sure where the Dorans lived, but I bet I'd find it.

I almost ran through the woods, my rage fueling every step as my feet crunched the dried leaves littering the ground to bits. *How dare she?* repeated over and over in my head as I strode past trees and bushes, up the hills and down the hills.

Finally I came to a gravel road and turned right, leading me up the valley. In a short time I found what I was looking for—a battered mailbox with DORAN lettered on its side.

Shoving the poppet in the pocket of my sweatshirt, I marched up the lane next to the mailbox.

A rambled-down house and two trailers sat in a yard overgrown with weeds. A rusty refrigerator with no doors tipped precariously against one corner of the house, and two skinny hounds, tied with long chains, lounged beneath the branches of a crooked elm tree. Spotting me, they lunged to their feet and ran out the length of their chains, growling and snapping.

I wasn't in the mood.

Skidding to a stop, I whirled toward the dogs. My eyes narrowed and I fixed them with a menacing look. "Shut up," I said through clenched teeth.

Instantly the barking stopped and they both cowered. Dropping their heads and tails, they moved back underneath the tree and watched me from the corners of their eyes.

Satisfied that I wouldn't have a problem with them, I turned my attention to the house just as the screen door flew open and several men poured out from inside the old house.

I spotted Ethan among the group. His eyes showed alarm and he made a move to step forward. A quick glance at the man next to him made him stop. He lowered his chin, dropping his eyes, but I knew his attention was still on me.

The grizzled man from my vision starring Ethan and Sharon came forward. Zachary Doran, no doubt, and he was just as scummy as he'd been in my dream. He spat a long stream of tobacco juice in my direction before he spoke.

"You git on down the road," he called out.

I didn't move. "I'm here to see Sharon."

"Don't care why you're here, you'll git if—"

A hand on his shoulder stopped him and shoved him to the side. Sharon pushed past him, and the other men then sauntered down the porch steps.

"You'd better do as he says," she said with a smirk. "Or we'll set the dogs on you."

"Oh yeah?" I shot a look at the dogs. With a whine, they ran for cover behind the tree.

Turning my attention back to Sharon, I saw her eyes widen in surprise at the dogs' behavior.

"What do you want?"

"I don't want anything," I said, my voice quivering with anger. "I'm here to give *you* a warning." Reaching in my pocket, I withdrew the poppet and held it up in the air. Stepping forward, I waved it in front of her. "I suggest you stop your little parlor tricks."

"Or what?" she scoffed. "You and your wishy-washy relatives won't do nothing to me."

"I wouldn't count on it," I replied in a low voice.

Her lip lifted in a sneer. "Y'all are too soft. You don't believe in"—she made quotation marks in the air—"'negative energy.'"

"Right. But we also believe in protecting our own . . . " I paused, looking her square in the eyes. "Do you *really* want to see how far we'd go with that belief?"

She made a move toward me, but Zachary hurried down the porch steps and grabbed her arm. "Sharon, you'd better leave her be."

She whipped her head toward him and gave him a scathing glare. "Shut up."

The old man jerked his hand away.

"I'm the granddaughter of a seventh son of a seventh son," she said with a toss of her head. "I'm not afraid of you."

Crossing my arms over my chest, I stared her down. "You should be. Our magick is as old as the earth. We know things you can't even begin to understand."

I watched a flicker of uncertainty fly across her face, then she glanced over her shoulder at the men watching from the front porch. "Bull," she replied with a voice full of bravado.

"Fine," I answered with a shrug. "Keep it up and you're going to find every witch in my family lined up against not only you, but all the Dorans."

The old man's face slackened and fear shone in his eyes. "Sharon," he said hurriedly, "remember Pa and what they done to—"

She whirled on him. "I told you to shut up." Turning her attention back to me, she laughed. "You don't know what you're talking about. Your family made a vow not to break the truce."

I uncrossed my arms and looked down at the doll still in my hand. "We didn't. You did." I lifted my eyes to her face. "All bets are off."

Without a backward glance, I turned on my heel and walked away.

*   *   *

The door hit the wall with a bang, making Aunt Dot jump as I hurried into the house.

"Where's Great-Aunt Mary? Where's Abby?"

"Abby's still in bed," Aunt Dot said, fluttering over to me. "And Sister's down at Lydia's."

"Call Lydia," I commanded. "Get them up here right now."

Aunt Dot didn't argue and went immediately to the telephone and began dialing.

As I crossed the living room, headed back to the bedroom, I caught sight of Abby's carry-on. She never left home without her medicinal herbs. Maybe she had something that would help cure her flu. I changed direction and walked over to the bag. Picking it up, I placed it on the chair and unzipped it. The papers Abby had been reading lay on top. When I moved them to the side, big bold letters caught my attention and my heart froze.

THE LAST WILL AND TESTAMENT OF ABIGAIL CAMPBELL MCDONALD

"Abby!" I shrieked, and grabbing the papers, ran into the bedroom.

As I tore into the room, Abby stirred and sat up in bed. "What? What is it?" she asked, her voice thick with sleep.

"This," I said, crossing to her with the papers held tightly in my hand. "What's this?"

She sighed softly. "Oh."

I sank to the bed next to her, my knees suddenly weak. "Why did you bring your will with you on this trip?"

Her eyes wouldn't meet mine. "Be prepared for the worst and it'll never happen."

"Uh-uh," I replied with a shake of my head. "Clichés won't work, Abby. I want the truth."

"It all happened so long ago, it's not important," she said, evading me.

"It is if you think you're going to die," I cried. "That's

what our conversation on the mountain was all about, wasn't it? You were letting me know your wishes while you still had time?"

She didn't answer.

"You knew all along that Sharon Doran might try and hurt you, didn't you?" I persisted.

"Yes," she whispered.

I took both of her hands in mine and watched her intently. "Sympathetic magick can't kill you. You're too powerful to let that happen."

"So was my mother," she said as her eyes filled with tears, "and the Dorans killed her."

Nineteen

I was still sitting on the bed when Lydia rushed into the room. Noticing my alarm, she misjudged the situation and went quickly to Abby. She placed her hand on Abby's forehead.

"No fever," she said. "Her color's pale, but not too bad." She stepped away from the bed and looked down at me. "She looks better than you do, though. What's going on?"

I stuck my hand in my pocket and pulled out the poppet. "This."

Lydia and Abby both gasped.

"I knew it," Abby said, turning her head away. "The price will finally be paid. Blood for blood."

"Bullshit." I shot angrily to my feet. "If you think I'm going to let that so-called witch win, you've got another think coming."

"You can't use magick against someone," Abby said in a weary voice.

"I don't see why not," I shot back. "She's using it against you and I have the right to protect you."

The runescript.

"Abby, you're strong enough to sit in the chair, aren't you?" I looked quickly at Lydia to judge her opinion.

She gave her head a slight nod.

Without waiting for Abby to answer, I pulled back the

covers and helped her out. After settling her in the chair, I covered her legs with the quilt and went back to the edge of the bed.

Both Lydia and Abby watched me with puzzled looks as I lifted the mattress. The piece of lath was gone.

Disheartened, I let the corner drop and sat on the now rumpled bed. With my hands dangling uselessly between my knees, I studied my grandmother. She really believed that Sharon Doran was slowly killing her. I had to convince her otherwise.

She lifted a trembling hand to her face and stroked her forehead. "I can't let you use magick against the Dorans," she said in a weary voice. "What you send out comes back three times over."

"Ha—what about Sharon and what she's sending our way? If that statement were true, she ought to be roasting by now," I replied. "And I hope she does."

Her hand fell away and her green eyes narrowed. "Ophelia," she said, irritated, "I taught you better than to wish something like that."

Her remark sounded more like the old Abby.

"You said she caused your mother's death," I argued. "Why hasn't that come back to haunt her?"

"Sharon didn't cause Mother's death . . . her granny did." Abby stroked the quilt covering her legs. "Mother took to her bed—"

"You mean like you're doing now?" I asked, not letting her finish.

She ignored my question and continued. "A week later, she'd passed." Leaning her head on the back of the chair, she sighed. "I'd always feared Granny Doran would eventually get her revenge. I wanted Mother to come back to Iowa and live with us, but she refused."

I remembered Mom talking about the argument she'd witnessed between Abby and Annie. Wait a minute. Mom had mentioned another argument . . . one between Abby and Great-Aunt Mary. Now I knew the reason.

"You wanted to go after the Dorans when Annie died, didn't you?" I demanded. "But Great-Aunt Mary wouldn't let you."

"Yes." Her voice sounded stronger. "And she was right in insisting that I didn't. Who knows where it might have led and who would've suffered. It was such a hard time . . . we didn't even go through Mother's things . . . just packed them in boxes and threw them in the attic." Her eyes filled with pain. "The Dorans got their pound of flesh *and* their ounce of blood. The truce has held ever since."

"Until now, don't you mean?" Her acceptance infuriated me. "I don't know why anyone thought the Dorans were entitled to either 'flesh' or 'blood.' They were the ones who committed the crime. They should've been the ones to pay."

Her eyes flew to my face. "You know?" she whispered.

Not meeting her eyes, I scuffed the toe of my shoe on the wood floor. "Yeah," I confessed reluctantly. "I went to the clearing. I saw them rape Annie." Moving quickly to the chair, I knelt at her feet and took both her hands in mine. "Abby, I'm so sorry for what they did to your mother," I murmured.

She pulled her hands out of my grasp and clutched the arms of the chair as her eyes flashed fire. "It wasn't my mother . . . it was me."

I heard a soft plop as Lydia's butt suddenly hit the bed. A quick glance over my shoulder told me that the disbelief on her face mirrored mine.

Abby's eyes traveled to Lydia and then to me. "Oh, they didn't succeed," she said in a clear, firm voice. "I stopped them."

"How?" I whispered, feeling as if my stomach was about to heave.

"I called forth the Elements." Her face tightened with long ago vengeance. "You should've seen their fear," she spat out. "The younger one—"

"Sharon's uncle . . . Zachary?" I asked as all the pieces of the vision gelled in my mind.

"Yes, he couldn't hold his bowels. He ran from the stones like a rabbit, leaving his father to face my wrath alone."

Rising, I stumbled backward and joined the silent Lydia on the edge of the bed. We both stared raptly at Abby.

Her head turned, her eyes focusing on the mountains towering above the valley.

"The standing stones are ancient," she said in a whisper, "but you've been there, you already know that."

"I figured as much," I replied. "They're tied to the burial mound that Tink and Dad found, aren't they?"

She nodded, her eyes never leaving the window. "Mother had taken me there all my life." A wistful smile formed on her face. "I played among those stones as a child and I'd always felt a strong bond with the gentle spirits lingering there." Her smile faded. "Until that day, it was a beautiful, peaceful spot."

The first dream I had—I'd witnessed a scene from Abby's childhood. She'd been the little girl curled on the blanket, and Annie was the young woman singing.

"I used that connection when I called the Elements. I drew on the primal magick that I'd always felt and added it to my own." She winced and shuddered. "Only what I tapped into was not gentle. It was savage."

I, too, had called the Elements—twice. Once, not so long ago, I used the power of Earth, Air, Fire, and Water to seek enlightenment, and the other time? For retaliation. I'd gathered the power inside me and was ready to loose it against a killer, but Abby's mind touching mine at the last moment stopped me. I still remembered what it felt like—of being able to stretch out my hand and crush those who inflicted harm. And Abby had not only drawn on the Elements, but added the magick of the ancients. The power would've been magnified a hundredfold.

I could see her now in my mind . . . battered but not beaten, her arms outstretched, the wind whipping her auburn hair, ringing down all that raw power on the sorry heads of the

Dorans. It would've been truly frightening, and as far as I was concerned, they deserved it.

"Why, Abby? Why did they attack you?"

She opened her eyes and exhaled slowly. "It was the old man's idea. He thought if Zachary dishonored me, it would force Mother to agree to a marriage between me and his son." Her face twisted in a grimace. "Ever since they'd moved to this valley, both the old man and his wife had been jealous of our family's influence. They wanted folks to come to them, not Mother. They tried to undermine her at every opportunity, but their plan didn't work." Plucking at the quilt covering her lap, she turned her attention to me. "Then he came up with the idea of joining our blood with theirs. He saw it as a way to unlimited power. But no matter how hard he bullied her, Mother wouldn't do it."

"Why didn't one of the men in the family step forward and tell the old man to back off?"

Crossing her hands in her lap, she sat forward. "Our family has always produced more girls than boys. And the few men who did have blood ties to us were either still in the service or working jobs away from the mountain."

"What about the in-laws?" I asked.

"No," she replied with a slight shake. "Mother was afraid of starting a war between the Dorans and us, so she handled it alone."

"Great-Aunt Mary and Aunt Dot?"

"Great-Aunt Mary was teaching school down by Raleigh, and Aunt Dot was working over in Asheville. She hid what was happening from them. They only learned of it after the attack."

"You know the attack wasn't your fault, don't you?" I asked gently.

The idea of Abby carrying around the feeling that she had somehow caused the attack sickened me . . . so many women in similar situations did. I couldn't bear it if Abby were one of them.

"Yes . . . I know. What they did was on their heads," she said, sagging back against the chair. Lydia made a move to go to her, but Abby waved her back. "I'm fine. This is hard for me—"

I started to rise to my feet. "We can talk about this late—"

"No," she said, interrupting me. "You need to hear the rest of the story."

I sank down and waited for her to continue.

"I should've stopped when Zachary ran. I was safe. The old man wasn't going to hurt me. He was as frightened as his son . . . He huddled by the stones, cowering as the rain poured down on him," she continued sadly, "but I didn't . . . I was so angry."

"What did you do?" I whispered, shocked by her confession.

Abby's eyes looked directly into mine before her gaze drifted to the window. "I focused not only my magick, but that of the ancients on the old man. I cursed him . . . Two weeks later he died." Her eyes came back to me. "I killed him as surely as if I'd used a knife."

Twenty

"I don't believe it," I cried, shooting to my feet. "Everyone said he died of a fever. *Was* there a fever going around?"

"Yes . . . " She hesitated. "The Robbins' boy almost died from it, but Mother saved him."

I slapped my leg. "There you go . . . you didn't kill him . . . if anything he died from his own wickedness," I insisted.

Abby reached out and took my hand. "But I'll never know for sure, will I?" She squeezed my hand tightly. "I've lived with the uncertainty all of my life, and it's one of the reasons why I've tried so hard to teach you restraint."

"And you have," I exclaimed, dropping to my knees in front of her. "When Brian's killer came after us, I wanted to use the powers to hunt him down, but I didn't. You stopped me." I stared at her intently. "Now Sharon Doran wants to harm you. Don't you have the right to protect yourself?"

She let go of my hand and stroked my cheek, her eyes full of love. "Protect, but not destroy. I want you to always remember the difference. I didn't."

"Yes, you did. They tried to destroy you," I argued, "and you were simply protecting yourself."

"No, I wasn't. I wanted the old man dead, I wished for him to die, and he did," she answered, convinced her words were true.

I rose to my feet and began pacing the room. "I don't care

what you say. I don't believe you can kill someone just by wishing."

"Ah-hem," Lydia cleared her throat to get my attention. "What about Oscar?"

Abby's eyes flew to Lydia. "What about him?"

Lydia nervously fingered her amulet. "Ophelia found a poppet right before she discovered him dead. It had a nail through the stomach."

"Poohey," I exclaimed, sliding to a stop. "Great-Aunt Mary said he'd had stomach problems for years and died of a hemorrhage."

Lydia lifted an eyebrow and said nothing.

I resumed my pacing. "Even if Sharon did hex him to death, he wasn't a witch . . . he couldn't defend himself like you can," I said, spinning toward Abby.

She seemed to shrink in the chair in defeat. "I committed a crime against that family," she said with resignation. "If Sharon wins now, maybe this feud will finally end."

"You'd sacrifice yourself?"

"Yes," she whispered.

I was so angry at her and her selflessness that I wanted to throw a childish temper tantrum, but I knew it wouldn't do any good. I tried another argument.

"If Sharon wins, what do you think is going to happen to the people in this valley and in these mountains? They're already scared of her, and by besting this family, it will only add to her reputation." I stared at Abby in defiance. "She will do *what* she wants, *when* she wants, and nobody will say a word against her. Is that what *you* want?"

"She'll be punished in the end," Abby said meekly.

I felt like shaking her. Nothing I said seemed to penetrate what she believed was inevitable. What could I say that would put the fighting spirit back in her?

I had it.

Throwing up my hands, I stopped my pacing. "If this is the way magick works, I wash my hands of it once and for all."

"It's your heritage. You're one of the chosen," Abby hissed. "You can't ignore it."

"Oh yes I can . . . I walked away from it once before, remember?" I said, reminding her of the time following Brian's murder and my struggle to come to terms with his death. "Magick didn't save him and now, if we can't use it to save you, I want nothing to do with it."

"What about Tink?" she asked, distressed. "You have to help her learn how to use her gift."

I shook my head. "No, I don't. We'll ignore that she can contact the dead—eventually she'll get over it."

"Being a medium isn't something one 'gets over,'" she insisted, with more strength in her voice now.

"I'll teach her how to suppress her talent . . . I'm good at bottling things up—I have experience."

"You must *not* do that. You've grown so much over the past couple of years. You *can't* go back to the way you were after Brian died."

I watched her eyes cloud with fear. Good, she believed I'd do what I said.

"Why not?"

"If you deny your gifts again and force Tink to do the same, that child will never know a day of happiness in her life. She must be allowed to follow her path." She frowned. "And you must help her. You can't give up."

I shrugged, looking down at her. "Why not? That's what you're doing."

Turning on my heel, I did one of the hardest things I've ever done . . . I walked away from my grandmother.

My bravado failed when I crossed the living room and saw Aunt Dot and Great-Aunt Mary sitting at the kitchen table. Great-Aunt Mary's head whipped toward me and her resentful blue eyes caused my steps to falter.

"What have you gotten yourself up to now, girl?" she demanded. "More trouble, I suppose."

Terrific. Another battle. Taking a deep breath, I lifted my chin and walked over to the table to face her.

"I didn't start anything," I insisted, "but I intend to end it."

"Humph, I told you to stay out of it." She looked me up and down, and I saw in her eyes that she found me lacking. "I'll protect this family."

Abby had always required that I show respect to my elders, but I'd had it with her. "You're not doing a very good job," I said, pulling out a chair.

At my words, I heard Aunt Dot's sharp breath.

I glanced over at her as I plopped down. "I'm sorry, Aunt Dot, but she's not," I said, tossing the poppet on the table.

Seeing the poppet lying there, she began to wring her hands while Great-Aunt Mary stared at it as if she were looking at another snake.

"Where did you get this?" Great-Aunt Mary asked through clenched teeth.

"On the outcrop overlooking the valley," I replied.

She poked at it with a crooked finger. "Explains Abby's illness."

I was tired of hearing it. "Oh, please," I scoffed. "A figure made of clay can't kill." I gave her a level look. "Or as you pointed out, one made from a potato." I turned my attention to Aunt Dot, then back to Great-Aunt Mary. "You've both said Sharon Doran's magick didn't amount to much, so why think her tricks would work against Abby?" I leaned forward. "Especially when I made . . ."

My voice trailed away as a thought occurred to me. The disappearing runescript.

Hooking my arm over the back of my chair, I stared at Great-Aunt Mary, and for once she looked away first.

"You wouldn't know anything about a little piece of wood with carvings on it, would you?" I asked, already knowing the answer.

"I told you," she grumbled, "*I* protect this family."

Looking up at the ceiling, I rolled my eyes. "Of all the shortsighted—" I cut myself off and looked at her again.

"The runescript wasn't an attempt to usurp your position in this family. I was only trying to help." I kept my voice even. "How did you find it?"

"One of Gladys's boys was helping me change the bedding."

"What did you do with it?"

"I had him bury it," she huffed.

"That's just peachy, isn't it?" I asked, leaning forward. "Why wouldn't you let me try and keep Abby safe?"

"It's not your place, it's mine," she said with vehemence.

"Look," I said, scrubbing the side of my face in frustration. "I'll say it one more time . . . this isn't some kind of competition. And don't you think we have enough of a challenge fighting Sharon without fighting each other?"

"You're a novice," she uttered, the contempt she felt coloring her words. "And if you expect me to trust you when all you've done is let—"

She broke off as Lydia and Abby entered the kitchen. Lydia, with one hand on Abby's arm, reached out with the other and moved a chair away from the table. After settling Abby on the chair, she took her own place at the table.

Aunt Dot sprang to her feet and hurried over to the stove to fetch Abby a cup of tea. Her face was wreathed with a smile as she placed it in front of Abby. "I'm so happy to see you out of bed," she cried, taking her seat again next to Great-Aunt Mary.

"Are you feeling better?" Great-Aunt Mary asked in a voice much kinder than the one she used with me.

"A little," Abby answered with a smile of her own. "I'm sorry to have worried y'all, and I'm sure I'll be feeling my old self again soon." She turned her smile toward me. "Ophelia wouldn't have it any other way," she finished with a note of pride.

Great-Aunt Mary let out a snort.

Abby ignored her as her attention moved to the poppet still lying on the table. "I see Ophelia showed you what she found."

Great-Aunt Mary's hand shot out and grabbed the poppet. "I'll take care of it," she said, slipping it in the pocket of her apron.

With a shake of my head, I leaned back in my chair. "I want to know everything about the Dorans," I said, addressing her.

A frown crossed her face. "I think you already know more than you need to."

Not letting her rile me, I waited her out.

The silence grew until finally Abby leaned forward, looking at Great-Aunt Mary with unwavering eyes. "Please . . . you know more about what happened after the attack than I do. Tell her. You may not have faith in her, but I do."

Great-Aunt Mary shifted uneasily as she made a tsking sound. "I suppose I don't have any choice," she said with a glance at Abby's determined face. "I take it you know about the standing stones."

I nodded. "Why did the family deed it to the Dorans?"

Turning her gaze from Abby, her eyes hardened as she stared at me. "After the incident, I came home right away. If she only would've told me . . . " She paused. "Annie was beside herself. She was so afraid that if anyone learned about what the Dorans had done, the valley would erupt in violence." Her eyes moved once again to Abby and her voice softened. "You know your mother wanted them to pay for what they did, don't you?"

Abby nodded. "But she didn't want innocent blood shed over it."

"That's right." Turning back to me, all the softness slipped away. "We thought when the old man died, that would be the end of it. And it was . . . until Granny Doran showed up on our doorstep one day with her snot-nosed youngest on her hip, demanding retribution for the death of her husband."

I was shocked. "She knew about what happened at the standing stones?"

"Yes." Great-Aunt Mary answered curtly. "She probably had been the one to encourage them."

I felt my eyes round with amazement.

"She said she'd sic the law on us, that she'd see to it Abby was driven from the valley." Great-Aunt Mary swallowed hard. "We couldn't let her go around telling tales, getting people all riled up."

"You weren't afraid of something like Salem happening here, were you? Witch hunts ended—"

She held up a hand. "There'd always been those that'd looked sideways at us. We didn't know what she might talk them into doing. We feared a mob coming for Abby in the middle of the night, so . . . " She shrugged a thin shoulder. ". . . we gave her what she wanted."

"The clearing with the standing stones," I stated.

"Yes. Everyone knew it had always been a special place to our family, a place of power. She thought she could take that power for herself."

"Ack, it didn't work," Aunt Dot piped in, her distaste sounding loud and clear. "Once the land passed out of our hands, the clearing changed from a benevolent place to something just as evil as the Dorans."

"Sharon mentioned a vow . . . what was that about?" I asked.

"When did you talk to her?" Great-Aunt Mary asked quickly.

"After I found the poppet," I replied calmly.

"You confronted her?" Her voice carried a rising note of alarm.

"Of course I did." I cocked my head, with a look of determination on my face. "I'm not going to ignore her threatening Abby."

"What did you say to her?"

"I told her that we would protect our own."

Great-Aunt Mary's eyebrows shot up. "We took an oath never to harm their family, and we've stuck by it . . . "

"We have the right to defend ourselves."

"We've had peace in this valley for over fifty years . . ." She paused, her eyes flashing with anger. " . . . until *you* came along and stirred everything up."

"Hey," I said, defending myself, "we're here because you wanted us here."

"Well, I didn't expect this to happen—old wounds getting picked apart—I thought you'd mind your business."

"Great-Aunt Mary," I said as I leaned forward, "this family *is* my business." My eyes traveled to each one of the four witches gathered at the table with me. Sitting back, I crossed my arms over my chest. "So ladies, what are *we* going to do about Sharon Doran?"

Twenty-One

Our little council of war reached a stalemate. It had developed into a standoff between Great-Aunt Mary and me. *She* wanted to simply reinforce the protective spells that she'd cast. *I* wanted to take a more proactive approach and find out more about Sharon Doran. She fought me on every point. Honestly, I didn't know what the woman's problem was. Did she worry that I might abandon my life in Iowa, uproot Tink and move here in an attempt to challenge her for the leadership of the family? Why did she see me as the threat and not Abby? Oh, *yeah*, she liked Abby.

Finally, fed up with all the arguing, I rose to my feet and left the house. My presence had just seemed to inflame the situation. Maybe without me there, Abby could get Great-Aunt Mary to listen to reason.

As I crossed to the kitchen door and grabbed my sweatshirt, I saw a small look of triumph cross Great-Aunt Mary's face. She thought she'd won, that I'd given up. She thought she could browbeat Abby into agreeing with her on how to handle Sharon Doran.

Well, she underestimated my grandmother and she underestimated me. Either with her cooperation or without it, I intended to find a way to stop Sharon Doran.

This mess began years ago, at the clearing with the standing stones. What ancient people had built the circle and why?

Had their understanding of magick been so strong that even now, centuries later, their power still lingered in the stones? Was it their power that Abby had tapped into? Was it enough to kill? What if Sharon was now using it to fuel her own magick?

All I had were questions, but I needed answers. I couldn't fight her if I didn't understand her power, and although I'd sworn never to return to that cursed place, I found myself headed in that direction.

As I tramped along, the vision I'd had of Abby's attack nettled me. I didn't want to go through it again. I needed to see a time long before the violence I'd witnessed. But could I do it? Was I strong enough to control what vision came through?

"Jeez, Jensen," I muttered to myself, "quit worrying about it and just do it."

When I reached the clearing, the same unease pricked at me. I stopped and once again imagined a golden bubble, only this time it wasn't as fragile as a bubble. No, I imagined an impenetrable shield.

Keeping my eyes down, I took my first hesitant step, then another and another, until finally I was at the standing stones. I paused between two of the upright stones and took a deep breath.

Energy pinged against my shield like rocks hitting a window, and I felt a shiver of fear tickle the back of my neck. What would happen once I dropped it?

Looking down, I noticed a small group of red pebbles lying at my feet. I bent down and selected seven. Seven pebbles—seven standing stones. A protective circle. It might work.

I walked to the center of the standing stones and carefully made a second circle with the small stones. Satisfied, I stepped inside and sat cross-legged in the center. With a deep breath, I tried to connect with the energy coursing below me.

The images sprang forth in my mind. Night . . . stars

slowly fading overhead as the sun began its journey across the sky. A soft summer breeze stirred the air. The first sounds of birdsong mingled with voices chanting in an unknown tongue. Shadows just beyond the edges of the stones. They shifted and took shape.

An old man, his face weathered by the elements, stood in the center of the circle. Long white hair drifted over shoulders covered in buckskin. Seven dark red feathers of a hawk fluttered on the side of his head. In his outstretched hands he held a gourd rattle, and in the other a hoop. As the rays slowly inched across the center of the circle, the chanting rose in volume and intensity. Suddenly the rays shone directly on the old man, making his hair appear to glow with a light of its own. A cheer rang throughout the clearing.

Solemnly, he lowered his arms, and two young men, also dressed in buckskin, approached the center, heads bowed. Their extended hands carried bows and arrows as if they were offering them to the old man. Silently, he touched the weapons with his hoop.

Next to approach the shaman was a young couple. Their moccasined feet silently crossed the hard ground, and their hands were tightly clasped together. A benign smile crossed the old man's face as he lightly rested the hoop on the young man's head. Turning, he did the same thing to the young woman.

Slowly, reverently, other shadows formed as they approached the old man and received his blessing. And as they did, a sense of peace surrounded me.

I let my eyes drift open and the vision vanished.

Looking around, I felt a deep weariness that this sacred place had been used for violence. The people who had once conducted their most scared ceremonies here knew of its defilement, and it was their rage that hummed in the air, weighing down on anyone who ventured near. That's what Abby had called forth, and it was still there, waiting just beyond the edge of the standing stones.

* * *

Shaken by my vision, I didn't want to face Great-Aunt Mary, so I kept walking, past the Aunts' down the road to Lydia's. As I neared the edge of Lydia's yard, I saw Dad and Tink sitting on the porch playing some kind of board game. Mother was nowhere to be seen, but Lydia was tossing a ball to Jasper. Seeing me, she gave the ball one last throw and walked toward me.

Lydia stopped and looked me over. "Don't y'all worry," she said, sensing my tension, and misunderstanding the reason. "Abby's confession snapped her out of that fatalistic attitude that's been weighing her down." She shook her head. "I don't see her taking to her bed again. And with the spells Great-Aunt Mary's going to—"

"Lydia," I said, interrupting her. "I think it's going to take more than a circle of salt and cooking up a few potions on the stove to stop Sharon."

"It will be okay," she insisted.

That's what everyone kept saying . . . why didn't I believe them?

With a smile, Lydia linked her arm with mine and together we crossed the yard to join Tink and Dad.

"Y'all playing Chinese checkers?" she asked, noticing the star-shaped board.

"Yes," Dad replied tersely, "and I'm getting whipped."

I did see that Tink's pile of captured marbles was much bigger than Dad's. Placing a kiss on the top of her head, I sprawled in the chair next to her. "Good job, kid!" I said, giving her a high five. I smiled over at my father. "It's a payback for all the times you beat me at Chutes and Ladders."

"Humph," he answered as he steepled his fingers and studied the board. "I think she's reading my mind."

"Grandpa," Tink said with a giggle. "Mediums can't read minds."

"Well then the spirits are helping you," he answered with a teasing glint in his eye. "It's the only explanation." He carefully picked up one of his green marbles and hopped two spaces.

Tink, giving Dad a cagey grin, promptly jumped three spaces and captured two more of his marbles.

Dad groaned.

Lydia gave him a comforting pat on his shoulder. "If she wins, Edward—and it surely does look like she will—I'll give you an extra big piece of pie at supper. Kind of a consolation prize."

Dad answered her with a chuckle. "It would be worth it to lose, then."

"Ophelia," she said as she focused on me. "You're more than welcome to stay for supper, and the night, if you want."

The idea of not going back to the Aunts and facing Great-Aunt Mary did have its appeal, but staying here also meant dealing with Mom. After arguing with Great-Aunt Mary, I didn't feel up to answering all of Mom's questions.

"Thanks, Lydia, but I think I'd like to avoid Mom, too," I answered, crossing my ankles. "Maybe I'll just hide out in the barn all night."

With a laugh, Lydia gave me a little wave and went inside.

Dad watched her go then turned to me. "What was that all about? Rough afternoon?"

"You might say that," I replied with a sigh. "I'm sure you'll hear all about it later."

"But you don't want to talk about it now?" he asked, moving one of his marbles.

I shook my head.

On her next move, Tink snapped up another green marble.

Narrowing his eyes, he tried giving her a stern look, but she laughed and smiled sweetly at him. "Your move, Grandpa."

"In a minute, in a minute," he replied, focusing on the board. "How's Abby?"

"Better. She was out of bed when I left and Aunt Dot was plying her with more tea."

Dad chuckled. "All the women in this family do see tea as a cure-all, don't they? Lydia's forced me to drink gallons."

"How is the foot?"

He moved another marble. "I can put a bit of weight on it now, so tomorrow," he said with a wink at Tink, "I think we can do a little more exploring."

I jerked forward. "I don't think that's a good idea, Dad."

"Why not? It's more fun that getting beat at Chinese checkers."

"There's more going on here than meets the eye . . . I'd feel better if you and Tink stick close to either here or the Aunts."

Dad's eyebrows drew together in a frown and Tink shifted in her chair to look at me. Curiosity was written all over her face.

I didn't like the way this conversation was headed. Tink didn't need to know what had happened to Abby all those years ago. She was too young. Maybe someday she'd hear the story, but not now.

While I searched for an answer, Tink's expression changed. "This is about the feud with the Dorans, isn't it?" she asked.

My eyes flew wide. "How do you know about that?"

She rolled her eyes. "I stayed with the Aunts, remember?"

I did a slow burn. Great-Aunt Mary had no right to bring Tink into the situation. "Great-Aunt Mary told you about it?"

Leaning back in her chair with a sigh, she gave me a look that told me how dense I really was. "No, all she said was that the Dorans weren't nice people and that I should avoid them. One of the younger cousins told me about the feud. And she said Sharon Doran—"

My hand on her wrist stopped her. "I don't care what she said. I want you to stay out of it," I said firmly. "I'm your mother and I know what's best."

"But—"

"No 'buts.' " Even though I had my doubts about whether Sharon could hurt someone via a poppet, I didn't want to find a clay doll with lavender eyes on my next trip up the mountain.

"I mean it, Tink. You and Dad hang out here, or go shopping with Mom, anything but wandering around the mountains on your own."

"You sound like Great-Aunt Mary," she grumbled.

I didn't appreciate the comparison, but I let it pass.

Dad, after years of practice observing Mom and me, wisely stayed neutral by keeping silent.

Ignoring the pout on Tink's face, I tried changing the subject. "Where is Mom, by the way?"

"She went with one of the cousins to an antique shop . . . thank goodness," Dad exclaimed. "All her hovering was driving me crazy." He looked back down at the Chinese checker board and moved another marble.

Still upset with me for pulling the "Mom" card, Tink halfheartedly captured it.

With a grimace over another lost marble, Dad looked over at me. "Your mother had wanted to spend the day at the Aunts, sitting with Abby, but Great-Aunt Mary discouraged her. She said she'd take care of Abby."

Wouldn't you know it? I thought. Great-Aunt Mary probably saw Mom as encroaching on her territory, too. And I thought I had control issues. Great-Aunt Mary made me look mellow.

Who knows, said a little voice in my head, *at her age, maybe you'll be just like her?*

"No way," I muttered aloud.

"What did you say, sweetie?" Dad asked.

"Nothing, Dad." I turned to Tink. I'd treated her the same way Great-Aunt Mary had been treating me—giving her orders without an explanation. "I know you hate feeling left out, but I'm not sure what's happening myself. This feud—"

"When you find out, will you tell me?" she asked.

"Yes," I promised. I'd worry about how to explain the past later. "This feud," I repeated, "is serious, and I need you to follow Great-Aunt Mary's advice. Stay away from the Dorans, okay?"

"Okay," she agreed grudgingly, and turned her attention back to the game. Dad had made another move, and Tink, sizing up the situation, took one of her marbles and deftly cleared the board of Dad's remaining green ones.

"I give up," he said, throwing up his hands. He held one out to Tink. "Good game."

"Thanks," she said, taking his hand and giving it a vigorous shake. "Want to play again?"

"If I do?" A grin spread across his face. "Do you suppose Lydia will give me *two* extra big pieces of pie?"

"Oh, Grandpa," she chuckled, and handed him back his green marbles.

Reaching out, I tweaked her blond ponytail. "Hey, after supper, are you spending the night here?"

She nodded, making her hair dance. "Lydia said I could if it's okay with you." She gave me a sideways look. "Is it?"

My eyes slid over to Dad.

Catching my expression, he smiled and nodded. "Don't worry," he assured me, "I'll make sure we stay out of trouble."

"All righty then," I said, standing, "I suppose I'd better head back to the Aunts."

I gave Tink a kiss and Dad a quick hug then started trudging down the road. My steps were heavy. I hadn't been kidding about hiding out in the barn. I didn't want to talk to Great-Aunt Mary, at least not tonight. The weather was mild, I told myself, the barn had hay. I could make a comfy little nest for the night. On second thought, did I really want to share a space with creatures that only came out at night? Bugs, mice, and, God forbid, rats? I shuddered. Not in this lifetime.

My thoughts were chased away by the sound of a motorcycle roaring down the gravel road. I watched as it slowed and came to a stop beside me.

Twenty-Two

The rider placed both feet on the ground, his long legs balancing the heavy bike, and turned his head toward me. His helmet and visor blocked his face, but I recognized Ethan immediately.

"What do you want?" I asked.

Without lifting his visor, he handed me a helmet. "Hop on," he said, his voice muffled.

I considered arguing, but the tension I saw in his shoulders made me reconsider. I put on the helmet and climbed on behind him. In an instant we were cruising down the gravel road, away from Lydia's, the Aunts, and the Dorans.

It felt wonderful. The stress of the last few days fled in the rush of the wind tugging at me. I gripped Ethan's waist tighter.

We rode down the valley and out onto a paved road. When Ethan goosed the gas, the bike bucked and we sped off down the ribbon of highway. The lines on the road flashed faster and faster beneath us, almost hypnotizing me. Free, I felt free, and I laughed with the joy of it.

I don't know how long we rode in silence, but finally Ethan slowed the bike as he approached a small restaurant on our right. Turning into an almost empty parking lot, he drove the bike around to the back of the building and came to a stop. After cutting the engine, he balanced it again, allowing me to climb off.

While I removed my helmet and fluffed my now flattened hair, he took off his own helmet and put the kickstand down.

I glanced nervously around the parking lot. "Isn't this dangerous?"

"My driving?" he asked in mock surprise.

Handing him my helmet, I shook my head. "What if one of the Dorans sees us?"

"They won't. They never come here, and the owner is a . . . friend."

There was something funny about the way he said "friend."

"A friend or a snitch?"

"Never mind," he said with a chuckle as he led me toward the back door.

He knocked twice and a big, burly man wearing a dingy apron answered.

"Jack?" the man said, his voice full of surprise. "What are you doing here?" He quickly reached out a beefy hand and drew us inside, locking the door behind us. "And who's she?" He eyed me suspiciously.

Ethan smacked him playfully on the shoulder. "She's okay. She's one of us. We need a quiet place to talk. Where we wouldn't be interrupted." He motioned to a door on the left. "Is the meeting room free?"

"Ah, yeah," he replied, shambling ahead of us. "You want something to eat?" he called back to us.

"That'd be great, Barney," Ethan replied.

As we followed, I leaned close to Ethan. "I presume *you're* 'Jack'?" I asked softly.

"This time I am," he whispered back. "Try to remember to call me by the right name, okay, Jensen?"

This time? I shook my head. All this cloak and dagger stuff. I paused as a thought hit me: Was *Ethan* his real name?

Catching my hesitation, he looked at me and smiled. "Don't worry, Jensen," he mumbled out of the corner of his mouth. "I *am* 'Ethan,' but only when we're alone."

My brows knitted together. "You've had so many names," I said, keeping my voice low. "How do you keep it all straight?"

Taking my arm, he chuckled as he guided me down the hall. "Easy . . . since my life can depend on it."

But with me, he used his real name. He trusted me enough to do that. A warm glow spread over me at the thought.

Before Barney left us alone in the little room, Ethan ordered the special and two Bud Lights. Surprised, I glanced up at him as he held my chair. "You remembered what I drink," I stated.

"Of course I do," he said as he took a place across the small table from me. "I remember a lot of things about you, Jensen. For example . . . " He paused and his eyes narrowed. " . . . your habit of letting your mouth get ahead of your brain."

Uh-oh, here it comes. I glanced up at a spot on the stained ceiling.

"What did you think you were doing facing off with Sharon like that?" His voice quivered with a hint of anger.

Barney, shuffling into the room with our beers, saved me from answering right away. But I should've known that it would take more than a measly beer to distract Ethan, or Jack, or Cobra, or whatever other alias he wanted me to use.

He leaned forward, and I tried to look innocent, but it didn't work. "Well?" he said, crossing his arms on the table, his gray eyes drilling into mine.

Quickly I explained why I'd confronted Sharon.

"That thing you were waving around in front of Sharon's nose is called a poppet? And she's using it to try and kill Abby?"

"She's giving it her best shot," I answered, watching him closely.

I didn't see amusement or doubt in his gray eyes, only puzzlement.

"Can someone do that?" he asked.

Sliding my finger down the side of my beer, I shrugged. "I don't know, but Abby believes it's possible. She thinks Granny Doran used one to kill Annie, her mother."

Ethan sat back. "You're kidding?"

"No, I'm not . . . I know this all sounds really weird, but—" I turned my head while I debated whether I should tell him about Oscar Nelson. Would he laugh at me?

Decision made, I faced him. "My cousin, Lydia, believes Sharon used a poppet to kill Oscar Nelson," I blurted out, and waited for his reaction.

"I thought he died of a stomach hemorrhage."

"According to Lydia, it was brought about by a nail stuck through a likeness of him."

He tugged on the corner of his mouth before speaking. "You know that wouldn't stand up in court," he replied evenly.

"Of course I do," I said, irritation creeping into my voice. "What I want to know is whether or not you believe me?"

"That Sharon would harm Abby?" His lip curled in disgust. "You bet I believe it," he said with passion. "She hates your family, but is she using magick?" Rubbing his chin, his face became thoughtful. "It wouldn't surprise me—I've been here long enough to know her reputation—I know everyone believes she's a witch. Hell, the love spell thing made my blood run cold." He stopped and took a long swig of his beer. "Even her own family's scared of her."

"Well, then," I said, sitting back and crossing my arms, "you understand now why I had to confront her."

He placed his bottle on the table. "No, I don't."

I scooted forward. "Ethan—"

"Jack," he corrected me with a grin.

I waved a hand at him. "Whatever . . . my family believes, I believe," I insisted, "in magick. I know what it can do when someone misuses the power. I can't let Sharon get away with working her spells against my grandmother."

"Can't you do some kind of counterspell?"

"I have . . . we have, but she's done other things, too."

I explained to him about the snake coiled under Abby's bed. At the end of my story, he just sat shaking his head.

"I don't care what you think," I huffed. "She snuck that snake in the house . . . I know she did."

He held up both hands. "I'm not saying you're wrong," he replied defensively. "I'm confused, that's all."

"About what?" I shot back.

His eyes narrowed as he traced an invisible line across the table. "Think about it, Jensen. Why would she risk planting the rattler in the bedroom? She could've been caught."

My forehead wrinkled. "I don't understand what you're getting at."

"Remember when you threatened me with a case of boils?"

"Yes." I felt a blush creep up my neck and I shook my head. "I really wouldn't have done that."

"But if you had, would I have gotten boils?"

"You bet, slick," I replied with a glint in my eye.

"Why?"

I leaned back in my chair. "'Cause I'm good, that's why."

"Then if Sharon's good, why didn't she just cast the spell, knowing it would work, and let it go at that? Why put the snake in your room?"

"Because she wanted to make sure Abby—or one of us—were hurt," I said, stating the obvious.

"Do you follow through with your spells?"

"I don't need to," I replied, a little insulted that he questioned my ability.

Wait, he wasn't questioning mine—he was questioning Sharon's.

Amazed, I stared at him. "She hid the snake because she

didn't know if the spell would work," I cried. "You think she's a fake, don't you?"

On the ride home our conversation replayed in my head while I huddled behind Ethan's body. I'd never questioned that Sharon's abilities were lacking. Everyone said she was a witch so I took it to be true. Ethan's questions opened all kinds of possibilities. I knew she wasn't psychic, but you don't have to be a psychic, or a medium, or talk to fairies in order to practice magick.

However, you do have to believe in the power of magick in order for your spells to work. If you carry even the slightest niggle of doubt, your spell can fail. So was Sharon's witchery all an act? An act she used to intimidate the community around her? Was she using fear and happenstance to validate her reputation?

The young girl who visited Aunt Dot, convinced that Sharon placed a curse on her, had certainly been afraid. Had the girl really had a black cloud following her, or was it her own guilt over trying to manipulate another that weighed her down? And Oscar—what about him? Had it been a fluke that his stomach ailment caused his death just when Sharon had made the poppet?

Right now all I had were questions.

Ethan stopped down the road from the Aunts. It wouldn't do for me to come tearing up the road with a stranger, like some teenager who'd picked up a guy at a dance.

"I'll walk you as far as the barn," he said, taking the helmets and strapping them to the handlebars.

"You don't need to," I protested.

He gave my arm a tug. "I want to make sure you get inside."

With a shrug, I let him pull me down the lane toward the barn. We stopped in its shadow.

Lights blazed from the Aunts' windows and I could see the flickering of the TV set. Boy, I sure hoped that they'd assumed I was staying at Lydia's. I didn't want to have to explain to them where I'd been.

"I'd better get inside," I said with a slight dip of my head. "Thanks for dinner."

"Any time, Jensen," he replied with a touch of humor in his voice.

Raising my head, I looked up at him and gave the collar of his jacket a playful yank. "Be careful, will you?"

In the faint light, I saw his face grow serious. "If you do the same."

"I'm always careful."

He gave a soft snort. "No, you're not. You rush in where others fear to tread."

"I do not," I answered with a lift of my chin.

"Yes, you do," he said, and placed his hands on my shoulders. "And although I don't like seeing you in danger, I do admire your courage."

My eyes flew wide in surprise. A compliment from Ethan? Suddenly shy, I looked quickly down at the ground. "I'm not brave, not really."

His hand lifted my chin until our eyes met. "You're also argumentative, but I can live with that."

"Um, well, ah—" I stuttered, unnerved by his close proximity.

He didn't seem to notice my nervousness. "I have a question," he said softly. "You said you'd never do a love spell. Why?"

"I told you, it's wrong," I mumbled.

"Have you ever been tempted?"

"No."

"You said your spells don't fail," he persisted. "If you cast one on me, do you think it would work?"

"I'd never do that," I answered, squirming a little.

"But if you did?"

Okay, I got it . . . his questions were just another one of his jokes. Well, I could dish it out, too. I squared my shoulders and stood tall, shoving my nerves aside.

"You were worried about Sharon's spells?" I said, arching an eyebrow and looking him straight in the eyes. "Ha—my family history goes back over a hundred years." I gave him a poke in the chest. "If I decided to cast a spell on you, you'd find yourself standing in front of a preacher, slick."

He caught my hand in his and pulled me closer. "Really? Now that's an interesting thought," he murmured as he lowered his head toward mine.

At the touch of his mouth on my lips, every nerve in my body flamed. I literally fell into him and his kiss. His arms came around my waist and I felt myself lifted off my feet while my arms wrapped around his neck. The heat of his body seemed to reach out and consume me. I heard a groan, but I didn't know if it was me or him.

I don't know what would've happened next if the screen door hadn't suddenly slammed open. Ethan set me on my feet and pulled me deeper into the shadows as we watched Aunt Dot sling a basin of wash water onto the ground.

An uncomfortable silence followed.

I broke it first. "Ah, gee, that was, ah, unexpected," I finished lamely.

I sensed rather than saw his smile. Taking a step closer, he bent his head close to mine. "Not really, Jensen," he whispered in my ear. "Someday a time will come when I'm not pretending to be someone else, and you're not tripping over bodies." He stepped away from me. "We'll see how 'unexpected' it is then."

With a salute, he turned and sauntered down the road, leaving me standing there stunned.

Twenty-Three

When I entered the house, I was relieved to see that Great-Aunt Mary had retired for the night. Aunt Dot sat in her recliner, already snoring softly, with her crocheting lying in a ball in her lap, and Abby was curled on the couch, staring mindlessly at the TV.

Turning at the sound of the door opening, she looked over her shoulder and gave me an old familiar smile as I came into the room. I hesitated and placed a hand on my cheek. Was my face flushed? Would she pick up on what had just happened with Ethan? Brother, I hoped not.

I crossed the room and joined her on the couch. Her hair lay in a thick coil over her shoulder and I could see that she had rebraided it. She had also changed into a different pair of sweatpants and sweatshirt. Both were very good signs that our crisis had passed. She still looked a little pinched around the lips, but her color was good. She definitely looked more like the old Abby. I let out a sigh of relief.

"You look much better," I said as I placed a hand on her knee.

Putting her hand on mine, she smiled again. "I am. I'm sorry for worrying you."

"Forget it," I said, giving her knee a light squeeze. "As long as you're okay . . . that's all I care about."

She took her hand away while her eyes drifted toward

the TV. "I never wanted you to know. I never wanted to lose your—"

"Stop," I said, holding up my hand. "You haven't lost a thing. Nothing could change the way I feel about you, Abby."

Her eyes met mine, and I saw the glimmer of fear hiding in them fade. "In a way, I'm relieved that this is all out in the open now. It's like a great weight has been lifted."

"Has it been eating at you all these years?"

"At times." She lifted her shoulder in a shrug. "Shortly after old man Doran died, your grandfather came to the mountains—"

"Did you ever tell Grandpa about the attack?"

"Of course I did. Right after he proposed to me. I couldn't marry him without being honest." A small smile lifted the corners of her mouth. "I thought he'd run, but he didn't. He was like you, he didn't believe that my curse had killed the old man."

"Ha," I said, "I always knew Grandpa was smart."

"Yes, he was," she replied fondly. "After we married and moved to Iowa, I wasn't constantly reminded of the Dorans and the memory and the guilt eased," she continued. "When your mother was born and it was obvious that she hadn't inherited the gift, I saw it as retribution for what I'd done. I accepted that my legacy would end with me and made what peace I could." Leaning forward, she laid a hand on my cheek. "Then you were born . . . From the moment you opened your little eyes and looked up at me, I saw the gift burning bright in them. You were my symbol of forgiveness, and I made pledge never to allow you to make the same mistake that I had."

"And when I denied my gift after Brian's death . . . " I felt my eyes fill with tears and my throat clogged. "I never understood how much that must've hurt—"

"My dear child," she said, stroking my cheek, "it was a lesson that you had to learn." She dropped her hand and gave me a comforting smile. "We've both had hard lessons, haven't we?"

Swallowing hard, I wiped my eyes. "Yeah." I leaned the back of my neck against the couch. "So what do we do now?" I asked, rolling my head to the side and looking at her.

Her smile faded while the old fire sprang back into her eyes. "Stop Sharon."

I don't know if it was the conversation with Abby or the incident with Ethan that caused it, but I couldn't sleep. I tried, I really did. I fluffed my pillow; I rearranged the blankets; I scooted up in the bed; I scooted down in the bed. Nothing worked. My mind would jump from Ethan to Abby and then back again. I could *not* focus.

The easiest thing would have been to simply ride out the rest of our visit. Use combined magick to protect Abby— that is, if Great-Aunt Mary deigned to let me be involved— then go home. I doubted Sharon had enough oomph to cast a spell that would carry from North Carolina to Iowa.

By the end of our talk, Abby seemed determined to stop Sharon. And I shared her feelings. If we didn't do something, Sharon would be left to continue as she always had: misuse magick to spread fear throughout the valley. Only one problem—Abby would never agree to giving Sharon a dose of her own medicine, she wouldn't allow us to use our talent against her.

So how did one stop a witch? Was there a spell I could cast that would strip her of her abilities? Did she even have ability? Ethan suspected she was a fake.

Ethan. When he brought the Dorans to justice, which I was convinced he would, would Sharon also get caught in his net? A nice long prison term for the manufacture and distribution of an illegal substance would end her reign of terror in this valley. But what if she put a curse on him? Even if I didn't believe that she could kill him with magick, she could bring him bad luck. And in his line of work, that could be just as fatal.

I rolled over onto my side and stared at the alarm clock. Sighing, thoughts of Ethan brought back memories of his kiss. I was surprised at the strength of my reaction. Not a prude by any means, I still didn't launch myself at men as I had him. I felt the heat infuse my cheeks at the memory.

And how should I take his last remark . . . the one about the future? Was it a threat or a promise? Which did I want it to be?

Flipping onto my back, I looked up at the ceiling. I'd worked hard to balance my life. My job, motherhood, exploring my gifts, all required a lot of time, patience, and energy. Would Ethan just complicate my life that much more? Was that how Great-Aunt Mary had viewed romance? A complication?

Jeez, Jensen, why had Great-Aunt Mary popped up in the little chat I was having with myself? I winced at the comparison between me and her, even though I was the one making it.

I needed Darci. She had far more experience in matters of the heart than I did, and she could help me reason this all out.

But thanks to the crappy cell phone reception in the mountains, I couldn't even call her.

My eyes flared open in the darkness. If I talked Mom, Abby, and Tink into taking a shopping trip into Asheville, I bet I could get reception. Lydia would probably take us if I asked her.

"Great idea," I whispered to myself, fluttering my feet under the quilt.

With a contented sigh, I flipped onto my stomach and finally slept.

I pitched my idea the next morning at breakfast. Great-Aunt Mary huffed about running off into town, wasting gas, blah, blah, blah. I ignored her and kept my mouth shut. She may have been happy spending most of her hundred years hemmed in by these mountains, but they were beginning to make me feel claustrophobic. I needed some space, from not only the mountains, but all the problems that seemed to be facing us. The jaunt with Ethan on his bike had helped, but it hadn't lasted long enough for me to gain perspective. A day spent away from this place would.

And I'd have a chance to call Darci.

Lydia and Mom quickly agreed, and soon the five of us were heading toward Asheville.

Lydia was the perfect tour guide. She pointed out places of interest along the way and stopped at a couple of the scenic views. We hopped out of her SUV and snapped several photos—Tink, Mom, Lydia, and Abby with their arms linked, standing against the backdrop of the fall-colored mountains; Tink and me making silly faces; Mom and Tink posed like movie stars against a rock wall. And one that I knew would be my favorite: Mom, Abby, Tink, and I smiling happily into the camera as if we didn't have a care in the world. A moment to savor.

When we arrived at downtown Asheville, we wandered down the broad sidewalks, passed street performers—a juggler dressed in outlandish colors tossing brightly colored pins into the air, a guy with dreadlocks and an open guitar case, sitting on the sidewalk and playing music. We admired dusky pottery and gleaming glassware displayed in the shop windows. We drifted into art galleries and looked over paintings done by local artists.

But the best was when we strayed into one of the many New Age shops. I watched as Abby's eyes roamed the collection of crystals, pentagrams, incense, and books about magick and witchcraft. Her eyes stopped when they landed on the young woman behind the counter.

She was dressed in a long flowing robe and her flat black hair had broad streaks of blond around her face. She looked at the five of us with eyes heavily rimmed in black above lips painted bright red. A large silver pentagram hung on a chain around her neck.

Abby leaned her head close to mine. "Is she supposed to be a witch?" she whispered.

"Different strokes, Abby, different strokes," I said with a chuckle.

After purchasing a few crystals and some incense, we left the shop. Once on the sidewalk, we agreed to split up. Tink would go off with Mom, while Lydia and I went with Abby to a small café for tea. After spending a day in bed, Abby needed to take things easy. We'd meet up at one for lunch at the Grove Arcade, a historic building containing restaurants, boutiques, and galleries.

I wondered at the wisdom of letting Tink go shopping with Mom, so I drew my mother aside.

"Listen, Mom, Tink has her own money for souvenirs. Don't let her con you into giving her more," I lectured.

Mom's eyebrows arched. "I guess I can give my grand-daughter money if I want," she informed me.

All righty then. Shaking my head, I walked back to Abby and Lydia, while Tink and Mom took off down the street, giggling and whispering together.

Twenty-Four

After settling Abby and Lydia at a nearby café and placing my order, I excused myself and stepped outside. I took my cell phone out of my bag and dialed Darci's number.

The phone rang and rang, and I hoped I hadn't called while she was in class. Finally she answered.

"Ophelia!" she squealed. "How are you? Are you enjoying your vacation? Have you found any bodies? Ha ha!"

"Actually . . . yes," I replied curtly.

The merriment on the other end died. "No fooling," she gasped.

It took me several minutes to tell my tale, and for once Darci listened without interrupting.

"Do you know what started the feud?" she asked when I'd finished.

"Yes, but it's not my story to tell, it's Abby's."

"Hmm, sound's like this Sharon's really nasty," she replied, letting my statement drop. "What are you going to do?"

"I don't know."

"I'll be on the first plane."

"No, you won't," I said stridently, "you have classes."

"I can take a break," she argued back.

"I'll handle it."

"How?"

"Something will come to me. You're *not* flying down here."

The sound of Darci exhaling slowly sounded in my ear. "Have you tried your runes?"

I quickly explained what happened when I'd tried.

"Wow," she said softly. "That's weird. Are you going to try it again?"

"Yeah, but I don't know when." I paused. "I don't know what course to take. My talent seems to be on the fritz ever since I arrived. No dreams are guiding me; my runes won't let me touch them. I—"

"Have you tried some old-fashioned snooping?" she broke in.

Master snoop that she was, I should have figured she'd suggest that.

"You need to know about Sharon Doran," she continued.

"Like what?"

"Well—" She stopped, and I could almost hear the wheels turning. "What else has she done, or what do they assume she's done? Other than the poppets and the love spells, what other trouble has she caused?"

"I don't know," I said, searching my memory. "All Lydia said was that people are afraid of crossing her."

"That's pretty vague, isn't it? There must be a reason for their fear."

"You mean other than Lydia thinks Sharon killed Oscar with magick," I answered with a tinge of irony. "That seems like a good reason to me for people to be scared of her."

"But he recently died. She must've done other spells, curses, whatever, and you need to know what they were and when."

"Okay, so start asking questions. What else should—"

She interrupted me. "And be diplomatic about it, will you? Don't go blundering about like usual."

"I don't blunder."

"Really? Bill," she said, referring to our local sheriff,

the one who liked to threaten me with protective custody, "might argue with you on that one."

"Okay, okay," I grumbled, "I'll be tactful."

"Are you sure you don't want me to come?" she asked in a hopeful voice.

"Yes, I'm sure," I answered with a chuckle. "I don't think the men down here would know what to make of you, Darce."

And speaking of men—now would be a good time to bring up Ethan. But I couldn't mention him specifically.

"Ah, there's one more thing . . . there's this . . . ah . . . "

She made an exasperated sound. "Would you just spit it out?"

"Guy." The word came out in a rush.

"Oooh," she purred into the phone. "What's his name? How did you meet him?" she fired off.

"Never mind, he's just a guy I met. And I'm, well, kind of attracted to him," I mumbled.

"You're not thinking of moving down there, are you?" she exclaimed.

"No."

"Long distance romances usually don't work," she said cautiously.

"He has to travel a lot in his line of work."

"Sooo," she said, drawing the word out. "He might show up in Iowa?"

Remembering Ethan's remark about the future, I nervously tapped my leg with my other hand. "I think so."

"Go for it."

"Go for what?"

"You know, *it*!" she explained. "You're attracted to him, evidently he's attracted to you, just let . . . " Her voice trailed away.

"Don't you think the timing's bad?"

She snorted. "With a life like yours? Give me a break. The timing's never going to be good, and you'll wind up alone just like your Great-Aunt Mary."

I groaned. I wished people would quit comparing us. And why did the comparison always have to be with Great-Aunt Mary? Why couldn't they compare me to Aunt Dot? She was nice, kind, maybe a little off with the fairy thing. Okay, so I wasn't like Aunt Dot, but Great-Aunt Mary? It made me defensive.

"You know," I said into the phone, fisting a hand on my hip, "I don't need a guy to make my life complete."

"I know, but wouldn't it be nice to have someone you could always count on?"

"I have you, and Abby, and Tink," I argued back.

"That's not what I meant." Her voice softened. "Someone to share your thoughts, your desires, your—"

I cut her off before she waxed too romantic on me. "I get it."

"Good," she said, her voice firm. "Now don't chase him away, let him pursue you, but at the same time, let him know that you're interested. And dress nice the next time you see him. Wear a little makeup, too, while you're at it."

"Is that all, O Great Love Guru?" I asked sarcastically.

Her chuckle rang in my ear. "Just let it happen, Ophelia. If it's meant to be, it will."

I blew out a long breath. She sounded just like Abby.

"But I don't know if I want it to happen. I mean, gee, with Tink, Abby, and all, I worry—"

"That's part of your problem. You worry too much. Go with the flow."

"Should I go with the flow before or *after* I stop the evil witch?"

Darci laughed. "That's up to you. You'll figure it out."

I hoped she was right, and not just about Ethan.

When we met up with Tink and Mom for lunch, it was as I'd feared. They were both loaded down with shopping bags. And it wasn't just the bags—Tink looked different. Her normal pink baseball cap had been replaced with a black beret, worn at a jaunty angle over her blond hair. Draped around her neck was a loosely knit purple scarf. She looked at least four years older.

I wasn't sure that I liked it.

"You look quite stylish," I said, giving her a peck on her cheek.

Her eyes went skyward at the word "stylish."

"'Awesome' is more acceptable," Mom piped in.

"Okay," I said and playfully gave the beret a tug, "awesome."

Tink beamed. "You should see the rest of the outfit Grandma bought me, Ophelia," she said, her voice full of excitement. "Black skinny jeans, boots." She took a breath. "I can't wait to wear them to school. All the girls are just going to die."

I took a step back and studied her. She had a slight blush on her cheeks and her long eyelashes looked abnormally dark. "Are you wearing makeup?"

Her cheeks grew pinker. "Ah, yeah. Grandma and I let a lady show us some samples at one of the cosmetic counters."

One of the cosmetic counters? Just how many had they visited? I shot a look at Mom and she smiled.

"Don't you think that you're a little young to be wearing makeup?" I asked.

The question earned me another eye-roll.

I glanced over at Abby for assistance, but the bemused expression on her face told me that I could expect no help from that quarter.

With a shrug of defeat, I took my place at the table and ordered lunch.

All during the meal, Tink kept up a steady stream of chatter about her shopping experience with my mother. "Awesome" and "amazing" peppered her litany.

The one to blame for Tink's enthusiasm sat with a self-satisfied look on her face the whole time. My total lack of interest in shopping, clothes, hair, and makeup had always been a heavy cross for my mother to bear. Now she had the chance to create a "mini-me" of herself, and she was loving every minute of it.

Ah, well. Tink lived in Iowa—Mom lived in Florida. How much damage could she do?

By the time we'd finished lunch, we all saw that Abby's energy was flagging, so we left Asheville and headed back to the valley. We were tired but relaxed. Mom, Abby, and Tink sat in the back while I sat on the passenger side in front.

On the drive home I listened to Mom and Tink plotting their next shopping extravaganza, with Abby interjecting a remark or two every now and again. I was happy we'd taken this excursion—it was a welcome break from the problems that surrounded us in the valley. I had to figure out a way to follow Darci's advice and do a little snooping.

It wouldn't be easy. People in this part of the world tended to be close-mouthed around strangers. And I was a stranger, even though my family had lived there for over a century. The ones who did believe in magick would be reluctant to talk about Sharon, and even the ones who didn't would still be superstitious enough that they wouldn't want to risk Sharon's ire.

I needed to be very, very careful.

"Y'all don't mind if I stop and get gas, do you?" Lydia asked, breaking into my thoughts. "I like to have a full tank in case I get called out in the middle of the night."

Tink suddenly leaned forward. "I'm dying for a Mountain Dew. Can I have one?"

"'May I,'" I corrected without thinking, "and yes, you may."

"Thanks," she said, sitting back.

I shook my head with a chuckle. The Aunts might make their sweet tea with enough sugar to rot your teeth, but they didn't approve of soda pop—too many additives, artificial coloring, preservatives, etcetera. Tink had been in withdrawal ever since we arrived.

Lydia pulled off the highway and into a small service station next to the gravel road leading up the valley. It was a real service station. When the bell dinged, a young man wearing grease-stained blue jeans trotted out of the building and began to fill the SUV. While the pump ran, he lifted the hood and, using the oily rag hanging from his back pocket, checked the oil. Finished, he washed the windows.

Tink and I watched him for a moment before leaving the SUV and going into the small building. Another bell dinged as we opened the door.

The station was small, no bigger than my garage at home. A battered counter stood at one end, next to a cooler holding a variety of soft drinks. A glass jar holding sticks of beef jerky sat on the chipped Formica top next to a Plexiglas stand holding glazed doughnuts. Racks of candy bars and beer nuts hung below.

I bought three teas—one for Mom, Abby, and Lydia—a Mountain Dew for Tink, and a Pepsi for me. Joining Lydia at the SUV, I handed her the tea and she smiled her thanks as she handed the young man two twenties.

"Keep the change, Billy," she said.

He dipped his head and gave a shy grin. "Thanks, Miz Lydia." After wiping a greasy hand on his pants, he helped Lydia into the driver's seat, then rushed around the front of the vehicle and opened the passenger door for me.

"What a polite young man," I commented as Lydia pulled onto the gravel road.

"He is that," she replied with a chuckle, "but unfortunately it's going to take more than good manners to get him out of this valley."

"What do you mean?" I asked.

"Oh, he has big dreams." Her face grew serious. "The problem is he expects them just to happen without any effort on his part."

"He's still young, maybe he'll learn."

"I hope so, but his mama's always spoiled him. He's the only boy with five sisters, and they've waited on him all of his life." She gave her head a firm nod. "He needs to get off his duff and get an education. Otherwise he's going to be working in that gas station for the rest of his life."

"Are the jobs scarce around here?" I asked.

"That they are, but Billy Parnell's a smart—"

My hand shot out, interrupting her. "What did you say his name was?"

"Billy Parnell." Her eyes darted in my direction and she lowered her voice. "He's the one Sharon bewitched."

I looked in the side mirror, back at the little station. Not *too* far, I thought, unscrewing the cap on my bottle of pop and taking a long drink. Maybe tomorrow I'd walk down for another Pepsi.

Twenty-Five

The next morning, once I was reassured that Abby had suffered no ill effects from our outing yesterday, I decided to walk down to the station and talk to Billy Parnell. As I passed by Lydia's, I noticed her out in her garden. Seeing me, she called out with a wave. I veered off the road and walked over to her, passing Jasper on my way. Opening one eye, he sized me up. Convinced that I didn't pose a threat, he laid his head back on his paws with a contented sigh and went back to sleep.

"Where are you off to so early in morning?" Lydia asked, stripping off one of her gloves and giving me a one-armed hug.

"Oh," I replied, scuffing the ground with the toe of my tennis shoe. "I thought I'd take a walk. I need the exercise after all the food Aunt Dot's been shoveling at me."

She turned back to her garden, and sticking her hand back in her glove, clipped off a seed pod from one of the plants. "How's Abby?"

"Good," I answered with a smile. "When I left, she was up and dressed. She's going to help Aunt Dot through the family albums and make some kind of a display for Great-Aunt Mary's party."

Lydia snipped off another pod and dropped it in the basket. "Won't that be nice?" She paused and smiled over her shoulder at me. "Land sakes, I haven't looked at those old pictures in ages. Is Great-Aunt Mary going to help them?"

I snorted. "As much as she likes to be in charge? You know it," I exclaimed. "*And* I imagine she'll have plenty to say about their selections."

Twirling clippers on her finger, she studied me. "You mustn't mind her, Ophelia. She means well."

"Yeah?" I kicked at a clod of dirt lying at my feet. "Did you know that she got rid of the runescript that I'd made to protect Abby?"

"Yes," she said with a frown. "Aunt Dot told me. It was wrong of her to do that."

"And you saw how she acted during our talk yesterday . . . she's not going to let me do anything to stop Sharon."

Lydia let out a long sigh. "Ophelia, you have to understand. All she's ever had is her position as head of the family. No kids of her own, no husband—"

"Her choice," I pointed out, cutting her off.

"That may be, but I think she resents anyone she sees as trying to test her authority. And how she feels about the Dorans, well . . . " She paused, gathering her thoughts. " . . . it's personal."

"Since it's *my* grandmother," I stressed, "who Sharon's trying to kill, it makes it kind of personal for me, too, Lydia."

"I know, but Great-Aunt Mary has always seen Abby as her surrogate daughter. She and Annie were very close, you know."

"That's what Aunt Dot said." I bent down and picked up a small gray stone lying at the edge of the garden. "Why didn't she go after them when Annie died? You heard Abby—Great-Aunt Mary was afraid of stirring things up, just like she is now."

"I'm not so sure," Lydia said thoughtfully.

I slipped the small stone in my pocket. "You think she did do something and Abby doesn't know?"

Lydia's eyes narrowed. "After our talk, I remembered a

remark that my mother once made. It had something to do about an argument between Granny Doran and Great-Aunt Mary." Her forehead crinkled in a frown. "It happened after Annie's funeral, after Abby had left for Iowa."

"Do you know what it was about?"

"No, but I do know Granny Doran never left home much after Annie died. It was rare to see her, and when you did, Sharon was always with her."

"She must've felt like a prisoner in her own home."

She nodded. "I guess if what Abby believes is true—that Granny Doran brought about Annie's death—she did pay a price."

"Lydia, you agree that Sharon has to be stopped, don't you?"

Lydia looked over at me with a shake of head. "I don't like her, that's for certain, but if Great-Aunt Mary thinks . . ." Her voice trailed away.

Her reluctance was obvious. All of her life Lydia had accepted what Great-Aunt Mary said as law, and it was going to be difficult for me to change her mind-set. Maybe if I proved that Sharon wasn't all she was cracked up to be, I could persuade her to help me.

I needed to talk to Billy Parnell.

While I continued my walk down to the station, I mulled over my approach.

So, Billy, do you know that Sharon Doran cast a love spell on you?

No, that wouldn't work.

Billy, I know why you're stalking . . . What was that girl's name? I couldn't remember. Ah well, that approach wasn't the best either. I'd just have to wing it.

When I reached the station, I noticed the small lot crowded with cars and pickup trucks. A different young man stood at the pumps, washing the windows of a beat-up Chevy. I sauntered toward the building, scanning the lot for Billy, but I didn't see him.

Inside the small station, two locals stood at the counter, sipping coffee, eating doughnuts, and talking to the man behind it. Billy wasn't there either. Their conversation stilled when the bell jangled, announcing my entrance, and three sets of eyes fastened on me with curiosity.

"'Morning," I called brightly as I headed toward the cooler.

"'Mornin'," they all said with identical nods.

Okay, so what do you do now, Jensen? I asked myself as I pretended to look over the selection of soft drinks.

"Say," the man from behind the counter said, "weren't you here yesterday with Lydia Wiley?"

I grabbed a bottle of Pepsi and turned. "Yes. I'm Ophelia Jensen."

The men exchanged looks. "You're her cousin, ain't ya?" one man, wearing a John Deere trucker hat, asked.

"Yes," I replied with a smile.

The man standing next to him, dressed in a pair of bib overalls, grinned. "The one from up North, right?" I nodded, and he nudged Mr. John Deere Hat in the ribs. "We heard about you," he said, turning his attention to me.

Oh goody . . . I wondered what he'd heard.

"Y'all are here for Miz Mary's birthday," Mr. Bib Overalls continued.

"That's right," I said, placing my Pepsi on the counter and laying down my money.

The man behind the counter chuckled. "She's a corker, that one."

Mr. John Deere Hat let out a laugh of his own. "My mama still goes on 'bout her talkin' to Daddy." His face sobered. "After he died, you know," he confided.

How does one respond to that? flashed through my mind. *Yes, I have an aunt who talks to dead people?*

My lips formed a tight smile as I nodded in agreement.

"How's she doin'?" Mr. Bib Overalls asked.

"Oh, fine," I responded, unscrewing the cap of my pop and taking a drink.

Mr. John Deere Cap took a bite of his doughnut and

chewed it thoughtfully. "I bet all this company has her excited, don't it?"

"Well," I said, lifting one shoulder, "with Great-Aunt Mary it's hard to tell."

They all chuckled again. "She's always been one to play her cards close," the man behind the counter said. "Miz Dot doin' well?"

"Yes."

"When you git home, y'all tell her that my boy sure appreciated those bottles of elderberry she sent down for his young'un's christenin'."

I just bet he did. Bottles? I wondered if anyone was left standing.

Mr. Bib Overall's eyes suddenly narrowed. "Say, aren't you the one who found old Oscar?"

"Ah . . . yeah." I took another swig of Pepsi, uncertain what would come next.

All three shook their heads at the same time. "Bad business that," Mr. John Deere Hat said.

"Yes, it was," I agreed. "Great-Aunt Mary said he'd been ill for a long time."

"Humph," Mr. Bib Overalls snorted. "Oscar's been complain' 'bout his stomach for as long as I can remember. His wife, when she was livin', always said he just done it to get outta work." He sucked on a tooth. "Guess now we shoulda believed him."

Okay, Jensen, maybe now would be a good time to ask your new best friends about Billy Parnell. But how?

"Ah, by the way, when I was here yesterday, I think I lost a lipstick."

All the men looked at me skeptically. Okay, so I didn't look like a woman who'd worry about a missing tube of lipstick, but I pressed on.

"My daughter gave it to me for Christmas, and she'd be so upset if she knew I'd lost it," I lied. "I think it might have fallen out when I got in Lydia's SUV. Any chance that young man, ah . . . "

I let my voice trail off.

"Billy?" the man behind the counter interjected.

"Yes, that's what Lydia called him. Did he happen to find it?"

He scratched his head. "Billy didn't say nothin' 'bout no lipstick." He dropped his hand. "I can ask him."

"That's okay, I can." I looked hopefully toward the door leading to the service bay. "Is he working today?"

"Nope."

Dang it. Now what?

Twenty-Six

Disheartened, I made a move to leave. "It was nice meeting you, and I'll be sure to give your regards to the Aunts," I said with a note of dejection in my voice.

The man behind the counter called out, "Wait, I said he wasn't workin', I didn't say he wasn't here. He's out back workin' on that old car of his."

I shot him a smile over my shoulder. "Thanks."

As I hurried out the door, I heard one of them say, "She's sure het up about that lipstick, ain't she?"

I found Billy in back of the station, wearing the same grease-stained blue jeans and an old letter jacket. He had his head stuck under the hood of a car that had more rust than paint on it. Letting down my shield for a moment, I sent out tiny fingers of energy toward the boy, trying to sense any bewitchment. None.

I continued toward him, and when he heard my approach, he suddenly raised his head and thumped it on the hood.

"Ouch."

"I'm sorry," I said. "I didn't mean to startle you."

"Ah, that's okay," he replied with a rueful grin as he rubbed the back of his head. "Mama always said it's so hard nothin' can hurt it. Can I help you, ma'am?"

"I'm Lydia Wiley's cousin, Ophelia Jensen."

"I remember you from yesterday." He wiped a grimy

hand on his jeans and held it out. "How do, Miz Jensen—Billy Parnell."

Shaking his hand, I replied, "Nice to meet you, Billy."

"What can I do for you?" he asked, leaning back against the front of his car.

"Umm, I seem to be missing the lipstick that my daughter gave me for Christmas," I said, repeating the same lie I'd told the men inside. "I was wondering if you might have found it lying on the ground after we left."

His face scrunched up in a frown as he thought about it. "No, ma'am, I sure didn't."

"Darn," I sighed, feigning disappointment over the imaginary lipstick. "That was my favorite."

"I'm sure sorry."

I gave Billy a big smile. "I know it sounds silly, to be so upset over a tube of lipstick, but you know how it is with women, you have a girlfriend—"

"I don't have no girlfriend," he said, breaking in.

"You don't?" I asked with mock surprise.

"No, ma'am, but I got five sisters."

"Ahh, well then," I said with a laugh, "you understand women."

He shook his head vigorously. "No, ma'am, I don't, not a'tall."

I let my laughter die. "That's hard to believe," I mused. "It's also hard to believe that a nice young man like you isn't courting some lucky young girl."

He looked down at the ground and shuffled his feet. "I aim to spark a girl, but she don't seem too interested."

"I wouldn't worry about it, Billy," I said with a comforting tone in my voice. "Great-Aunt Mary's always said there's more fish in the sea."

I'd never heard Great-Aunt Mary say that or anything like it, but he didn't know that. And throwing in Great-Aunt Mary's name couldn't hurt.

He raised his head and his face lit up. "That's right . . . y'all are related to Miz Mary and Miz Dot."

I nodded.

He looked down again. "Maybe I should go see them," he mumbled, then brought his eyes up to my face. "You think one of them might help me win my girl?"

"I don't know," I replied hesitantly. "What seems to be the problem?"

"She don't want nothin' to do with me is the problem," he said, his lips turning downward. "I can't figure it out . . . ever since we was kids, she's been hangin' 'round, but now . . . " He shoved his hands in his pockets. "I thought it'd be easy, 'specially after what that witch said—" His mouth snapped shut and he turned back around to his car.

Now I was getting somewhere. I stepped closer. "What did the witch say, Billy?"

"Nothin'," he answered, picking up a wrench and tightening a cap.

"Did Sharon Doran talk to you about your girl?" I persisted.

"I'm not supposed to say anything," he muttered.

After crossing the space between us, I leaned against the car. "It's okay . . . you can tell me. I'm a witch, too," I finished with a wink.

A stubborn frown tightened his mouth. "She said I'd better not tell."

Frustrated, I shoved my hands in my pockets. My fingers touched the small stone I'd found at Lydia's. Drawing it out, I stared at it lying in the center of my palm. It might work.

I closed my eyes and felt the earth's energy beneath my feet. Gripping the stone tightly, I envisioned that energy traveling through my body and into the stone. I saw it form a protective net around anyone who held it. When I was finished, I opened my hand and held it out to Billy.

"What?" he asked, his eyes moving from the stone to my face.

"Take it," I said, shoving my hand toward him.

His eyes narrowed as he studied me. "Why?" he asked suspiciously.

"I put a spell on it. The stone will protect you . . . um, well, in case anyone gets mad at you."

"Wow." His eyes opened wide. "Thanks," he said, slipping the stone in his pocket.

"Now will you tell me what Sharon said?"

He hesitated. "Are you sure the spell will work? I don't wanna come against the wrong side of that woman," he declared.

"Come on, Billy," I said reasonably. "You've lived around my family all of your life. Have you ever known one of our spells *not* working?"

"No, ma'am," he said, lowering his chin.

I could see the fight going on inside of him. On the one hand, he wanted to unburden himself, but on the other, he was still intimidated by Sharon. Finally, he nodded and gave in.

"She told me Cecilia was my soul mate. She said everything I've ever wanted would be mine. As long as I had Cecilia. I could get out of these mountains. Live in the city." The words rushed out. "I'd have money. A nice car. A good job—"

"Whoa," I said, holding up a hand. "All this will happen if you marry Cecilia?"

"Yeah." He gave a vigorous nod, sending a shock of dark hair over his eyes. He brushed it back. "And I've been tryin', tryin' real hard, but that Cecilia doesn't want to cooperate."

"And making your dreams come true doesn't require any effort on your part?"

"Nope, just Cecilia." He cocked his head and gazed at me. "Isn't that what magick's all about, gettin' what you wish for?"

I hated to burst his little bubble, but this kid needed to wise up.

"No, that's not what it's all about," I said, rolling my eyes. "What we want isn't always what's best for us, and true magick doesn't hand us all our wishes on a silver platter. It's about getting what we need to be better people and helping others."

His face fell. "You mean to tell me I been chasin' around after her, makin' a danged fool of myself for nothin'?"

I laid a hand on his shoulder. "Sorry, but, ah, *yeah*."

"Shoot!" he exclaimed, tossing the wrench on the ground. "She lied to me."

"Yes she did, but I wouldn't go spreading it around if I were you." I dropped my hand and moved away from the car. "And I think it would be best if you steered clear of her for a while."

"Oh, don't you worry," he said emphatically, "I'm staying away from her *and* Cecilia Kavanagh."

"Oh, and Billy," I called over my shoulder as I walked away. "If you want your dreams to come true—get an education."

"Yes," I said aloud, pumping a fist in the air. "Ophelia Jensen . . . have spells, will travel." I literally skipped down the gravel road.

With Billy convinced that the protective charm I'd given him would guard him from Sharon's anger, he'd told me exactly what I needed to know. She didn't believe in her own love spell, so she made it appear that it worked by manipulating poor Billy. He hadn't been bewitched, just stupid. And unfortunately, I didn't have a spell for that one.

I had a strong suspicion Sharon's true talent was for trickery, not magick. I couldn't wait to tell Abby. If we could destroy her reputation as a witch, it would strip her of the power she seemed to hold in the valley. But I needed more. How many other people had she conned? What had Darci suggested? Find out who, when, and where?

And who better to interrogate than Cousin Lydia? Cutting across the yard, I started jogging.

Twenty-Seven

As I neared the house, I caught Lydia coming out the side door and waved her down.

"Hey," I hollered. "Where are you going?"

"Up the mountain to the Jessups'. I'm taking Mrs. Jessup some Gilly Bud salve for her arthritis," she called back.

I hurried over to her, puffing and panting. "May I ride along?"

Lydia gave me a broad smile as she rummaged around in her bag for her keys. "'Course you may, darlin'."

Looking over her shoulder, she slapped her leg and whistled. A black streak darted from behind the house and headed toward the SUV. Jasper slid to a stop at Lydia's side, and with his long, pink tongue lolling out of the side of his mouth, watched her with expectation.

"Jasper goes with you?"

"You bet," she said, giving the dog a fond look and opening the back door.

Jasper didn't need to be told what was expected of him. He jumped in and circled twice before settling down on a blanket in the backseat.

Smiling, I joined Lydia and Jasper, and off we went. We bounced along the road, driving up the valley, past the Aunts', Oscar Nelson's homestead, the Doran place. When we drove by the Dorans', my eyes were automatically drawn toward the ramshackle house, and I couldn't help wondering how Ethan fared. Was he any closer to bringing his investigation to a close? Was he okay?

With a sideways glance, Lydia caught the anxiety on my face and misread the cause. A slight wrinkle gathered between her eyebrows, but she didn't ask any questions.

I suddenly felt bad about my intentions. Cousin Lydia was a kind, gentle woman. She probably assumed that I'd wanted to accompany her to learn more about mountain magick. She'd never suspect that I intended to grill her about the Dorans. Like everyone else in the valley, she preferred not to talk about them, and she wasn't going to appreciate my questions. But it couldn't be helped—I needed information and she was my best bet. But I wouldn't do it now. I'd wait until we were on our way back.

As we climbed out of the valley and up into the mountains, the gravel road narrowed and changed into more of a path than a road. Deep ruts marked the tire tracks, but the view from the passenger side was spectacular. The mountains, with their fall foliage, looked like someone had taken a brush and dabbed the slopes with bright swatches of yellow, red, orange, and green.

Yup, the view was great . . . just as long as I didn't look down. The narrow trail didn't have much of a shoulder, and I couldn't imagine traveling this in bad weather. A hard rain would reduce the dirt path to slippery mud. And without a shoulder . . .

"Do you travel this way often?" I asked, alarmed at the thought of Lydia out here alone.

"If I'm needed," she replied lightly.

"Don't you worry about driving these roads?"

"No," she answered, her voice calm as she concentrated on staying on the path. "If it's too nasty, Mac goes with me. I'm careful, and I have faith that all will be well."

The more I got to know Lydia, the more I admired her. She was so balanced, like a younger version of Abby. My eyes slid back to the window and the view. Now I felt really guilty about interrogating her, but I had no choice. I had to learn more about Sharon. Pushing away my thoughts, I glanced back at the dog.

"Jasper seems to have adjusted."

At hearing his name, his tail thumped the seat.

With a smile, Lydia took a quick look in rearview mirror. "He's a good dog, and I don't think he had much of a life living with Oscar. He loves going for car rides. Don't you, boy?"

At her words, I saw Jasper lift his head while his tail beat a faster rhythm on the car seat.

After giving him a scratch behind his ears, I turned back to Lydia. "You said you're taking 'Gilly Bud' salve? I don't think I've ever heard Abby mention that one."

"I'm sure she knows of it—it's one of Annie's remedies." Her hands gripped the wheel tighter as a bump jarred the SUV. "Balm of Gilead?"

"Oh yeah," I replied with a nod. "I've heard of that."

"I don't know how y'all make it in Iowa, but around here we take buds from the black poplar and boil them in olive oil." She jerked her head toward a stand of trees in the distance. "After it's strained, we mix it with beeswax. It's very soothing to inflamed joints."

We hit another bump, and I gripped the bar above the door to steady myself. "How long have you been a healer?"

"Probably for as long as you've been a psychic," she replied with a grin.

I shot her a wry look. "All of your life, just like me."

She nodded.

"The gift skipped Mom. How about yours? Was she gifted?"

"Yes, she was a weather witch like Flora," she said, referring to our joint ancestor.

"Aunt Dot told me a little about her. Could she cause it to rain like Flora did?"

"She surely could." Lydia chuckled. "But she didn't do

it very often. She never knew if it would be a sprinkle or a deluge."

I laughed. "Hard to control, huh?"

"That it was. She mainly used her gift to predict the best times for planting and harvesting, if it would be a hard winter, that kind of thing." She smiled proudly. "Her advice helped many around here get through some tough times." Giving me a quick glance and her smile broadened. "And when Mama said a storm was coming, you'd better head for the cellar."

"What a handy gift to have," I said a little wistfully.

"Better than being a psychic?"

I lifted a shoulder in a shrug and said nothing.

"We all have our own gifts, darlin'." Her voice was soft and comforting. "Each carries with it the good and the bad. Mama may have been a witch who could predict the weather, but she couldn't stop the destruction caused by a bad storm tearing through the valley. It made her feel helpless, and it hurt."

"Like when you know someone is beyond your gift of healing?"

"Yes, and when you see a future full of pain."

"Or a past," I said in a low voice, thinking of Abby.

We'd reached the end of the path and Lydia pulled over into a yard. Rolling to a slow stop, she shut off the SUV and turned toward me. "If you could give away your gift right this instant, would you?" she asked abruptly.

Her question took me off guard. Would I? There'd been many a time when I bitched and complained about my heritage, but without it, who would I be? And to be honest, deep down inside I kind of liked me, warts and all.

I shook my head. "No, Lydia, I wouldn't."

"Me either," she said with a grin. "Come on, let's go get Mrs. Jessup fixed up."

With that, we both got out of the SUV, and leaving Jasper staring out the window after us, walked up a tidy brick path to a small cottage surrounded by fall mums. Lydia knocked on the door, and after a minute or two it was opened by a woman stooped with arthritis. As she greeted us and drew us inside, I noticed her swollen hands and twisted fingers.

But it was her face that surprised me. I had expected someone as old as Aunt Dot or Great-Aunt Mary, but she wasn't. She was closer to Abby in age.

After introductions were made, I followed Lydia and Mrs. Jessup into the living room. I took a seat in one of the threadbare armchairs while Lydia and Mrs. Jessup sat on the couch.

Lydia opened her bag and removed a small jar of yellow salve. When she unscrewed the top, the sweet smell of lavender filled the room. Her eyelids drifted shut and she fingered her amulet. As she did, a shimmering green haze seemed to emanate from the center of her chest. The haze strengthened until it encompassed Mrs. Jessup.

Did Mrs. Jessup see it, too? Maybe not, but as it surrounded her, she visibly relaxed. With a sigh, she leaned back against the couch while Lydia, her eyes open now, settled one of Mrs. Jessup's gnarled hands in her lap.

Lydia took a small scoop of the salve and began to massage one of the woman's twisted hands, murmuring softly.

I felt myself relax, too, listening to her quiet voice, and again was amazed at her talent.

When she finished with one hand, she repeated the process on the other. Never rushing, taking all the time she needed to smooth and stroke each joint, each finger.

I knew women who would pay an outrageous price to have the same thing done for them—women who didn't suffer like Mrs. Jessup did. And if Lydia chose to take her gift to the city, she would be a rich woman. But I had a feeling she already knew that. Instead, it was apparent that she'd made her choice to stay here and help those who needed her.

Yup, my cousin was one admirable lady. And I was probably going to make her mad enough never to speak to me again. Great.

Lydia patted Mrs. Jessup's knee. "How do your hands feel now, Hazel?"

Opening and closing her hands, Mrs. Jessup smiled. "So much better," she sighed.

"Good," Lydia said, screwing the cap back on the jar and handing it to her. "Have Missy give you a massage at least once a day, all right?"

"I surely will." She focused on the jar in her hands. "Ah—"

Lydia rose and gave her a look filled with kindness. "It's fine, Hazel."

Still focused on the jar, Mrs. Jessup shook her head. "I don't like being beholden."

"You're not. We still have plenty of the salt pork that you gave me the last time I visited."

"You sure?" she asked skeptically.

"Yes," Lydia said as she helped Mrs. Jessup to her feet.

"Y'all at least stay for coffee? I've sweet rolls."

"Hazel," Lydia declared, "I'd never pass up some of your cooking, but let us help."

A short time later the rolls and coffee, in gray granite-ware cups, sat on the table.

Each bite of my roll, gooey with melted brown sugar and butter, seemed to dissolve in my mouth, and I fought the urge to smack my lips. Folks in these mountains might not have much, but they sure made good use of what they had. One couldn't find tastier food in a five star restaurant.

I was curious about the salve Lydia had used. "You put lavender in the Balm of Gilead?" I asked between bites.

Lydia grinned and nodded. "Yes, and your father doesn't care for it one bit," she said with a laugh. "He said it made him smell like a perfume factory."

"Your father has arthritis, Ophelia?" Mrs. Jessup asked.

"No, but he took a tumble in the woods and sprained his foot." I jerked my head in Lydia's direction. "Lydia's been nursing him."

"What a pity," Mrs. Jessup commented. "Where did he fall?"

"In the clearing north of the Aunts'," I replied.

Her eyes widened and darted toward Lydia. "But nobody—" She broke off. "Have another roll?" she asked, scooting the plate toward me.

No, but some answers to my questions would be nice, I thought.

After letting Jasper out to take care of any necessary business, we drove back down the mountain path. I remained silent. Inside, I stewed about how to bring up the subject of Sharon Doran to Lydia. I truly did not want to make her angry. Finally, she broke the silence.

"So what do you want to know about Sharon?" she asked with a lift of her eyebrow.

My cousin was not only admirable . . . she was smart.

Twenty-Eight

I turned sideways in my seat. "How did you know?" I asked in a shocked voice.

A smirk tugged at her mouth. "A sudden interest in healing? Going to visit a complete stranger?" She shook her head. "Not your style, darlin'."

Whew, I exhaled loudly. "You're making it a lot easier on me. I thought I'd have to pry the information from you."

Lydia's face grew serious. "I haven't really known you and Abby that long, but I feel like I have. Aunt Dot *and* Great-Aunt Mary," she said pointedly, "have always talked about y'all so much." She sat tall in her seat. "Besides, you're family. I'll help any way that I can."

"Thanks, Lydia," I said, laying a hand on her shoulder. "Got any paper and a pen? Wait." I lifted my purse onto my lap. "I've a pen."

She motioned to the back with a jerk of her head. "There's paper in my bag."

I pulled the bag to the front and grabbed a small notebook. Poising the pen over the paper, I thought about my conversation with Billy. He'd confirmed what Lydia had already told me—everyone who caused problems for Sharon had paid a price.

"You've told me that trouble plagued anyone who crossed

Sharon. I need to know their names and what happened to them," I finally said.

Lydia's finger tapped the steering wheel and her eyes narrowed. "Let's see . . . Martin Thomas . . . he owns pasture next to the Dorans. It's their responsibility to maintain part of the fence line, and when they didn't, he complained. Shortly thereafter, ten of his sheep were found dead."

"Okay, Martin Thomas—dead sheep." I wrote, struggling to keep my handwriting legible. "Next."

"Doran's cows wandered into George McCleary's field and trampled his corn. When he asked for restitution, his well went bad. He not only had the expense of replanting, but of digging a new well."

"George McCleary—bad well." My pen went sliding across the paper when we hit a bump. Brother, I hoped I'd be able to read these notes.

"Are the McClearys related to us?" I asked.

"No, like I said, we've always stayed away from them."

Until you came along seemed to hang in the air.

"I'm sorry, Lydia," I replied earnestly. "I didn't come here to cause trouble. Honest."

"I know you didn't, sweetie." Her mouth turned down in a frown. "This has been a long time coming. Sharon's rode roughshod over this valley enough. It's time someone stopped her." Tightening her hands on the steering wheel, she gave me a sideways glance. "And if you can figure out a way, more power to you."

"Even if Great-Aunt Mary doesn't approve?" I asked, cocking my head and watching her. "Earlier today you seemed reluctant to go against Great-Aunt Mary's wishes."

She tugged on her bottom lip as the road smoothed out and the path changed to the gravel road. "Well, I thought about it after you left this morning. You know folks—like Mrs. Jessup, for one—have enough problems without living in fear of the Dorans. I only ask one thing." She looked at me quickly. "You don't do anything without discussing it with Great-Aunt Mary."

"Lydia," I gasped. "She's never going to agree to any idea of mine."

"Yes she will," she said with a nod of her head. "Regardless of what you think, Great-Aunt Mary has always been a reasonable woman, and if you explain to her . . . " Her voice trailed away.

"Okay," I said with hesitation. "Is there anyone else who's had problems with the Dorans?"

"Humph," she gave a derisive snort. "What I've told you? Those are things that have just happened in the last six months. I could go back for years."

"Whenever you're ready," I stated with a click of my pen.

She raised one finger. "Mrs. Abernathy's grandson broke his leg after a fight with one of Sharon's nephews." She raised another finger. "Matthew Carson's potatoes rotted in the field after he complained about the Doran boys racing their cars up and down his road." Another finger raised. "Eb Wilson got a bad case of food poisoning after he refused to sell the Dorans his prize milk cow. Pat—"

I held up a hand, stopping her. "I think that's enough for now."

Scanning the list, I tried to see a pattern, but couldn't find one. "Lydia," I said, my eyes still focused on the paper. "All these events could just be bad luck."

"Bad luck caused by Sharon and her granny," she replied with a snort.

"Have any other families had a series of misfortune? Families that *haven't* had a run-in with the Dorans?"

"Of course."

I turned in my seat and faced her. "Don't you see what's happening?" I said, leaning forward with excitement. "Sharon's taken credit for causing these calamities and used it to promote her rep as a witch. These events could've happened normally."

"Well," she said thoughtfully, "I suppose the sheep could've eaten some mountain laurel."

"Isn't that the shrub with the pretty flowers? Abby's mentioned it before."

Lydia bobbed her head. "Pretty and poisonous. I've heard stories of folks who've used juice from the leaves to commit suicide."

"Wow . . . it's that deadly?"

She nodded again.

"How long does it take for the poison to work?"

"Less than a day," she replied, her tone short.

"What are the symptoms?"

"Convulsions, paralysis, watery eyes," she ticked them off, "bowels voiding, hemorrhaging."

"Is there any antidote?"

"A stomach pump—but it has to be done right away."

"Is there anything else that could've caused the sheep to die?"

She snickered. "The woods are full of things a body doesn't want to eat. Bloodroot, Dutchman's breeches, snow-berries."

"Would livestock eat that stuff?" I asked, running a finger down my list.

"I don't know—maybe."

I stopped next to Mrs. Abernathy's name. "What about the grandson? How did he break his leg?"

"He tripped down the basement stairs going to fetch something for his grandma."

"That could happen to anyone," I said reasonably. I read my notation about the McClearys. "What about the well? Do you suppose it could've been caused by runoff? We've had that problem in Iowa. Herbicides, insecticides, manure leeching into the groundwater."

"It never happened before," she argued. "For as long as I can remember that well has been crystal clear. Suddenly it turned bad and stunk to high heaven."

"Okay, forget the well. What about the potato blight? Did anyone else have the same problem?"

"No." Lydia shifted in her seat. "You honestly believe that the misfortune wasn't caused by a spell?"

"Yes, I do," I said with a frown.

"That Sharon didn't cast spells on them?"

I crossed my arms. "I didn't say that . . . she might have cast spells, but they didn't work."

"How can you say that?" she cried.

"Because . . . " and I quickly shared the conversation I'd had with Billy.

"She conned him into chasing Cecilia?"

"That's right." I gave a satisfied nod. "If Sharon believed in herself—"

"You've got to be kidding me," Lydia broke in. "You've seen how she acts, she's got an ego the size of Texas."

I leaned forward. "But don't you see, that's just what it is—an act. You know as well as I do that magick doesn't work if you don't have faith in yourself."

"You really think Sharon doesn't have enough faith to make her spells work, so she resorts to tricking everyone into believing that they do?" she asked, and I heard the skepticism in her voice.

"Yeah," I replied, scooting back in my seat.

"If that's what she's doing, it's really twisted."

I shrugged. "So is trying to destroy someone with magick just because."

"Okay, I get your point." Lydia's eyes narrowed. "She might have poisoned the sheep and the well, but I don't know how you're going to prove it." She sighed. "And I don't know how you're going to convince people who've always feared the Dorans that you're right."

There was one victim we hadn't discussed—Oscar Nelson.

"Lydia, what about Oscar Nelson?"

"And the poppet?"

"Right. Great-Aunt Mary said he suffered from a stomach ailment for years, but the way the men at the station talked, they'd always assumed he was faking it." I studied Lydia's profile. "Do you know? Did you ever treat him?"

She shook her head. "Oscar never held with our ways. He preferred to doctor down in Asheville."

I turned toward the window. "Boy, I wish I could look at his medical records," I commented.

I considered my options. I had been known to climb through a few windows, browse a couple of confidential files, but the idea of breaking and entering a medical plaza? I didn't think so. No, there had to be another way.

I looked back at Lydia. "I don't know . . . maybe this whole thing is crazy. Maybe I should just let Great-Aunt Mary handle Sharon."

Lydia suddenly whipped the SUV into a strange driveway.

"What are you doing?" I cried in alarm.

"I have an idea," she said as we sped up the lane. "We'll ask Cousin Elsie."

Lydia was driving like a woman possessed, and I braced my hand on the dash.

"Who's Cousin Elsie and what are we going to ask her?"

"Her mother was a daughter of Flora and Jens. She's about the same age as Aunt Dot, maybe a little younger."

"Have I met her?"

"She doesn't get out much, but you might have seen her at Oscar's funeral."

I shook my head. "I don't remember meeting a Cousin Elsie."

Lydia's lips twisted in a grin. "If you had, you'd remember."

"Why?"

"Never mind . . . you'll understand when you meet her."

"Will she be at Great-Aunt Mary's birthday celebration?"

Lydia snickered. "Not likely—they don't see eye-to-eye on a lot of things, so it would be best if you left Great-Aunt Mary out of the conversation," she said, coming to a stop and putting the transmission in park. "Oh, and another thing . . . don't stare at her wart."

With a groan, I climbed out of the vehicle. Lydia opened the back door, and after strapping a leash to Jasper's collar, let him climb out. Together the three of us crossed the weed-choked yard to the small house.

"So what's Cousin Elsie's talent?" I asked as Lydia lifted her hand to knock.

"Poisons," she whispered, wiggling her eyebrows.

The door swung open, and I swear, except for having a normal skin tone, I looked into the face of the Wicked Witch of the West. Wart, hooked nose, scraggly gray hair . . . Cousin Elsie looked like every caricature I'd seen of witches. Any minute I expected to see flying monkeys, the creatures who'd caused my worst childhood nightmares, to swoop down from the high ceilings. I almost turned and ran.

Lydia sensed my thoughts. Her hand shot out and grabbed my arm. Propelling me toward Cousin Elsie, she smiled pleasantly at the old woman. "Good afternoon, Elsie. This here's Annie's great-granddaughter, Ophelia."

At Lydia's words, I tore my eyes away from Elsie's face and finally noticed how she was dressed. A bright fuchsia dress with a ratty silk flower pinned at the neck. I tried not to let my jaw drop. She was the woman who'd been staring at me from across Oscar's open grave.

Elsie did some observing of her own and looked me up and down. "Saw you at Oscar's funeral."

Robbed of speech, I could only nod like an idiot.

"Here for Mary's birthday, are you?" she snorted, bending down and scratching Jasper's ears.

I cleared my throat. "Ah, yes, ma'am."

"Well, come on in. Always did like Annie, so you're welcome in my house."

Reluctantly, I followed her as she hobbled down the hall to the back of the house. My wide eyes took in everything, from the faded wallpaper to the swaths of spiderwebs hanging in the corners. Finally we stepped out of the gloomy hall into a bright kitchen. A wood-burning stove sat against one wall, with a huge cauldron bubbling merrily on the back burner. Bundles of herbs hung from the ceiling, and on the opposite wall, rows and rows of books were piled on shelves. On the topmost shelf a big yellow tabby lay watching us with amber eyes. He stared at Jasper with some curiosity. With a great yawn, he stretched out his front feet and extended his claws as if to say, *Try it, bud, and you'll be sorry.*

Jasper got the message and obediently stayed at Lydia's side.

Elsie pulled out a chair and motioned for me to sit. I did as she wanted. Lydia sat next to me, while Jasper curled on the floor.

"I'm just getting ready to eat my dinner," Elsie said, shuffling over to the stove and the boiling cauldron. "Would you girls like to join me?"

Under the table, I clutched Lydia's knee. She'd said Elsie's talent was poisons. Did I really want to eat something she'd cooked?

She pried my fingers loose. "Thank you, Elsie," she said, giving me a warning glance. "We'd love to, wouldn't we, Ophelia?"

I numbly nodded.

Lydia rose and crossed to the stove to help Elsie serve the soup. Returning with two steaming bowls, she placed one in front of me. I looked at it suspiciously. Lydia caught my expression and frowned. She picked up a spoon and handed it to me then pointed at the bowl.

Carefully, I dipped the spoon in the brown liquid swimming with vegetables and, lifting it to my mouth, took a cautious sip. It was terrific.

"This is very good, Elsie," I said, trying to keep the surprise out of my voice.

"'Course it is," she grumbled, taking her place at the table. "Didn't think I'd poison y'all, did ya?" She let out a creaky laugh.

Twenty-Nine

Once I'd gotten past the way Cousin Elsie looked and the way her voice sounded like a door needing oil, I liked her. She was a nice woman—a little different, but still nice. She kept us amused throughout the meal with stories about growing up in the mountains and the pranks that she and the other cousins played.

"You and Aunt Dot really put your grandmother's chickens to sleep by tucking their heads under their wings?" I asked.

She gave a deep, hoarse chortle. "We surely did. And Grandma Flora wasn't pleased to look out the window and see all her chickens lying like lumps on the ground. I think we were put in the corner for that one." She slid a plate of homemade bread toward me. "But the most trouble we got into was the time Annie and me camped out all night at the Seven Sisters." She cocked her head to the side. "Let's see—we must've been about ten at the time."

I picked up a slice of the bread and, taking my knife, smeared it with sweet butter. "The Seven Sisters?"

"That's what Annie always called them. They're in the clearing north of the old home place."

My knife paused over my bread. "The standing stones?"

"That'd be them." She pushed her empty bowl away and leaned against the table. "Annie loved that place and we were always sneaking off to play among the stones." She folded her hands. "Our folks didn't approve . . . said the place had too much magick . . . but Annie never feared it. She told me the spirits liked having us there." She cackled again. "Mary, on the other hand, was scared spitless every time we talked her into coming with us."

"How did Annie know about the spirits? I thought Annie was a healer, not a medium."

"She wasn't, but she always claimed she felt their presence. She said they protected her."

They'd certainly lent their power to help Abby when she needed it, I thought.

Elsie's lips twisted in a smile. "Annie loved that place so much she took some of the red pebbles, same stone as the Sisters, home to her ma. I can't remember now what she called them, but my aunt made those funny little signs on the pebbles—"

I dropped my knife. "Runes?"

She snapped her fingers. "That's it. Grandpa Jens had taught both her and Annie how to use them. And, before she died, she gave them back to Annie."

I couldn't believe it—all this time I'd assumed that my great-great-grandmother had made my runes from river rock, but she hadn't. The stones had come from the clearing. Did Abby know?

Elsie's smile faded. "I surely do miss that Annie," she said quietly.

I took a deep breath and looked directly into her moist eyes. "Elsie, did Granny Doran wish Annie dead?" I asked abruptly.

Her eyes narrowed and she studied me in silence for a moment. "You heard that old story, hey?"

"Yes, and Sharon's tried the same thing with Abby," I replied.

Elsie shoved back in her chair. "Pshaw," she exclaimed. "That girl could no more cast a death spell than I could ride a broom."

I wasn't too sure she couldn't, but I kept my mouth shut and let her continue.

"Annie had a bad heart. She doctored herself for years, but finally it went beyond even her healing and just gave out."

Shooting a wide-eyed look at Lydia, I saw her face wore the same expression as mine. "But why—"

Elsie flapped a hand at me, cutting me off. "Annie didn't want anyone to know, not even Abby. When she told me about it, she made me promise not to say anything."

I shook my head. "I don't understand," I mumbled. "Wouldn't it have been—"

"Annie didn't want to be treated like an invalid," she said in a rush. "All of her life, Mary had fussed over her, and Annie was afraid if Mary knew of her condition, she'd take over. Annie didn't want to spend her days being waited on and bossed around. She wanted to live her life on her terms, not Mary's."

I thought about all the years Abby had spent convinced that the Dorans killed her mother and the pain that it had caused.

"But after she died, why didn't you say something?" I cried in an angry voice.

Elsie scowled at me as her own anger gathered in her eyes. "I did!" she exclaimed. "The night Annie died, I tried to tell Mary, but she wouldn't listen. She didn't want to believe that her beloved sister would keep such a secret from her. She said the spirits would have told her if Annie was sick. And then she told me to git and I did. I've not talked to the woman since."

With a groan, I covered my face with my hands and tried to calm down. "Elsie, you have no idea the problems that secret has caused," I muttered. Dropping my hands, I looked over at her and she glanced away.

"Well," she huffed, "maybe I should've told Abby."

"You think?" I asked with a glare.

Lydia's hand gently touched my knee under the table, and

I took a deep breath. "Did Annie tell you anything about old man Doran and his son?"

"No, all I know is for some reason she deeded over the Seven Sisters to them after the old man died." She traced a circle on the tablecloth. "I never could figure out why, and when I asked, Annie wouldn't say."

I looked at Lydia and she gave me an encouraging nod. As succinctly as I could, I laid out the situation between our family and the Dorans to Elsie. I explained what had happened to Abby at the standing stones and why they'd come into the possession of the Dorans. By the time I was finished, I felt her skinny frame vibrating with indignation.

"That dirty bast—" She snapped her mouth shut and rose to her feet. "He never was worth the powder it'd take to blow him to hell. And her . . . " She hobbled over to the bookshelf and grabbed a couple of books. "She was just as bad." Crossing back to the table, she smacked them down.

A cloud of dust rose in the air.

"There"—she waved a crooked finger at the books lying on the table—"if that old biddy and her granddaughter have been using the gifts of the forest for their trickery . . . " Her voice faded as she tapped the worn cover of the top book. ". . . how they done it will be in there. And if it's not," she said with a nod of her head and a wave at the shelves behind her, "it'll be in one of those. I've spent most of my life studying what grows in these mountains, and I wrote everything I learned in them books."

Two hours later I'd learned Elsie had spoken the truth. The table was covered with stacks of her journals, as Lydia, Elsie, and I poured over them.

"What about this?" My eyes skimmed over Elsie's spidery handwriting. "You wrote that bloodroot could irritate the skin?"

"That it can," she said with a nod. "The red sap causes a rash."

"Hmm?" I looked over at Lydia. "Any of Sharon's victims ever think she hexed them with sores?"

"Maybelle, over at the beauty shop, once broke out in a rash all over her hands and arms after Sharon was unhappy with the way she had cut her hair." Lydia's eyes narrowed skeptically. "But how would Sharon manage to get the sap on Maybelle's hands and arms?"

"Hand cream. Beauticians use a lot of hand lotion, don't they? Sharon could've slipped in some poison." I turned to Elsie. "That would work, wouldn't it?"

"It might," she replied.

Lydia looked down at the journal in front of her and flipped one of the pages. "I haven't found anything that would sour a well, though." She glanced at me. "Have you?"

"No."

Elsie gave another one of her low cackles. "I declare— you girls." Sitting back in her chair, she crossed her thin arms. "You don't need poison to ruin water. A five gallon bucket of hog manure will do just as well."

"Would it make them sick?"

"No, it'd stink so bad no one would be stupid enough to drink it."

I thought about Martin Thomas and his dead sheep. "Would sheep eat mountain laurel, Elsie?"

"Sheep will eat anything you give them," she said with a snort. "So will most livestock." She pulled one of the books toward her and opened it. "I think it's in here . . . yes, here it is . . . lambkill. It's a cousin of mountain laurel."

I shut the book in front of me and folded my hands on top of it. "In other words, there are plenty of ways that Sharon could've poisoned livestock, caused rashes, and soured wells." My eyes slid to Lydia. "But what about Oscar Nelson? Did she poison him, or did he just conveniently die of natural causes?"

Elsie brushed a straggly gray hair away from her face. "If she's been practicing on livestock, it wouldn't take her long to learn what would work on a man."

"Any ideas?" I asked.

"Water hemlock is the deadliest. There's been many who've mistaken it for parsnips and died for their mistake." She bit on her lip. "But that's usually in the spring."

Lydia flipped her book shut. "What would cause hemorrhaging?"

"Jeweled death cap would give you a bellyache before it killed you."

"Jeweled death cap?"

"Poison mushrooms. Nasty way to die," she said with a shiver. "One of the poisons shows up in the bloodstream right away."

"What else?" Lydia asked.

"Cottonmouth venom."

"Ha," I snorted. "I already know Sharon has a fondness for snakes." I explained finding the rattler in the bedroom to Elsie.

"Venom from a cottonmouth destroys tissue." She frowned. "So if a snake would've bit him, or if she'd have stuck him with something containing the venom, there'd have been marks on the body."

"I haven't heard anything about an autopsy—did they do one?" I asked, looking over at Lydia.

She shook her head. "I don't think so. Everyone, including the sheriff, just assumed Oscar's stomach ailment finally killed him."

"And if they didn't do an autopsy, they probably didn't do any blood tests." I pulled my dusty hands through my hair in frustration. "Without tests, we have no way of knowing what really killed him, do we?"

Lydia shook her head sadly. "No, we don't. If Sharon did poison him, she could've used any number of things."

Elsie picked up one of the books and carried it over to the bookshelf. "Why don't you ask him?" she said over her shoulder.

"Huh?" Lydia and I blurted out simultaneously.

Elsie turned and fisted her hands on her hips. "And you

girls call yourselves witches?" Shaking her head, she joined us back at the table. "First thing you should've thought of was using a circle. Make one and have Mary ask him how he died. She's always been mighty proud of her ability to talk to the dead. Not that she'd have a problem with him." She gave a little snicker. "Oscar always did go on about his health in life . . . don't imagine he's changed in death."

Thirty

Staring out the window, I thought over all the things we'd learned from Elsie. A lot to absorb in one afternoon. "She won't do it," I muttered.

"Great-Aunt Mary?" Lydia asked.

"Yeah." I turned and faced her. "All these years . . . what a waste. I can't believe she didn't tell Abby about Annie's illness."

Lydia lifted a shoulder. "She didn't think Elsie was telling the truth."

"But shouldn't she have told Abby what Elsie said and let her decide whether or not it was the truth?"

"I don't know," Lydia replied, her voice full of unhappiness. "Great-Aunt Mary has always had her blind spots, and one of those is accepting that someone knows more than she does."

"It's called pride," I snorted. "And her pride has caused too much pain for others."

She gave me a sideways glance. "You have to give her a chance, Ophelia. All of her life she's relied on her gift to guide her. Often to the exclusion of all else."

"And if the spirits say no, then that's it?"

"Yes."

"Even if the facts say different?"

Lydia nodded.

"That's nuts. I know she doesn't think much of me, but at least I've grown to accept that what I see isn't always right. That my interpretation might be off."

She gave a big sigh. "I guess that's something she never learned. Mama once told me that Great-Aunt Mary was only eight years old when people started coming to her."

"That's young," I exclaimed.

"I know . . . Mama always said the same thing. And even back then, Great-Aunt Mary was right more often than wrong. I guess over the years she just learned to assume that she was always right."

I turned back to the window. I'd never had that problem. All my life I'd second-guessed myself, especially after Brian's murder and my inability to prevent it. I'd always wished for more confidence, but looking at the way Great-Aunt Mary had behaved, maybe my doubts hadn't been such a bad thing. They'd left me open to consider other possibilities, they'd kept me honest. Maybe in the end it was all about balance—having faith in yourself, yet at the same time not letting that faith con you into thinking that you were never wrong.

"Are you going to tell Abby about her mother?" Lydia asked, breaking into my thoughts.

"Yeah, but not in front of the Aunts."

"Good idea," she said as she pulled into their driveway.

With Lydia and Jasper following behind, I walked slowly up the path to the Aunts' door. I dreaded talking to Abby. Would she be relieved that there was an explanation for her mother's death? That Annie had passed on because it was her time, and not because Granny Doran had put a death spell on her? Or would she be upset to learn that her mother had been ill and hid it from her? I didn't know, but after all these years, Abby deserved the truth.

After entering the house, the first thing we saw were stacks of boxes. Mom, Dad, Abby, Great-Aunt Mary, Aunt Dot, and Tink were all gathered in the living room, and the floor around them was littered with old newspaper clippings, photographs, and memorabilia.

Tink sat at Great-Aunt Mary's feet, wearing a hat that had to date back to the thirties. The floppy felt brim framed her young face as she read a yellowed newspaper article. Seeing me, she looked up.

"Look what I found," she said, fingering the brim. "Great-Aunt Mary said I could keep it. Isn't it cool?"

I forced a smile. "Sure is, kid. What are you doing and what's all this stuff?"

Placing the paper on the floor, she picked up an old sepia photograph and handed it to me. "Abby and I are making a display for Great-Aunt Mary's party. This is a picture of Abby's grandparents."

I looked down at the picture. An elderly man sat stiffly in a high-backed chair, his hands resting on his knees. Next to him stood a woman wearing a long black dress with a high collar. Her hand rested on his shoulder. They both looked rather grim.

"When was this taken?" I asked, handing the picture back to her.

"About 1920, I think," Abby replied from her place on the couch. "Come here," she said, patting a spot next to her.

I joined her, and she held out another photograph. "You wanted to see a picture of Daddy," she said as I took the picture from her.

A young man dressed in an Army uniform stared up at me. A half smile lit his face and a familiar twinkle shone in his eyes. It was the same twinkle I'd seen many times in Abby's green eyes. He looked so young, with his smooth skin unmarred by wrinkles. And his dark hair peeking out from under a cap set at a jaunty angle had no gray. I felt my throat tighten. Robert hadn't had a chance to get wrinkles or gray hair. His life had ended too soon on a battlefield in France.

But Abby had been right—I saw my mother in the face of the man staring up at me.

"He was very handsome," I said, clearing my throat and handing the picture back to her.

"Yes, he was," she replied as she gently traced her finger over his face. "He was a good man."

"Look at this picture," Tink said, scooting across the floor on her knees. "This is Abby's mom."

I looked down at the picture, then over at Abby. The resemblance was remarkable. Same high cheekbones, same mouth, same eyes—Abby was the spitting image of her mother.

She took the picture from my hand and held it next to the one of her father, as if she was seeing her parents together once again.

"I'd forgotten about this one of Mother," she said, her eyes misting over. "It was taken the same day as the one of Daddy. Mother didn't want to spend the money, but Daddy insisted." She looked at Tink. "Now that I think of it—there should be one of the three of us together. Are there any more boxes upstairs, Tink?"

"Tons," she exaggerated, rolling her eyes.

Abby chuckled. "Would you like to bring them down, please?"

"Sure." Tink hopped to her feet and skipped toward the stairway door.

"Wait a minute," Great-Aunt Mary grumbled. "I think we've drug out enough old stuff."

I stiffened and felt my eyes harden as I glanced over at her. Abby laid a hand on my knee. "Don't worry—we'll clean it up," she said to Great-Aunt Mary. "Tink's having fun digging through all these family memories. Just let her bring one more box down."

"Oh all right," Great-Aunt Mary said reluctantly as she shifted in her chair. "Better make sure you put it all away. I don't want to be tripping over anything in the dark."

As Tink disappeared up the stairs, I nudged Abby with my shoulder. "Want to go for a walk?"

Turning her attention to me, a puzzled look crossed her face. "I suppose." I heard the unspoken question in her voice.

Great-Aunt Mary abruptly leaned forward. "Don't y'all be running off and leaving this mess."

"I'll take care of it," Mom piped in.

The two of us rose, and leaving the rest of them in the living room, crossed to the door. Abby grabbed a sweatshirt from the coat hook. "Where are we going?" she asked softly as we went out the door.

"I'd like to go to the outcrop, if you don't mind," I answered.

"Okay."

We hiked along in silence, and as we did, I tried to frame how I would tell Abby about her mother. She seemed happy as she linked her arm with mine, and I hated to spoil her mood, but she had to know.

When we reached the outcrop, I pointed to the boulder. "Have a seat."

With a small smile, she squinted up at me. "What's this all about?"

I shoved my hands in my pockets. "Do you remember Cousin Elsie?"

Her sudden laugh rang out over the valley. "The poison lady? I sure do. Why, I haven't thought of her in years," she mused. "She and Mother were close. I take it you met her?"

"Yeah, Lydia and I had dinner with her."

"I should go see her."

"Don't mention Great-Aunt Mary," I muttered.

"I know. Great-Aunt Mary had always been a little jealous of her relationship with Mother, but I think there was some kind of blow-up when Mother passed." A slight frown wrinkled Abby's forehead. "It's silly. At their age, they should let go of old hurts and bitterness."

I really hoped she meant that.

Abby took a deep breath and tilted her head back, letting the late afternoon sun warm her face. And considering what had happened over the last few days, she seemed to be at peace. I hated the idea of shattering it.

"Ah . . . " I said, and plopped down on the rock next to her. "Speaking of Elsie . . . Lydia and I spent the day snooping."

The corner of Abby's mouth lifted in a grin as she opened her eyes and turned her attention to me. "Why doesn't that surprise me? Why were you snooping at Elsie's?"

I rubbed my legs. "I don't believe Sharon Doran can cast spells."

Abby's grin faded. "You don't?"

"I know she has everyone convinced that she can, and it's evident that she's *trying* to use magick to harm," I said, remembering Sharon's poppets, "but I don't believe her spells work."

"I don't know, Ophelia," Abby said, slowly shaking her head. "Everyone says bad luck follows those who cross her."

I pivoted toward her. "But she's making sure that bad luck happens," I said, not keeping the excitement out of my voice.

"How—" She stopped. "You were at Elsie's? Poison?"

I nodded. "I think she's doing other stuff, too, but poison seems to be the biggy."

Abby bowed her head as she mulled over my idea. Suddenly, she lifted her head and I saw anger gathering on her face. "Mother? If Sharon's using poison," she clutched my knee, "do you suppose—"

I grabbed her wrist, stopping her. "No, Abby, Granny Doran did not poison your mother," I said flatly.

"You can't know for certain," she cried, "and if she did, I'll—"

"Abby," I said sharply, "Annie had heart disease."

Her eyes flew wide. "What? No!"

I took her hand in mine and I felt her pain. "I'm sorry . . . I know what a shock this must be."

"Why didn't she tell me?" she gasped, bowing her head.

"She didn't want anyone to know. She didn't want anyone treating her like an invalid."

Lifting her head, she stared out over the valley. "But if you know . . . " She turned, fastening her green eyes on me. " . . . then she had to have told someone . . . " Her voice dropped to a whisper. "Elsie."

"Yeah."

"Elsie should have told us, instead of letting us all think Mother died from one of Granny Doran's spells," she said through clenched teeth.

"Um . . . " I couldn't look at her. " . . . she did. She told Great-Aunt Mary, but—"

Abby shot to her feet and I felt her staring down at me. "You mean to tell me that all these years, Great-Aunt Mary has known why Mother died?" she yelled. "She let me go on thinking that I was indirectly responsible for my mother's death!"

She spun on her heel and headed back down the path. I jumped to my feet to go after her. In my haste, I tripped and wound up sprawled on the hard rock. Quickly, I scrambled up and took off down the winding path.

"Wait!" I cried, but she was either too far away to hear me or ignoring me.

She was pulling too far ahead. I tried running, but kept stumbling over the rocks littered along the trail.

"Hey!" I yelled.

Again no response.

I'd just cleared the base of the mountain when I heard rustling behind me. Had Abby veered off the path and I'd somehow passed her? I stopped, my side aching, and listened. I heard the crack of a branch ahead of me and caught sight of Abby's red sweatshirt. I started running again.

So did someone else. Behind me. The sound of feet moving quickly through dead leaves. I didn't stop to look, but felt the sudden shiver of unseen eyes watching me. I had to reach Abby.

Finally, I saw her, and hearing my pounding feet, she

stopped. I closed the distance between us and had almost reached her when I heard a thrumming sound and felt a rush of air past my cheek. I watched in horror as an arrow whacked into a branch, right above Abby's head.

"Down!" I screamed as I dove for her.

Thirty-One

As we scrambled behind the nearest tree, the adrenaline rushed through my system. Crap—what do we do now? I glanced over at Abby. A thin trickle of blood marred her left cheek.

"You're hurt," I whispered in a harsh voice as I clutched her arm.

Her fingertips traveled to her cheek and she swiped at the blood. Holding her hand in front of her face, she looked at the smear on her fingers. "I'm okay. It's just a small cut. I think a flying piece of bark hit me." She peeked around the base of the tree.

I grabbed her and pulled her back. "What are you doing?" I hissed. "Get over here."

"We have to see where they are," she whispered back in an angry voice. "I don't intend to just sit here and let them skewer me with an arrow."

"What do you suggest we do? If we try and make it to the house, we're going to be an easy target. We can't—"

The sound of a branch breaking cut my words off and almost made my heart stop. They were coming for us! I had to get Abby out of there. I moved to a crouching position and grabbed her arm. "When I say run, run, and don't look back. I'm going to try and lead them—"

A shadow fell across us. Throwing myself in front of

Abby, I looked up expecting to see our killer staring down at us. I was so relieved, all the blood rushed from my head. Ethan.

Flipping on the safety, he shoved his gun in the waistband of his jeans and helped Abby to stand. I scrambled to my feet.

Gently lifting her chin, he studied the cut. "It's not deep," he said, dropping his hand.

I saw Abby's eyes narrow as she stared at Ethan and recognition dawned on her. "What are you doing—"

"Never mind, Abby, it's a long story," I said, and faced Ethan. "Did you see who it was?"

His forehead crinkled as he shook his head. "No, but we need to get you back to the house." He moved around to the other side of the tree and, using a handkerchief from his pocket, pulled the arrow out of the bark. "It's a hunting arrow," he said, studying the razor sharp point. "I'll take care of it," he added with a glance over his shoulder at me. "Right now, I want you both out of here."

Together we hurried through the woods, followed by Ethan, and stopped at the edge of the Aunts' yard.

"You go on," I said to Abby, "I'll be along in a minute. Oh, and Abby, don't mention Ethan."

With a nod, she left. When she was out of earshot, I turned and faced him. "Whoever shot that arrow might have seen you."

"I know," he replied with a grimace.

"You've risked your investigation."

"Hey," he said in a light voice, "I couldn't let them kill you."

I frowned up at him. "This isn't a joke. You've put yourself in a dangerous position. We both know who was shooting at us."

"Sharon."

"Yeah. And if she did see you, she's going to run back to her uncle and tell him." I tugged on the sleeve of his jacket. "You can't go back to the Dorans."

"I don't have a choice."

"Yes, you do," I insisted. "Let someone else handle the investigation."

A lopsided grin pulled at the corner of his mouth. "I appreciate your concern, Jensen, but that's not the way it works. I'll be okay." He gave my shoulder a playful punch. "You've already warned me about the love spells."

Grabbing his arm again, I gave it a hard shake. "Listen, slick, you've got a little more to worry about than just a couple of love spells," I exclaimed. "She poisons people."

"Do you have proof?"

My hand fell away. "Ah, no."

He tilted his head back and shook it. "Where do you get these ideas?"

I crossed my arms over my chest and glared at him. "I know I'm right—"

"Look," he said, not letting me finish, "I'd love to stand here and argue with you, but I've got to get back. We'll talk about your suspicions later."

He turned to leave, but my hand shot out and stopped him. "Wait—when?"

"Can you slip out tonight after everyone goes to bed?"

"Yes."

"Fine," he glanced over his shoulder toward the woods. "I don't want you to go wandering around in the dark." He looked back at me. "I'll meet you here."

"All right, but if you don't show, I'm going to come looking for you," I threatened.

His hands grabbed me before I could move, and the next thing I knew, he planted a quick, hard kiss on my mouth. With a chuckle, he turned and, with an easy stride, moved off into the woods.

"Later, Jensen," he called over his shoulder.

When I walked in the house, the tension slapped me in the face like a wet dish towel, almost knocking the air out of me. Everyone—Mom, Lydia, Great-Aunt Mary, Aunt Dot, and Abby—sat around the kitchen table. Dad and Tink had retreated to the safety of the living room and were pretending to look through the boxes. Aunt Dot hovered over Abby, dabbing at her cheek with a damp towel. Abby ignored her. She sat with eyes locked on Great-Aunt Mary, each of them wearing identical scowls. Lydia and Mom looked like they wished they were anywhere but at the table.

All eyes turned to me as I walked in and hesitated.

Great-Aunt Mary focused her wrath on me. "I warned you, didn't I?" she exclaimed. "I told you all your snooping would bring nothing but trouble." She waved a hand toward Abby. "Look what you've caused now—"

"That's enough," Abby said in a voice of pure steel as she pushed away Aunt Dot's hand. "This can be laid at your door, not Ophelia's. If you would have told me about your conversation with Elsie, the Dorans could've been stopped years ago."

"Elsie was lying!" she cried. "Annie would never have kept her illness from me."

I crossed to Abby and laid my hand on her shoulder, my eyes never leaving Great-Aunt Mary. "I believe Elsie," I replied, trying to keep my voice calm.

"Humph." Great-Aunt Mary's lips curled in distaste. "Who cares what you believe? You think you can waltz in—"

"That's it!" Abby shook off my hand and jumped to her feet. "*I* care what my granddaughter believes." Placing her hands on the table, she leaned forward as her eyes shot fire at Great-Aunt Mary. "I've respected you all of my life, but you've let your pride blind you to the truth. I want nothing more to do with you." Taking a deep breath, she straightened and turned toward Lydia. "I don't want to put you in the middle," she said, her voice trembling, "but would you mind driving us to Asheville? We're taking the next flight home." She jerked her head toward Great-Aunt Mary. "Let *her* deal with the Dorans."

She spun on her heel and strode across the kitchen, headed

toward the bedroom. As she passed Tink, she looked down at the mess on the floor. "Tink, darling, would you pick up then go pack?"

Without a word, Tink scrambled to her feet and began shoving clothes, purses, and pictures back into the cardboard boxes.

Twenty minutes later we were in Lydia's SUV heading to Asheville. Mom and Dad had returned to Lydia's to discuss whether they would go or stay. And Great-Aunt Mary had retreated to her bedroom, leaving a distraught Aunt Dot to say good-bye.

It broke my heart to see the sadness in her face. She had never been anything but kind to us, and she didn't deserve to see her family fighting like this. I almost tried pleading with Abby to stay, just for Aunt Dot's sake. But I'd known it wouldn't do any good . . . Abby was pissed. For years she'd believed that her actions so many years ago had eventually led to her mother's death. If only Great-Aunt Mary would've told Abby about her conversation with Elsie . . .

Shaking my head, I turned to Tink, sitting beside me in the backseat of the SUV. "What have you got there?" I asked as I watched her fiddling with what looked like an old straw purse.

"Aunt Dot gave it to me. She said it was Annie's and it was only right that I should have something of hers. Annie wove it from river cane." Tink ran her fingers over the fading herringbone pattern. "Isn't it pretty?" she asked, handing me the purse.

"Yes it is," I replied. "Abby, do you remember this?"

She turned and glanced at the purse in my hands. A soft smile tugged at the corners of her mouth. "Yes, I do. Mother loved that purse." She peeked around the corner of her seat at Tink. "Aunt Dot gave it to you?"

Tink nodded as she took the purse from my hand. "Since Annie made this, maybe you should have it," she said, holding it out to Abby.

Abby's smile widened. "No dear, you keep it. I agree with Aunt Dot . . . you should have something of Mother's. I'm sure it would please her to know it's now yours."

Tink, happy with her treasure, settled back in her seat and hugged it to her chest. Suddenly, her smile dropped away. "I think there's something in it." She quickly placed the purse on her lap and opened it.

"Is there?" I asked, peering across the seat.

"Yeah," she cried as she rummaged around in its depths. "This." She pulled out a folded handkerchief with blue violets stitched around the edges and handed it to Abby.

As Abby held the embroidered piece of cloth to her nose and sniffed, I saw tears gather in her eyes.

"It smells like Mother," she said in a quiet voice.

"Wait." Tink's voice rang with enthusiasm. "There's something else caught on the bottom."

I watched as her nimble fingers dug around the bottom of the purse and then, with a flourish, pulled out a yellowed envelope.

"Is it a letter? Who's it from?" I asked, not hiding my excitement at Tink's discovery.

With a puff, Tink blew the slit in the envelope open and withdrew a single sheet of typing paper. Quickly, her eyes scanned the faint writing. "It's from some lawyer, says something about a life estate." She cocked her head and gave me a perplexed look. "What's a life estate?"

"The use of property during a person's lifetime," I answered, holding out my hand. "May I see it?"

Tink handed me the letter and I skimmed over it. "Not much to it," I said, passing it to Abby. "All it says is Annie's wishes were followed, section such and such was set aside in a life estate, and that the papers were filed."

Abby took the paper from me and read it herself. "Lydia, do you know of any family property being set aside for the duration of someone's life?"

Lydia shook her head. "No, unless Annie put her share of the home place into one for Great-Aunt Mary and Aunt Dot.

That way the farmstead couldn't be divided until they were both gone."

"Hmm." Abby thoughtfully tapped her chin with the corner of the letter. "The law firm is a Petersen, Andrews, and Smith. Do you know of them, Lydia?"

"No, what's the address?"

Abby looked at the letterhead printed on top of the stationery. "Weaverville."

"We'll be passing right by it on our way to Asheville." Lydia gave Abby a quick glance. "Do you want to stop?"

She sighed deeply. "I don't know. The date on this letter is over fifty years ago. Do you think the lawyer would still be in business?"

"Who knows?" she replied with a shrug. "I say we check it out. You can't get a flight out of Asheville until tomorrow, so what would it hurt to take a little detour?"

A short time later we were stopped at a gas station in Weaverville, looking through the yellow pages under ATTORNEYS.

"I found it," I said, my finger stopping on the listing. "It's on Main Street."

"Come on," Lydia said as she gave my arm a tug. "If we're lucky, they're still open."

The clock in Cousin Lydia's SUV showed 5:00 P.M. just as we were sliding into a parking space. We hurried out of the vehicle and literally ran up to a redbrick building with the words *Petersen, Andrews, and Smith* painted in scrolly letters on a big plate-glass window.

My hand had just reached for the doorknob when it suddenly swung open and a man stepped onto the sidewalk. A look of surprise crossed his face.

"May I help you?" he asked.

"Um, well . . . " I shot a look at Abby over my shoulder. "I know this is a long shot, but we recently came across a letter from this firm to my great-grandmother, Mrs. Robert Campbell—"

"Annie Campbell?" he asked, interrupting me.

My jaw dropped as I looked the man over. He couldn't have been more than forty-five. He wouldn't have even been born when the letter was written, so how did he know about Annie?

"Y-Y-Yes," I stuttered.

He looked over my shoulder at Abby. "Are you Mrs. Campbell's daughter?"

"I am," Abby stated.

"Ah, good." He gave her a big smile. "You've saved me a drive up the mountain." He swung the door open and motioned the four of us inside. "I saw from my great-uncle's notes that you lived in Iowa, but there was no address," he said, following us inside. "I thought I'd have to pay a visit to Annie's sister in order to find you."

Once we were seated in front of the man's desk, he quickly introduced himself. "I'm Ben Robinson. My great-uncle, Jonathan Andrews, was the one who set up the life estate at your mother's request."

"It's a pleasure to meet you, Mr. Robinson," Abby said, extending her hand. "This is my cousin, Lydia Wiley, my granddaughter, Ophelia Jensen, and her daughter, Titania."

"It's nice to meet y'all," he said as he took his place behind his desk and opened a drawer. "Now, when I saw the death notice in the paper, I went through the files and—"

I held up my hand, stopping him. "I don't mean to interrupt, Mr. Robinson, but we don't know what you're talking about."

His eyebrows drew together. "Your great-grandmother didn't leave instructions?"

"No."

"I see." He sat forward and clasped his hands on top of his desk. "My great-uncle was in charge of creating a life estate for a small parcel of land adjacent to the property owned by Mrs. Campbell." He reached into the drawer and drew out a sheaf of papers. "The life estate was for one Mrs. Jonas Doran—"

I gasped. "Granny Doran?"

"Yes, I believe that's what the locals called her." He picked up the papers and thumbed through them. "Here it is—her obituary." He looked up and his eyes met Abby's. "Upon Mrs. Doran's death, the parcel of land she held as a gift from your mother reverted back to you, Abigail Campbell McDonald. I'll need to see your ID, of course, but—"

My hand shot out and I grabbed Abby's wrist. "Abby, you own the Seven Sisters!" I exclaimed.

Thirty-Two

After we went over the documents with Mr. Robinson, the four of us stood around Lydia's SUV trying to decide what to do. Did we go back to the mountain or did we go home?

"I should've known Mother wouldn't have just caved into Granny Doran's demands without a fight," Abby said with a shake of her head.

"Do you suppose Great-Aunt Mary knew about the life estate?" I asked.

"No," Lydia replied. "The Dorans owning that piece of land has always been a thorn in her side. If she knew it was to come back to Abby after Granny Doran died, she would've contacted the attorney herself by now."

I leaned against the SUV and exhaled a long breath. "Okay, so what do we do now? If we go home, Sharon's still going to act like she owns that land. And I doubt if Great-Aunt Mary or Aunt Dot would be able to stop her from using it as she sees fit."

Abby's eyes narrowed as a hard light shone in their depths.

"Well, I guess that settles it," she said, yanking the passenger door open. "We go back and take what is ours."

When we arrived back at the Aunts, I was surprised to see Mom and Dad talking with Aunt Dot. Relieved that she hadn't been left alone to deal with Great-Aunt Mary, I gave her a hug while I quickly explained what we'd learned in Weaverville.

"I must go tell Sister," Aunt Dot said, her face wreathed in a big smile.

Abby laid a hand on her arm, stopping her. "Let it wait until morning, Aunt Dot. I really don't want to talk to her tonight."

As she said it, I noticed the stress written on her face— her mouth looked pinched and dark circles shadowed her eyes. Crossing over to her, I placed both hands on her shoulders. "We'll take care of your bags, Abby, so why don't you go lie down? You look like you need a rest."

Her shoulders sagged. "Thank you, dear. I think I will. I need time to absorb everything that's happened today."

After Abby left the room, with Tink carrying her bags, no one spoke. The silence grew until Mom broke it.

"What in the devil is the Seven Sisters?"

"It's a circle of seven stones, kind of like Stonehenge, Mom," I replied, sinking down on a kitchen chair. "It's on the other side of the clearing where Dad fell, and Annie put it in a life estate for Granny Doran years ago."

I didn't know if she knew Abby's history with the place, so I kept my mouth shut.

"Have you seen it, Edward?" she asked suspiciously.

Dad's eyes lit up at the thought. "No, but I'd like to."

I blew out a long breath. "I think it was built by the same ancient culture that created the burial mound, but right now, Dad, it would be best if you stayed away."

Mom's eyebrows shot up. "Why? If Abby owns—"

"It's cursed, Maggie," Lydia broke in quietly. "Has been ever since the Dorans got their hands on it. No one goes there."

"If it's such a nasty place, why is everyone fighting over it?"

"Mom," I said, trying to explain, "it once was a very sacred place, a place of great power, and it was special to Annie. Granny Doran wanted it because of that."

"She tried using the power?"

"Yes."

"Against us?"

"I think she probably tried to use it against anyone who ticked her off, but it didn't work."

"Well," Mom said, rising to her feet, "I think it's obvious what needs to be done, then. All of you just go, do a little magick to cleanse the place, and take it back." She gave a satisfied nod at her solution.

I placed my hands over my eyes and gave my head a shake. "Mom, it's not that easy," I said, removing my hands. "It's complicated. Great-Aunt Mary should've stopped Sha—"

Aunt Dot suddenly shot out of her chair and hustled over to the stove. "I don't want to discuss this anymore. I'll make everyone some tea and then tomorrow morning Abby and Sister will talk and everything will be fine. They can't stay mad at each other."

I shot Mom and Lydia a skeptical look. I didn't want to upset Aunt Dot, but I'd never seen Abby so angry.

Aunt Dot saw me and gave me a mutinous stare. "They will work it out," she insisted. "Annie loved Sister, too, you know. She wouldn't want the family split."

"I know, Aunt Dot," I said gently, "but Great-Aunt Mary should've told Abby about her conversation with Elsie."

Her eyes filled with tears. "Sister wasn't thinking right. She was crushed when Annie died. You mustn't hold what she did against her," she pleaded.

I felt so sorry for her. Crossing to the stove, I threw my arm around her shoulder. "I'll talk to Abby tomorrow, okay?"

"You'll convince her to forgive Sister?" she asked with a sniff.

"I'll try."

She took a corner of her apron and wiped her eyes. "Y'all must be hungry."

Not really, I thought, but I didn't say it. Aunt Dot needed something to take her mind off the family fracas, and what better way than feeding everyone? She whirled around, stoked the stove, and set the kettle on to boil. Mom popped out of her chair and hurried over to help her.

I looked at Lydia and she just shook her head. "If y'all are going to be okay, I'll go on home now. Mac's probably wanting his supper. I'll check in tomorrow."

And with that she was gone.

After supper, Aunt Dot, Mom, Dad, and I spent the rest of the evening watching TV and trying to relax. Great-Aunt Mary and Abby didn't join us. Like two fighters going to their own corners, they stayed in their respective rooms.

And poor Tink—she'd grown close to Great-Aunt Mary, but she worshipped Abby. I saw her divided loyalty written on her face. She spent most of her time running back and forth, checking on one, then the other. Great-Aunt Mary may have been unkind to me, but part of me hoped Abby would forgive her.

And me? I had problems focusing. With all the drama that afternoon, I'd almost forgotten about my rendezvous with Ethan, but now I found myself stealing glances at the ticking clock. And with each passing hour, my nervousness increased.

How could I slip out of the house with everyone there? What if Ethan didn't show up? Did Sharon see him with us in the woods and rat him out to her uncle?

Finally, Mom gave Dad the high sign. "Come on, Edward, let's get back to Lydia's. All this excitement has worn me out."

I looked over at Tink, curled up in front of the TV. "Are you staying here or going with Grandma and Grandpa?"

"I think I should stay here."

Dad rose slowly to his feet, gave Tink a pat on the head, and Aunt Dot and I hugs. Together, he and Mom left.

I glanced at the clock again. Two down, two to go.

"You know," I said nonchalantly, "I think I need some fresh air—"

"I'll go with you," Tink said, popping up from the floor.

"Oh, no, you don't," I said quickly as I pointed to the clock. "It's past your bedtime."

Tink rolled her eyes. "I'm on vacation."

"I don't care. You still need a good night's sleep."

"She's right, darlin'," Aunt Dot piped in as she slowly rose to her feet. "Why don't you help me back to my room? All this sitting around tonight has caused my old knees to stiffen."

Without an argument, Tink took Aunt Dot's arm, and after a quick "Love ya," to me, escorted her back toward her bedroom.

Once they were out of sight, I crossed to the kitchen, grabbed my jacket, and quietly snuck out the door.

The full moon shining over the valley made it almost as bright as day, and I had no problems seeing my way over to the stand of trees where I'd agreed to meet Ethan. Once there, I paced back and forth while my fears raced through me.

What would I do if he didn't show up? Go to the Dorans? Go to the cave? You need a plan, Jensen, I thought.

Suddenly, Ethan stepped from the shadows. "You look like you're nervous."

I skidded to a halt. "How long have you been standing there?"

"Awhile," he said, and I saw him smile in the moonlight. "Now what's this about poisons?"

"I followed through with your idea—that Sharon isn't much of a witch . . . " The words poured out as I told him about the sheep, the well, Maybelle's rash, our visit with Elsie. "And," I finished breathlessly, "I think she poisoned Oscar Nelson."

"He died of a stomach hemorrhage."

I scuffed a toe of my tennis shoe in the dirt. "That's what everyone keeps saying, but I think she killed him."

"Do you have proof?"

"No, but wouldn't the arrow prove she took a shot at us?" I said hopefully.

"You can buy those arrows in any sporting goods store in the county."

"Wouldn't there be fingerprints?"

"Maybe, but unless hers are on file, we don't have a set to compare them to."

"Can't you get her prints?" I replied stubbornly.

"Not without a warrant."

"Details, details," I said with a wave of my hand. "What about the Dorans?"

"Huh? Are you asking me if I have their fingerprints?"

"No, I'm asking if you've noticed anything odd."

He chuckled. "You mean other than they're some of the biggest drug manufacturers around here?"

"Not that—poison."

"You've got a one-track mind, don't you, Jensen?" he asked with a shake of his head. "And what would I be looking for? A bunch of bottles with skulls and crossbones on them?"

"No," I said, my voice exasperated. "Bags of herbs, a few toadstools, a basket of snakes . . . hell, I don't know . . . I'm not an expert in poison."

"Just love spells, hey?" he teased.

I felt hot blood rush to my face. "Not those either." I gave a big sigh. "This is important. She's got to be cooking up her nasty brew somewhere, and I don't think she'd do it at home. Does she have—" I clapped my hands together and grabbed his arm. "Come on, I want to check something out." I took off at a fast clip, pulling him with me.

He stopped and I slid in the grass. "Where are we going?"

"I think I might know where she keeps her stuff . . . trust me." I gave his arm a tug.

He didn't budge. "The last time you said trust me, we found a basement full of bodies."

I yanked on his arm. "No bodies this time, I promise."

Turning away from him, I crossed my fingers and hoped I was right.

Thirty-Three

Dappled moonlight covered the forest floor as we made our way to the Seven Sisters. Sharon was fighting so hard to keep that little parcel of land in her family. There had to be a reason. I knew it wasn't the power that lay among those stones—she hadn't been able to tap into it. If she had, she wouldn't have needed to use dirty tricks and poison to strike fear throughout the valley. Her magick would've been strong enough to accomplish most anything.

No, she was using the fact that everyone was afraid of the clearing to hide her activities. She could try casting her spells, brew her noxious potions, and do pretty much whatever else she wanted without fear of discovery. Her only witnesses were the spirits of the ancient people who once lived and died here.

I shivered recalling their rage. The gentleness that Annie and Abby had sensed lurking among the stones was gone, and if that anger were ever released again . . . I shuddered once more.

Ethan suddenly turned. "Are you cold?"

"What, ah, no," I stammered. "I'm fine."

He chuckled. "My grandma always said a sudden shiver means someone just stepped on your grave."

"Do you mind?" I asked, giving his shoulder a nudge. "I'd rather not talk about graves right now."

His eyes scanned the forest, then he nodded. "It *is* spooky out here, isn't it?"

I snorted softly. "You ain't seen nothing yet, slick. Wait until we get to the Seven Sisters."

"Seven Sisters?"

"The stone circle."

"Right, in the clearing."

Together we continued our journey. Ethan walked ahead as quietly as a phantom, while I followed behind. And not silently. I seemed to step on every twig, every branch. Next to him, I felt clumsy.

Finally we reached the edge of the clearing. On the other side of the trees was the Seven Sisters. I reached out and touched Ethan's back.

"Wait a minute," I said, taking a deep breath.

He looked over his shoulder at me. "Is something wrong?"

"No . . ." My words faltered. How did I explain to him how this place made me feel? How did I explain the need to shield myself? "Um, I'm . . . ah . . . sensitive to the atmosphere here and I . . . need to gather my thoughts," I finished lamely.

His brows knitted while his eyes traveled around the clearing. "I see what you mean."

My eyes widened in surprise. "Really?"

"Yeah." He turned and faced me. "The air feels—I don't know how to describe it—well, smothering."

I was impressed at his sensitivity. Did he have his own intuitive gifts? I'd never considered that before. But I didn't have time to dwell on that now. I pushed away the thought and concentrated on the task at hand. Closing my eyes and taking another deep breath, I formed my psychic barrier as I had before, only this time I expanded it to also encompass Ethan.

With a smile, I jerked my head toward the trees. "Let's go."

When we cleared the trees surrounding the Seven Sisters, he abruptly stopped.

In the moonlight, the Seven Sisters, choked with kudzu, were even more ominous than during the day. Great hulking shapes desolate and abandoned, like giants bound to the earth by chains. Ethan tensed. "This is *not* a good place, is it?"

"No," I answered with a slight shake of my head. "Not anymore. This way, around to the back of the stones."

I had only gone as far as the center of the circle, and if Sharon were using this place, I suspected it would be in the grove of trees behind the circle.

While we edged around the Seven Sisters, the sense of heaviness that Ethan and I felt increased. As it sank down on us, I felt my shield buckle and wrinkle. Instinctively, I grabbed his arm. Instantly his energy—strong, even protective—joined with mine, and my shield held.

Finally, when we reached the trees, the tension lifted. I wiped the sweat that I hadn't felt until now from my forehead.

I dropped his arm while my eyes searched the woods for some kind of sign to guide me to Sharon's hideaway. But all I saw were the trees and the mountains looming over us.

"Where to now, Jensen?"

Throwing up my hands, I did a three sixty. "I don't—"

I ducked as something swooped past us. Covering my head, I looked sideways toward the trees. "Please tell me that wasn't a bat."

"Not unless bats have feathers," Ethan chuckled.

"Like you didn't duck, too," I replied with a sneer as I straightened and looked up at the nearest tree.

Yellow eyes glowed at me while the moonlight reflected off the creamy feathers covering the bird's breast and underbelly. Sharp talons clung to the low branch. He opened his hooked beak and let out a rasping scream that sent the leaves rustling as prey fled for cover.

I guess I had my sign.

The hawk suddenly spread his wings and effortlessly rode the air currents into the night sky.

Grabbing Ethan's hand, I tugged. "Come on before we lose him," I cried.

"We're following a *bird*?"

I shot him a look over my shoulder. "Yeah," I said full of excitement. "I'll explain later."

"Talk about a wild-goose chase," he muttered, but followed me anyway.

I kept the bird in sight, trying not to trip as I ran deeper into the grove of trees. When he veered to the left, I did the same. Slowly, the bird circled lower and lower until he came to rest on a low hanging branch.

A low hanging branch right next to a weathered shack. We'd found it.

I sent a silent thank-you, and once again the hawk took flight. With strong wings beating the air, he soared above me until finally he disappeared above the treetops.

Ethan came to a stop next to me and gave me a poke to draw my attention. "Don't you think we've more important things to do than bird watching?"

I felt like saying "ta-da" but didn't. Instead, I pointed at the weathered shack, no bigger than a storage shed, sitting in front of us.

"There," I said with a cocky grin. "Bet you anything it's Sharon's."

When we reached the shack, Ethan clutched the plywood door and gave it a firm yank. It swung open, its rusty hinges creaking.

Whatever was inside rushed at me with a whoosh. My arms flew to cover my face. Evil . . . decay. I fell two steps back and would've run had Ethan not grabbed me.

"What's wrong with you?" He gave my arm a little shake.

"I—I don't think I want to go in there," I stuttered.

"It's an abandoned shack."

"No, it's not," I insisted. "Bad things have happened in that shack."

Rolling his eyes, he tipped his head back and sighed. "I didn't come all this way not to check it out," he said, looking at me again. "I'm going in."

"Be careful."

With another roll of his eyes, he turned and crossed back to the shack. A moment later I saw the light of a lantern come through the open door. The shades on the two cracked windows suddenly dropped when Ethan closed them.

Curious, I took a tentative step toward the door and craned my neck to see inside. Nothing. I was too far away. *Oh what the heck.* I took a deep breath and joined Ethan inside.

"I thought you didn't want to come in," he said over his shoulder while he wandered around the small space, looking at the jars lined up on shelves.

"Well, I'm in now. Are you finding anything?"

"I don't know," he said, reaching out to touch a cast-iron pot sitting on the potbelly stove.

"Don't touch that!" I yelled.

He spun around.

"It might have residue on it." I wandered over to the shelves. Clear jars, some containing liquid, some containing dried herbs, sat in neat rows. I peered at the faint labels.

Angel's trumpet, black henbane, bloodroot, water hemlock—all names I recognized from Elsie's books. Sharon had quite a cornucopia of poisons. I turned and spied a terrarium sitting on an old table. It was half full of wood shavings. I stepped closer to have a look.

I backed up when I heard the hiss followed by the ominous sound of a rattle.

With a trembling finger, I pointed at the table. "There's a snake in there."

"It's okay. There's a screen nailed across the top. He can't get out."

Shuddering, I rubbed my arms. "Sharon's a real Lucretia Borgia of the mountains," I said, my lip curling. "She's got enough poison in here to make everyone in this valley sick, if not kill them." I crossed over to Ethan. "When are you going to arrest her?"

"Making poison isn't illegal," he said, crouching down and lifting the material hanging around the bottom of the table.

"It's not?" I said, disheartened.

"No." He reached under the table and pulled out a large plastic bag. "But this is," he said, holding it up to the light.

"Drugs?"

He opened the bag and sniffed. "Oh yeah." Shutting the bag, he shoved it underneath the table and let the material fall back into place.

"Does this mean you can arrest the Dorans tonight and close your case?"

"Not exactly. I don't have a warrant, so technically I'm breaking and entering."

I shook my head. "No, you're not, we're just entering. I've had this discussion with Darci."

His lips twisted in a smirk. "I just bet you have." Standing, he wiped his hands on his jeans. "We *are* trespassing. This land belongs to the Dorans."

"No, it doesn't. It belongs—"

Ethan grabbed my shoulders. "What? Not the Dorans?"

"No. Before you interrupted me, I was going to say it belongs to Abby." I cocked my head and stared up at him. "We found out Granny Doran only had the use of this land during her lifetime. When she died, it reverted back to Abby."

"Are the Dorans aware that you know?"

"I don't think so, we discovered it today. Tomorrow we're going to decide how to reclaim the property."

His fingers dug into my shoulders. "Can you wait?"

"I guess. Why?"

His face grew thoughtful. "I'll drop a hint that something's up. They'll want to mo—" He cut himself off and a big smile spread across his face. "Jensen, I could kiss you!"

When Ethan finally released me, I felt like some heroine in a romance novel—knees weak, heart racing, heat pooling in . . . well never mind.

Jeez, Jensen, get a grip, I argued with myself. *You're in a shack full of poison, snakes, and drugs belonging to a woman who'd like nothing better than to destroy your entire family. Now is not the time to get all dewy-eyed.*

I took two shaky steps back, putting some distance between us. Ethan had the ability to muddle my thoughts, and from the expression on his face in the pale light of the lantern, he enjoyed it.

"Let's go," I said, turning on my heel and heading for the door. "We've both found what we were looking for."

I heard his low, hoarse whisper behind me. "Yes, we have."

I hesitated, one foot over the threshold. *What's that supposed to mean?*

The shack was suddenly plunged into darkness as Ethan extinguished the lantern. I waited while he secured the door, and taking my arm, we headed back toward the stone circle.

Trying to compose myself, I dreaded walking around the Seven Sisters again. Dreaded the feeling of a tremendous weight pressing down on us. And as we approached, the feeling was still there, but different, not as heavy, somehow lighter.

"Until this is over and I've busted the Dorans, I want you and your family to stick close to home," he said after we'd passed the Seven Sisters and were heading through the woods back to the Aunts.

"I'll try."

"Not try." He squeezed my arm to make his point. "Do. Promise me."

When I released a long sigh, he pulled me to a stop. "I mean it, Jensen. The Dorans have everything to lose, and it makes them even more dangerous."

"What about you, then? Won't you be at a greater risk?"

"Don't worry about me. I'm going to be calling in reinforcements."

"What kind of reinforcements?"

He ignored my questions. With a tug on my arm, he continued walking. "For once in your life, listen. This will all be
over in a couple of days."

"You're sure?" I asked skeptically.

His eyes met mine and he gave me a cocky grin. "Hey,
have I ever lied to you?"

Now that he mentioned it . . .

Thirty-Four

Ethan and I parted at the edge of the trees, near the barn. I thought he was going to kiss me again, but by the time we'd reached the Aunts, his mind seemed far away. And to be honest, I felt a little disappointed as I snuck in the back door of the house. I quickly reminded myself that I didn't have time for romance either. I had to figure out a way to nail Sharon Doran.

Slipping quietly into the bedroom, I changed into my T-shirt and sweats, and slid into bed without disturbing Abby. I hadn't realized how tense I was until my muscles started to relax. They felt like a rubber band that had finally been released. My body melted into the thick feather bed.

I don't know how long I slept, but in the corner of my mind came an awareness of knocking. Not willing to surrender my sleep, I rolled over and buried my face in the pillow.

The rapping became louder, more insistent. Reluctantly, I flipped over and sat up, still half asleep. I opened my eyes and saw layers of gray floating in the moonlit room. My eyes began to sting and I took a deep breath. A coughing fit wracked my lungs.

Fire!

I bolted from the bed, shoving my feet into my tennis shoes. Scrambling over to Abby, I yanked her upright.

"Get up!" I choked. "Get the Aunts out of here!"

Bleary-eyed, she stared blankly at me for a second before she grabbed her robe and jumped from the bed. Together we tore down the hallway. Abby made for the Aunts' bedrooms while I flew to the attic, taking two stairs at a time. I rushed to Tink and pulled her from the bed.

"There's a fire!" I cried, wrapping an arm around her shoulders and guiding her to the stairs.

Once at the bottom, I gave her a shove toward the kitchen door. "Get out of here!"

"But—"

I stabbed a finger toward the door. "Go, wait for us by the barn."

Spinning around, I ran down toward the Aunts' bedrooms. "Abby—"

"In here," I heard her call out from Great-Aunt Mary's room.

I rushed up to the bed and helped her get Great-Aunt Mary to her feet. "Aunt Dot?"

"She's already outside. Tink?"

"Same."

Together, we half carried, half dragged Great-Aunt Mary across the living room and out the kitchen door.

I would've breathed a sigh of relief when I spotted Tink and Aunt Dot huddled together by the barn but my lungs felt too tight.

"Our house," Aunt Dot sobbed.

We couldn't just stand here and watch the house burn.

"Tink—run to Lydia's—call 911. Where's a hose?" I asked, grasping Aunt Dot's shoulders.

"There's a water hydrant around back," she said, waving a shaking hand toward the house.

Without waiting for further instruction, I beat it around the house and found the hydrant with the garden hose coiled next to it. Thank goodness the hose was already connected to the spigot and I didn't have to waste precious moments attaching it. Yanking the handle up, I grabbed the end of the hose and pulled it toward the flames creeping up the side of the back porch.

The heat warmed my face as I sprayed the old siding and the black smoke drifted my way, stinging my eyes. The water was stopping the fire's progress, but I didn't have enough pressure to extinguish the flames. Sooner or later the fire would get ahead of me and the whole house would go.

I needed help.

A hand on my shoulder almost made me drop the hose. I turned to see Lydia and Mac behind me. Mac took the end from me and continued spraying. Suddenly aware that I was freezing, I stepped back as Lydia wrapped a blanket around my shoulders.

"How did you get here so fast?" I asked through chattering teeth.

"I saw the smoke from my kitchen window and called it in. The fire trucks should be here soon."

No sooner were the words out of her mouth than I heard the sirens screaming down the road. She guided me to the edge of the yard just as the firemen came rushing around the corner of the house armed with a huge hose. In less than a minute water rushed out and poured over the burning porch. Another man came around the corner, carrying a medical bag and a small tank. When he tried to strap a mask over my face, I waved his hand away.

"Wait, my family?"

"They're fine. Another paramedic is treating them." He quickly checked my vitals. Finished, he glanced at Lydia and nodded. "She's okay—just some smoke inhalation." He picked up the tank, and together he and Lydia escorted me around the house to Lydia's SUV.

Looking inside, I saw Aunt Dot and Great-Aunt Mary huddled together in the back, while Abby and Tink sat in front. All of them had the same look of shock on their faces.

In less than a half hour it was over. The fire had been put out and the firemen were checking for any remaining hot spots.

Satisfied that the crisis was over, Lydia turned to me. "Y'all can't stay here tonight. I'm taking you back to my house."

"No," Great-Aunt Mary exclaimed. "I'm not leaving my home. I'll—"

Aunt Dot silenced her with a look. "No you won't, Sister," she commanded sharply. "We're doing as Lydia says."

Great-Aunt Mary's mouth clenched shut.

We all exchanged looks of amazement. I don't think anyone had ever heard gentle Aunt Dot countermand Great-Aunt Mary.

Once we grabbed some clothes and everyone had been transported back to Lydia's, Lydia, Mom, and I went about getting the Aunts settled down. When the fire chief stopped by, the rest of us were gathered at the kitchen table. After making introductions, Lydia quickly poured him a cup of coffee.

He smiled his thanks and took a drink. After he put his cup down, we began to pepper him with questions. Okay, *I* began to pepper him with questions.

"How did the fire start? Was it the wiring? Is there much damage?"

He held up one hand to stop me. "Other than a little smoke, there's not much damage to the main part of the house, but the ladies are going to need a new back porch. Y'all were lucky that you woke up when you did." He picked up his cup and took another sip of coffee. "In these old houses, it doesn't take much for a fire to spread."

"But how did it start?"

He leaned back and scratched his head. "I don't rightly know, but from the burn patterns, my guess is someone doused the porch with gasoline."

I exploded. "Yeah, and I know who!" I yelled at the poor man. "I want you to arrest Sharon Doran tonight!"

His eyes shifted nervously to Lydia before looking back at me. "I'm sorry, ma'am . . . I can't do that."

"Why not?" I asked, gritting my teeth.

"Because, ma'am, I'm not the sheriff. And y'all got to have proof."

"You said you think it was arson."

"You're right, I did, and I suspect the arson investigator will agree with me. But that still don't prove who did it." He shuffled to his feet, and I could see from the expression on his face that he couldn't wait to get away from Lydia's crazy Yankee cousin. Sliding his chair in, he gave me an apprehensive smile. "I'll be sure and tell the sheriff about your concerns, and maybe he can go on out to the Dorans' and question Sharon."

Sitting back, I crossed my arms and frowned. Sharon would laugh in the sheriff's face.

After the fire chief left, it was only Lydia's calm presence that kept me from dashing over to the Dorans', yanking Sharon out of bed, and forcing her to confess what she'd done. Dad had swallowed his own anger and taken Tink away to watch television in Lydia's rec room. Good thing—I was not setting an appropriate example for my daughter, but I was so angry that I couldn't contain it.

I fretted and fumed while I paced back and forth across Lydia's kitchen. Sharon had tried to kill us all—Great-Aunt Mary, Aunt Dot, Tink, Abby, and me. And I was helpless—I really hated that one. Unless Sharon had conveniently left a gas can with the name "Doran" written on it, there was no way anyone could prove she'd been the one to torch the house.

I stopped my pacing and looked at everyone still sitting at the table. "It's hopeless, and I give up," I said, tossing my hands in the air. "We're leaving for home tomorrow. I will not have my daughter's life put at risk." I faced Abby. "Get Ben Robinson," I said, referring to the Weaverville attorney, "to file some sort of an injunction to force the Dorans away from the Seven Sisters."

"So you're just going to run away and let Sharon win?" a voice from the doorway croaked.

Great-Aunt Mary shuffled into the room and plopped down on a chair next to Abby. Aunt Dot followed her.

"Look," I said with a glare, "don't talk to me about letting the Dorans win. Maybe you could've stopped them years ago."

"Maybe you're right. Maybe I could've, but I didn't, did I? Maybe I wasn't a good enough witch to stop her." Her eyes narrowed as she looked me up and down. "What I want to know . . . are you?"

Thirty-Five

"You're kidding me," I exclaimed. "You don't think I'm capable."

"Maybe I was wrong."

My mouth opened and shut—twice—I was speechless.

"I thought I was doing the right thing in trying to keep the truce Annie had made with the Dorans." She lifted a thin shoulder. "It was easier than to challenge them." Scratching at an invisible spot on Lydia's table, she dropped her eyes. "Sharon's caused a bunch of hurt in this valley. Annie never would've stood for it . . . she wouldn't have looked the other way.

Aunt Dot laid her hand on Great-Aunt Mary's.

Great-Aunt Mary lifted her eyes and looked directly at Abby. "I've made a lot of mistakes in my century of living," she said, turning her attention to me. "If you're smart, you won't make the same ones."

Amazed at this sudden turn of events, I sank onto the nearest chair. "What do you suggest we do? We can't prove a single thing that she's done," I said. "You know she's the one who set the fire?"

"I heard you whooping and hollering." She jerked her head in Aunt Dot's direction. "We've been talking, and you're going about this in the wrong way. You're trying to find evidence . . . why not use magick?"

"You won't let me," I forcefully pointed out.

"Not *against* her, but there's nothing stopping us from *taking* from her."

"Like what?"

"And here I was beginning to think you were a smart girl," she said with a glint in her eye. "What is she fighting so hard to keep?"

"The Seven Sisters, obviously," I replied. "But we know now that Abby already owns it. Which is why she's trying to kill us."

"They may belong to Abby now, but that alone isn't enough to break Sharon's hold on this valley," Great-Aunt Mary said.

I had to acknowledge that remark. "Maybe not," I answered with hesitation.

"Folks will still be scared of the place—"

"It's cursed now, remember?" Aunt Dot piped in suddenly.

"Yeah, I remember."

"Abby owns the land, but not the spirit. No one can, but if we free it of the curse . . . once folks around here learn of it—"

My face brightened and I jumped in. "They'll believe Sharon's powers are gone, and she won't be able to use their fear against them."

Aunt Dot nudged Great-Aunt Mary. "See, Sister, I've been telling you she can figure stuff out."

Great-Aunt Mary gave a soft snort.

I shifted toward Abby. "How do we do it, Abby?" Removing bad energy was more her bag than mine.

"I'm not sure," she said with a slight frown.

Elsie's séance idea popped into my head. "What about creating a circle and using energy to cleanse the clearing?"

"That might work . . ." She paused, and I knew she was thinking about the ancient spirits and the savageness she'd felt that day.

"Abby," I said slowly, "I have a confession to make. I went

back to the clearing after our talk. I wanted to understand what once was there."

Great-Aunt Mary leaned forward. "And?"

I explained the scene that had played out in my mind. "I think the spirits of the people who built the Seven Sisters will welcome us."

"This vision? What you saw was taking place at sunrise?" Great-Aunt Mary asked.

"Yes."

Her eyes traveled to the clock ticking above Lydia's stove. "We've three hours to prepare."

"Today? This morning? I haven't had any sleep, I don't know if I can banish—"

"There's no time like the present," she said, interrupting me.

I made a move to stand. "Well . . . okay . . . but I'm going to need some instructions."

"I didn't say 'you,'" she pointed out, "I said 'we.' You're not going alone, girl. All of us are, even Tink."

I shook my head vehemently. "Oh no she's not," I declared.

"She has to." Great-Aunt Mary studied me thoughtfully. "She's the child of your heart and that links her to Annie." Great-Aunt Mary turned her attention to Lydia. "And you, you're a healer, you've taken the role that Annie once played in this valley."

I tugged on my bottom lip. I understood what Great-Aunt Mary wanted to do. She wanted everyone who shared a link to Annie to join together to cleanse the clearing. But Tink?

"I still don't know about dragging Tink into this."

Great-Aunt Mary lifted a hand to her thin chest and she flattened it over her heart. "I swear on my sister's grave, I'll let no harm come to that child."

"But you won't be there—" I began, before she cut me off.

"Oh yes I will."

"How? Can you walk that far?"

"No, and that's why Maybelle's boys are going to help Sister and I get there," she said with a swift nod. "Two big fellows like them won't have a problem getting us to that clearing."

Aunt Dot leaned toward Great-Aunt Mary and whispered in her ear. She listened quietly for a moment, then her mouth settled into a hard line.

"No," she said firmly.

"You just said that you've made a lot of mistakes," Aunt Dot said, a stubborn light flashing in her eyes. "Here's a chance to fix one of them."

"She won't come," Great-Aunt Mary insisted.

"Yes, she will . . . if you ask her. She has a link to Annie, too."

"Humph," Great-Aunt Mary snorted. "Not as strong as mine. I never—"

Before she could finish, a knock at Lydia's back door interrupted her. Her eyes widened as Lydia opened the door and admitted the visitor.

"Mary," Elsie said with a curt nod of her head.

Great-Aunt Mary's jaw clenched. "Elsie."

The homey kitchen seemed to vibrate with tension as the two old women stared at each other across the small space. They reminded me of two gunslingers, waiting to see who drew first.

Aunt Dot broke the spell. "Elsie," she cried, jumping up from her chair and hurrying over to where Elsie still stood at the door. "I haven't seen you in a dog's age."

She gave Aunt Dot a wry look but allowed herself to be guided to the kitchen table. Once seated in her chair, she sniffed and lifted a hand to fluff the faded silk flower pinned at the neck of dress. "Seems you've had a spot of trouble, Mary."

Leaning back in her chair, Great-Aunt Mary crossed her arms. "Always one to state the obvious, aren't you, Elsie?" Her lips twisted into a bitter grin. "Since Sharon Doran tried to burn the house down around our ears tonight, I guess you could call it a 'spot' of trouble."

"So are you finally going to put a stop to her?" Elsie asked, leaning forward.

Great-Aunt Mary did the same. "Yes, *I* am."

Elsie nodded once, sending her scraggly hair floating around her face. "Good," she exclaimed. "Then I'm here to help."

"What makes you think I need your help?" Great-Aunt Mary shot back.

"Annie told me—"

Great-Aunt Mary gave a soft gasp. "You saw Annie? You're not a medium. You can't—"

Elsie held up a hand, stopping her. "Don't worry, Mary, I'm not stealing your thunder. Annie came to me in a dream tonight. She wants all this fussing and fighting to end . . . " She paused as her face took on a faraway look. "Annie never did cotton to holding grudges." The look fell away and her focus returned to Great-Aunt Mary.

"Annie told you to come here?"

"Yes, and it seems to me if you're going to clear away over fifty years of evil—" She stopped, and reaching in the pocket of her dress, withdrew a large plastic bag of herbs. Plopping it on the table, she stared at Great-Aunt Mary. "I think you could use my help."

Great-Aunt Mary turned to Aunt Dot, who bobbed her head in encouragement.

"We're going to the Seven Sisters. Think you're spry enough to make the trip?" Great-Aunt Mary challenged.

Elsie let out a low cackle. "As I recall, I'm younger than you, Mary. I'm guessing if you can make it, I can, too."

With a shake of her head, Great-Aunt Mary held up her gnarled hands and lifted a finger as she counted off each name. "Me, Sister, Lydia, Abby, Elsie, Tink." She dropped one hand and pointed at me. "And you, you're the seventh

witch, Ophelia. All you have to do is believe in your gift."
She gave a quick nod of her head. "Seven witches . . . Seven
Sisters."

Great-Aunt Mary was right about Maybelle's boys. They
were bigger than the two cousins who had helped Dad back
from the clearing the day he sprained his foot. And if they
thought it strange, getting called out at four in the morning
to carry two aged aunts out to the middle of the woods, they
never commented on it. Instead, they waited patiently while
we made our preparations.

Abby and Lydia set about gathering the supplies we
would need once we reached the Seven Sisters—crystals,
Elsie's bag of herbs, and a large sack of coarse salt.

Aunt Dot had referred to what lurked at the Seven Sisters
as a curse, and I didn't know if that was exactly right. From
what I'd experienced that night with Ethan at the hunter's
shack, I saw it more as negative energy that hung over the
entire place like a bad smell. Sharon had created that energy
with her attempts at magick.

I slapped my forehead—Ethan—I'd forgotten my promise to stay close to the house. If he caught us in the clearing,
he would be so pissed.

He won't catch us. He talked as if it would take time to
set up the Doran bust. He'd be busy working on that, not
wandering around the woods.

While everyone was busy, Great-Aunt Mary and Aunt
Dot were sitting at the table, talking quietly. I joined them. I
had a question for Great-Aunt Mary.

"Why did you change your mind about me?" I asked
without preamble.

"I didn't change my mind," she answered, "I always knew
the gift ran deep in you, girl. I just never thought you had the
will to use it. But since you've been here," she let out a low
cackle, "you've been like a terrier going after a mole . . . you
dig and dig until you get your answers."

I didn't know if I cared to be compared to a dog, but I let
it slide.

Aunt Dot tapped Great-Aunt Mary on her shoulder. "Go ahead, Sister, tell her," she urged.

"Annie didn't just visit Elsie. She was with us tonight, too," she said softly as her eyes dampened. "After all these years, she finally contacted me."

"How?"

"I was dreaming about her when Abby woke me up. She was trying to tell me something, but I didn't understand. Now I do."

"What?"

"That a body needs to let go of the past. It's what Abby needs to do, too." Her eyes drifted toward Elsie, standing at the counter with Lydia. "Maybe I do too," she continued softly. "Annie saved us tonight, you know."

That was a nice comforting thought, and I hated to argue, but it hadn't been Annie.

"I wasn't dreaming of Annie, Great-Aunt Mary. In fact, I wasn't dreaming at all." I shook my head. "I heard knocking."

She and Aunt Dot both nodded wisely.

"Annie? She was trying to get my attention?"

They nodded again.

"Have you told Abby? She'd like to know that her mother's still looking out for her."

"She already knows," Great-Aunt Mary said. "She was dreaming of Annie, too."

Wow. I wasn't a medium, but she was. I'd have to take her word about what had happened earlier.

The clock suddenly chimed five, and the Aunts turned to one another.

Time to go.

Thirty-Six

Dressed in white cowled robes borrowed from Lydia, our little troop neared the clearing. We were almost there when I hung back and linked my arm with Abby.

"Are you okay with this?" I asked.

"Yes," she said, her eyes on the broad back of the cousin carrying Great-Aunt Mary. "I've always told you to face your fears?"

"Uh-huh."

"Now it's time to face mine. I have a lot of happy memories of the Seven Sisters. Until the day the Dorans attacked me, it had always been a place of peace. I need to remember those memories if we're going to be successful."

"Are you sure?"

"Yes," she replied with a small smile. "And you need to focus on your vision of the shaman and his people. If you do, maybe we can finally end the influence the Dorans have had on this valley."

"Will Tink be okay?" I still questioned the wisdom of bringing her.

Abby's face grew serious. "If I didn't trust Great-Aunt Mary's word, I wouldn't have let her come." She stopped suddenly.

We reached the edge of the clearing and paused. As we'd passed the Aunts' house, I ran inside and grabbed my runes.

Even though they hadn't worked for me on this trip, I figured I needed all the help I could get. And now I sensed a warmth growing from where they nestled in the pocket of my robe. The feeling spread through me and chased away the morning chill. At the same time, I felt the oppressiveness of this place lift, and it was as if a sense of anticipation replaced it.

At the Seven Sisters, I heard Abby's small cry of dismay when she saw the stagnant pool, the choked stones. A small tear slid down her cheek.

"To see this . . ." She sniffed. "It would've caused Mother so much pain."

I tossed an arm around her shoulders. "Don't think about it. We're going to fix it," I said with a confidence I wasn't sure I really felt.

Maybelle's son set Great-Aunt Mary on her feet as she whispered something in his ear. He quickly left, only to return a few minutes later carrying pieces of wood and kindling. After handing them to Lydia, he and his brother faded into the woods beyond the circle. They'd been instructed to return after sunrise.

We fell into step, and one by one entered the circle. Lydia crossed to the center and laid out the wood while Abby handed each of us a piece of hematite for grounding and a piece of green fluorite for cleansing. We all slipped them into the deep pockets of our robes. Abby then opened Lydia's bag and withdrew the sack of salt. Opening it, she walked clockwise as she poured the salt in a large circle. Soon the circle was complete and the fire blazed.

One last thing . . . Lydia reached in her bag and grabbed the sack of herbs that Elsie had provided. When she cast it on the fire, the air immediately filled with the pungent smell of sage. She joined the rest of us, and with linked hands we all stepped over the circle of salt.

Closing her eyes, Abby called the Elements.

The dark richness of the Earth seemed to anchor us.

Air stirred the sage and its smoke drifted over and around us.

Bright flames of fire, fed by the breeze, leapt and danced.

From behind me, I heard the gurgle of water as if the stagnant pool had suddenly come to life once more.

Throughout the clearing, I felt a gentleness gather, forcing back the darkness that clung to this place.

I opened my eyes and looked at Lydia, facing me from across the fire. And I swear, she glowed with a soft green light while her amulet shone so bright it almost hurt my eyes. My attention traveled to Tink and Great-Aunt Mary. I saw shadows, shifting and moving behind them, drawing closer to the warmth of Lydia's fire.

And Aunt Dot? Little sparks of light zigged and zagged above her head. Was it her fairies lending their energy to ours?

I felt the rays of the morning sun begin to warm the back of my neck. Just a few more minutes before its light hit the center of the circle. It would be done, finished, all the evil banished forever.

The warmth vanished. A chill, like icy fingers, moved down my back. No, no, this was not supposed to happen.

I dropped Abby's and Elsie's hands and spun around as Sharon Doran stepped from the shadow of one of the standing stones.

With a rifle pointed directly at Abby.

"What in the hell are you doing?" she said, her eyes flicking in my direction.

Without thinking, I broke the circle and stepped in front of Abby. "We're taking back what's ours."

I heard a soft rustle on either side of me, and I glanced to my left then to my right. Still inside the circle of salt, everyone had moved to form a straight line. Now the seven of us faced Sharon.

A hint of fear flared in her brown eyes, and I pressed my advantage.

"It's over, Sharon," I said, keeping my voice calm.

Her hands on the gun tightened. "No, it's not," she replied

softly, and I saw the fear in her eyes vanish as a madness seemed to take hold.

Above us, clouds tumbled and rolled across the sun, blocking it. The heaviness that had been almost gone oozed around Sharon like a poisonous gas. I felt a darkening, building as it waited just beyond the edge of the Seven Sisters.

"Put the gun down and leave," I commanded, taking one step forward. "Before it's too late."

Her jaw clenched. "No, I vowed you'd pay, and you will." She slowly lifted the gun and sighted down the barrel.

I jerked up my hands. "Wait—let the others go. I'll stay."

Abby grabbed my sleeve, but I shook her off and crossed over the salt.

"You have nothing to gain by killing us. If you want revenge, take it out on me, not them."

Her eyes narrowed and the gun lowered as she thought it over. I took another step.

She caught my movement and jerked the gun back to her shoulder. "She killed my grandpa," she hissed with a slight wave of the barrel in Abby's direction. "Granny said she cursed him."

I shook my head. "Your grandfather cursed himself . . . I saw it, Sharon. He cowered before the spirits that dwell here."

"There ain't no ghosts here," she scoffed.

I moved closer. "Yes there are. And they don't like the way your family has defiled their sacred spot."

As if to affirm my words, a crack of lightning crisscrossed the sky above us, and the low rumble of thunder shook the clearing, the sound bouncing off the standing stones.

A thin bead of sweat glimmered on Sharon's top lip.

"They were the ones who caused your grandfather's death. He insulted them, like you're doing right now." I crossed my arms. "Do you want to die like he did, Sharon?"

"Are you cursing me?" The end of her gun wavered.

If I could just get close enough to grab the gun. I slid one foot forward. "I—"

The ground beneath my feet seemed to tremble, and I thought I saw the standing stones vibrate, as if they were trying to shake off the vines choking them. Suddenly, Sharon screamed, and I watched in horror as a jagged slash appeared on her cheek.

"Stop it!" she screamed again, her gun swinging in a wild arc as another gash marked her forehead.

My God, she was being cut to ribbons before our eyes.

"Run!" I shouted over my shoulder as I lurched for the gun.

She fired wildly and I hit the ground. The sky opened and a torrent of rain poured down on us. Scrambling to my knees, I tried crawling toward her, but the gun kept barking bullets as she tried to shoot the unseen forces attacking her.

I heard the sound of pounding feet, and lifting my head, I saw three men, wearing deputy sheriff jackets, come running toward us. And sprinting out in front of them? Ethan.

Sharon heard them, too, and spun, her gun still firing.

"No!" I screamed as Ethan crumpled to the ground.

The two men with him launched themselves at Sharon, tackling her to the ground.

The gunfire stopped and a deadly silence filled the circle. With my robe tangling around my knees, I crawled over to where Ethan lay.

"Lydia, Lydia!" I called. "Help me!"

I raised my head, my eyes scanning the clearing through the rain.

I saw her . . . she sat cradling Abby in her arms.

My scream echoed again and again.

Thirty-Seven

I thought the pain in my heart would kill me. We'd won, but at what price?

Then I saw Abby lift her head.

I almost fainted. "Is she hurt?" I called out.

With Lydia's help, Abby raised herself to a sitting position and flapped a hand in my direction. After Elsie and Lydia helped Abby to her feet, Lydia rushed to my side.

Ethan had rolled over onto his back and rain poured down on his still face. I leaned over him, trying to shield him with my body as best I could.

"Ethan, open your eyes," I said, bending close.

His eyes fluttered open and he groaned. "My leg," he gasped, his breath coming in short quick pants.

I looked over my shoulder at Lydia. She knelt by his knee carefully inspecting the crimson stain slowly spreading down the leg of his jeans.

"Abby?" I said to her.

"When the bullets started flying, Elsie shoved her to the ground and it knocked the wind out of her. She's fine."

"The rest?"

"They're all huddled under one of the lintels. No one was hit."

"Ethan?" I asked.

"The bullet hit his knee. It's not fatal, but I've got to stop the bleeding," she said, moving her hand over the ever widening stain.

Just like on the day when Dad had injured his foot, the air around us hummed with Lydia's healing energy as she used it to stop the bleeding.

Abruptly, she stopped and shook her head. "It's not working. His body is in too much pain and he's blocking the healing."

I turned back to Ethan, his eyes tightly shut as he rolled his head from side to side. "Ethan, listen to me . . . you're going to be fine . . . Lydia and I are going to help you."

Closing my eyes, I placed my hand on his forehead and concentrated on my mind touching his. His pain shot up my arm, and I almost lost the connection. Breathing deeply, I let it wash through me, absorbing it with my mind.

Slowly, Ethan calmed. His head stopped rolling and his muscles seemed to relax.

I don't know how long Lydia and I knelt by his side, but finally I heard the sound of all-terrain vehicles ripping through the woods. They came to a stop and two men jumped off, running toward us. Lydia moved aside as one of the men ripped Ethan's pant leg and assessed the wound. With quick sure motions, he opened the bag he'd carried and began treating Ethan's leg. The other man knelt across from me, and after tearing Ethan's shirt, started an IV.

He took a moment to glance at me. "We'll take it from here," he said.

I stumbled to my feet and slowly crossed the circle to where the rest of my family waited, their sodden robes hanging off their shoulders. As I did, out of the corner of my eye, I spied Sharon being led away in handcuffs.

From across the clearing her eyes met mine, and I staggered from the hatred I saw there.

Once they got us all out of the woods, I insisted that I be allowed to accompany Ethan in the ambulance. They didn't argue. I guess even DEA agents didn't want to take on a group of women dressed in soggy white robes. Shoving mine into Lydia's waiting arms, I hopped in the back and we took off.

On the ride to the hospital in Asheville, Ethan kept drifting in and out of consciousness. I didn't even know if he realized I was there. Finally his cool, gray eyes opened and he stared up at me.

He frowned as they focused on my face. "Jensen?"

"Hey, slick, how ya doing?" I said with forced brightness.

"Haven't I told you to keep your head down?" he asked, his voice slurred from the medication.

"I believe you have," I agreed.

He winced as he shifted his body. "Next time listen."

"I will, cross my heart."

A slight grin tugged at his lips. "Right."

"Ethan, you saved our lives . . . " I leaned in close. "Thanks."

"Anytime, Jensen." His eyes drifted shut. "Only next time, I'm going to try to not get shot doing it."

When we arrived at the hospital, they rushed him into surgery while I kept a vigil in one of the waiting rooms. I'd called Lydia and everyone was fine. She asked if I wanted her to join me at the hospital, but I declined. I was on my third cup of coffee when a man dressed in a DEA jacket walked into the waiting room.

A big man—he looked like a football player and carried with him an air of authority. He crossed the room and extended his hand.

"You must be Ophelia," he said smiling down at me. "I'm Ted Rivers."

"You're Ethan's boss," I replied, shaking his hand.

As he took a seat next to me, he chuckled. "How did you know?"

"A lucky guess?"

He chuckled again. "From what I hear, you have those frequently."

I clutched my cup a little tighter. "Ethan's told you about me?"

"A little," he replied with a wry grin, "but I went to school with Bill Wilson. I believe you're acquainted with him?"

"*Sheriff* Bill Wilson?" I gave him a nervous glance.

"That would be the one."

Peachy, I thought, rolling my eyes. Well at least he wasn't reaching for his handcuffs. I'd take that as a good sign.

"Bill speaks very highly of you," he continued.

I almost spilled my coffee. "Really?"

"You sound surprised?"

"Um . . . well . . . it's . . . " I babbled. Clamping my jaw shut, I turned toward him. "Ethan's still in surgery."

"I know. I spoke with a nurse when I arrived. He should be out soon."

"Is he going to be okay?"

His face grew serious. "The bullet shattered his knee and it's going to require time to heal. We're transferring him to the Mayo Clinic as soon as the surgeon gives the go-ahead."

The Mayo Clinic? I took a sharp breath. It had some of the best doctors in the country, and people from all over the world went to the specialists there.

"That bad?"

"No, no," he said, quickly facing me. "I didn't mean to worry you. His family lives in Rochester, it will be easier for them if he's nearby."

Family? Ethan had family? I'd never thought about it. Wife? Kids?

Mr. Rivers continued. "His parents and a brother live there," he said, filling me in. "His dad's a retired police officer, and his mother, well—" He broke off with a chuckle. "She runs a New Age shop. She's some kind of an astrologer."

Thirty-Eight

Two days later I walked into Ethan's hospital room to say good-bye. Sitting by the door were two large plastic sacks containing his belongings. Seeing them, I felt a tinge of unhappiness—Ethan would be going home to his family, back to the life he knew. For a long time he'd popped in and out of my life with some regularity. But now he had a long road of recovery ahead of him. He wouldn't have time to worry about my latest scrape. Or have the time to come to my rescue. The thought of him *not* being there bothered me.

Hearing my footsteps, Ethan turned his attention toward me. "Hey, slick, I hear you're taking a trip," I said with forced brightness.

"Yeah, back to Minnesota." He winced as he shifted uneasily in the bed.

Crossing quickly to the side of his bed, I pulled a chair close. "Are you in pain?"

"I'm okay," he replied, resting his head back on the pillow while his eyes drifted shut for a moment. "They've got me pretty doped up right now."

I started to rise. "Well . . . " I hesitated. "Maybe now's not a good time . . . I just wanted to stop by to say good-bye and—"

He opened his eyes and a smile flitted across his face.

"Jensen," he said, cutting me off. "Don't worry about it. I'm doing fine. Six months from now I'll be as good as new."

Right, I thought, sinking back down into the chair. After the surgery, the doctors had explained to his boss and me what they'd had to do. He had more plates and screws in his leg than the Frankenstein monster, and I knew he faced several months, maybe even a year, of rehab if he were to get the full use of his leg back.

I felt the tears gather in my eyes. "I'm so sorry, Ethan. This is my fault." Swallowing hard, I blinked quickly. "You were hurt saving us."

Cocking his head, he smiled again. "Didn't I tell you that there's just something about you that makes me want to play the white knight?" he teased. His voice suddenly grew serious. "I have a dangerous job, Jensen, there's always a risk. The important thing . . . the good guys won this time."

"Thanks to you."

"You helped," he said with a wink. "Ahh, I've been lying here thinking . . . and . . . " He paused. "Rochester isn't that far from Summerset . . . about a four hour drive, isn't it?"

"Yeah." I nodded. "That sounds about right."

"Well, you know, I'm going to be pretty bored, lying around, not doing anything except rehab . . . " He plucked at the edge of the blanket covering his legs. "It would be nice to have visitors."

"Are you inviting me to Minnesota?" I asked with a grin.

He returned my grin and held out his hand. "Yeah."

Without hesitation, I rose and crossed the short space between the chair and the bed. I placed my hand in his. In spite of his injuries, the drugs, his grip was firm as he pulled me down to sit on the edge of the bed. Neither of us spoke for a moment as his thumb traced a lazy pattern across my knuckles. With each stroke, I felt a charge race up my arm and feed a little bubble of happiness growing inside my heart.

"Mom would love to meet you," he said, breaking the silence. "She'll be so proud that I brought home a *real* witch," he finished with a laugh.

"That's not exactly the normal reaction," I replied with a shake of my head.

Ethan chuckled. "The words 'normal' and 'Mom' usually don't occur in the same sentence." He gave my hand a tug, bringing me closer, and staring into my eyes, his voice grew husky. "I'd really like you to come to Rochester. Will you?"

Everything that Ethan had done for me, for my family, flitted through my mind, but it wasn't just gratitude that I felt. This guy was a real life hero. How could a girl resist someone like that? I let the bubble of happiness show on my face as I leaned closer. "I'd like that."

Then without thinking, without worrying, without wondering if I was doing the right thing, I bent down and pressed my mouth to his.

I felt more than heard the groan that came from deep in his throat as his hands moved up to my shoulders and squeezed. All the want and need that being with Ethan seemed to cause came rushing to the surface, and my lips parted.

A sharp rap on the door suddenly ended the kiss, and looking over my shoulder, I saw a nurse standing just inside the doorway. A blush crept up my neck and into my face while Ethan's laugh echoed in the small room.

Noticing the wheelchair that the nurse had brought with her, I turned my attention back to Ethan. "Looks like your ride's here," I commented, feeling suddenly shy. "I'd better get going."

I began to rise, but Ethan's hand on my shoulder stopped me.

"I'll see you in Minnesota," he said firmly.

With a bob of my head, I gave him a quick kiss and stood. Smiling at the nurse, I crossed the room, heading for the door. I'd just stepped into the hallway when I heard the nurse's voice.

"Was that your girlfriend, Mr. Clement?"

A soft chuckle followed her question.

"I'm working on it."

Finally ready to celebrate Great-Aunt Mary's 100th birthday, the old farmhouse had bustled with activity all morning as everyone hurried about. With a clipboard and list in hand, Mom took over organizing everything that needed to be carted down to Lydia's. She reminded me of a general marshaling her troops right before a big battle, and not wanting to be one of the troops, I slipped back to the bedroom to change.

Crossing to the dresser, I pulled open the top drawer and was surprised to see all my undies neatly folded with a fresh sprig of lavender lying on top of them.

How sweet, I thought picking up the lavender and inhaling deeply. Aunt Dot left me a present.

I went to the bedroom door and popped my head around the corner. "Thanks for the lavender, Aunt Dot," I called out.

She appeared in the doorway of her bedroom. "What was that?" she asked, holding a comb paused in midair.

"Thank you for straightening out my clothes and for the lavender," I repeated.

"I wasn't in your room."

"Somebody was and they left this." I held out the sprig.

"Thank the stars," she said with a huge smile. "He's forgiven you."

"Who's forgiven me?" I asked, my voice perplexed.

"Our Nisse." She raked the comb through her thin hair. "He appreciates everything you've done for the family and the lavender is a peace offering."

As she ducked back into her bedroom, I thought I heard her mutter something about an extra pat of butter on the grits.

If I had thought the dinner Lydia served the first day we were there was something, Great-Aunt Mary's birthday put it to shame. I think everyone in the valley had turned out. I even saw young Cecilia Kavanagh studiously avoiding Billy Parnell. And he was doing the same to her.

Everyone wore a smile that day. There was a lightness of spirit, not only within my family, but the whole valley. All the Dorans were safely locked away. Cousin Lydia had heard through the grapevine that Sharon's snarky uncle had cut a deal with the district attorney and the Feds. In order to get his own sentence for the manufacturing and sale of illegal drugs reduced, he agreed to testify against Sharon. All her dirty deeds would be revealed at her trial, and the ensuing scandal would keep the gossip mill running for months. Yup, I thought with a nod of satisfaction, Sharon Doran would be spending a long time behind bars.

After the DEA had released the clearing as a crime scene, Abby and I went to the Seven Sisters one last time. Together we'd lit the torch and watched as Sharon's shack of poisons burned completely to the ground. The cousins that Great-Aunt Mary had given the task of clearing the kudzu away from the standing stones looked at us as if we were crazy, but we didn't care. It gave them just one more story to tell about their nutty Northern relatives. And when I'd looked back at the proud stones, I hoped that by next spring it would look as it had in my first dream.

Carrying a plate laden with food, I wandered over to where Abby and Tink sat. This would be my last chance to enjoy all the wonderful Southern food that I'd grown fond of, and I intended to make the most of it.

As I joined them, I noticed how much younger Abby looked now than she had on the day she showed me the outcrop. The stress and the strain I'd seen had vanished.

"Hey, I've got a question," Tink said waving a chicken leg at us. "Did either of you see the man at the Seven Sisters?"

"You mean the sheriff's deputies?" I asked, balancing my plate on my knees. "Of course we saw them."

She shook her head, her ponytail flying. "No, not them

. . . the old guy. He had some kind of feathers in his hair. He was the one who stopped Sharon from shooting you."

The shaman who'd once blessed his people. He had helped us reclaim their land.

Tink wasn't finished with her revelations. "I saw a woman, too, Abby. She stood right behind you." She hopped to her feet when one of the younger cousins called to her. "I think it was your mom."

The tone of voice she used made it sound as if it were the most common thing in the world to spot people who'd been dead for years.

I closed my eyes and shook my head as Abby chuckled. Placing her hand on my arm, she smiled. "She's going to be fine," she said with pride. "She's accepting her gift." Abby turned to face me. "You're doing a good job with her."

"Thanks," I replied, and shoveled a forkful of mashed potatoes and gravy into my mouth.

She rose to her feet. "It's almost time for the cake. I'm going to go help Lydia."

I nodded, unable to speak with my cheeks puffed out like a chipmunk's.

Her chair didn't stay vacated long. A minute later Elsie shuffled over and took the chair next to me.

I swallowed and looked at her in surprise. "Elsie, it's nice to see you here."

"Humph," she said as her attention wandered over to where Great-Aunt Mary sat. "That woman always was full of surprises. She came by yesterday with Dot and apologized for not believing me about Annie." She fixed her watery eyes on me. "Never thought I'd live long enough to see the day Mary apologized for anything."

I reached out and patted her hand. "That's good you've made peace with her. I'm glad."

"Are you coming back someday?"

"Oh probably, Tink thinks the world of the Aunts, so I want to maintain her connection with them."

Elsie gave her head a firm nod. "Good. I'd like to see you again. You'll be sure and stop by," she gave me a sly look, "for dinner."

I laughed. "That I will, Elsie. I promise."

She leaned back in her chair. "Yes, sirree, you remind me a lot of . . . "

Uh-oh, here it comes. I'm going to be told I'm just like Great-Aunt Mary.

" . . . Annie," she finished.

I felt my plate start to slide and I made a grab for it. "Annie? Really? But I don't look a thing like her."

"Not on the outside, but you surely do on the inside. She never backed away from a fight either. You have the same spirit."

I leaned over and laid a hand on her wrist. "That's one of the nicest compliments I've ever received. Thank you."

"You're like her in other ways, too." She pursed her lips. "Her talent didn't come easy to her either when she was young, regardless of how Mary might tell it."

"It didn't?"

"No. When Annie was a girl, she always wished she was 'normal.'" Elsie chuckled softly. "Whatever that is. She spent most of her early years fighting her nature." She slid a glance my way. "Sound familiar?"

"A little," I admitted reluctantly.

"But once she got over that, her life just fell into place." Elsie paused to watch Abby and Lydia slowly crossing the yard, carrying a cake blazing with one hundred candles over to where Great-Aunt Mary sat, surrounded by kin. "Those were good years," she continued with a half smile. "She met a man who understood how special she was and treated her as such."

"They had quite a love story, didn't they?" I asked a little wistfully.

"They sure did," she nodded empathically, "but it wasn't all Robert. Annie was brave enough to risk her heart for a man like him. Not everyone has the courage to do that." I watched as her gaze focused on Great-Aunt Mary blowing out her candles.

I turned my attention to Great-Aunt Mary, too. Tink stood on her left with her hand resting on Great-Aunt Mary's shoulder. She wore a big smile and her lavender eyes danced. Mom stood next to Tink with her arm carelessly draped over Tink's shoulder. Her attention wasn't on Great-Aunt Mary but on Tink, and I could see the pride written on her face as she gazed at my daughter.

Aunt Dot was on Great-Aunt Mary's right, taking the scene in with her sharp old eyes. As the last of the hundred candles sputtered and flickered out, she bobbed her head with satisfaction as if to say, *Well, we've made it this far.* I felt a grin tug at my lips while the crowd erupted with applause.

The grin became a smile of pure happiness as I studied the little group gathered under the big elm tree. Great-Aunt Mary, Aunt Dot, Tink, Cousin Lydia, Abby . . . all with their own unique talents . . . all witches. Standing, I held out my hand to Elsie and helped her to her feet. Together we crossed the sun-dappled yard to join *my* family.

**Sign up for the FREE
HarperCollins monthly
mystery newsletter,**

The Scene of the Crime,

**and get to know your favorite authors,
win free books, and be the first to learn
about the best new mysteries going on sale.**

To register, simply go to www.HarperCollins.com, visit our mystery channel
page, and at the bottom of the page, enter your email address where it
states "Sign up for our mystery newsletter." Then you can tap into monthly
Hot Reads, check out our award nominees, sneak a peek at upcoming
titles, and discover the best whodunits each and every month.

*Get to know the magnificent mystery authors
of HarperCollins and sign up today!*